THE IMPACT
of a
SINGLE EVENT

R. L. PRENDERGAST

Dekko Publishing

Published in Canada by Dekko Publishing, Edmonton.

First printing, August 2008
Second printing, February 2009
Third printing, April 2009
Fourth printing, July 2009

Library and Archives Canada Cataloguing in Publication

Prendergast, R. L., 1970-
The impact of a single event / R.L. Prendergast.

ISBN 978-0-9784548-0-7

I. Title.

PS8631.R45I56 2008   C813'.6   C2008-903170-9

www.theimpact.ca

Art by Ausilia J. Corso
Printed and bound in Canada.

 Printed on 100% post-consumer recycled paper.

For S. L. Prendergast,
my wife, my friend, my love.

Journal History and Family Tree

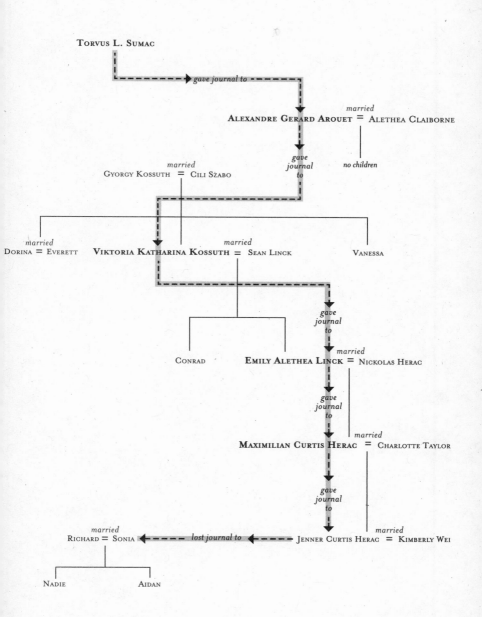

Author's Note

The journal entries that follow have, in general, been left unedited. For the purpose of clarity, minor mistakes of punctuation have been corrected; however, the language, spelling, and grammar presented in this book accurately reflect the time periods in which the journal entries were written.

Richard

Half a kilometre ahead of us, I see a car's tail lights glowing at an odd angle. As we draw nearer, I understand why. The car has flipped over into the ditch and the roof is crushed in on the driver's side. Clothes lie scattered over the highway.

"Oh no!" Sonia exclaims in a horrified whisper.

Quickly, I pull over onto the shoulder and beam our headlights at the upturned car. The doors are flung wide open, the trunk is unhinged, and one of the rear tires spins impotently. Flames burn where the missing front axle should be.

"Someone's inside!" Sonia shouts.

An arm dangles lifelessly from the driver's side. I run to the overturned car and find a man jammed into the seat. Blood covers his face, the steering wheel pushes into his chest, the crushed roof bends his neck forward. Beside him, a woman hangs limply from her seatbelt like a broken marionette. Shattered glass is everywhere. I notice folk music: the car radio is still playing, the sound obscene in the nightmarish setting. Conscious of the flames, I manage to reach inside and turn off the ignition.

"*Monsieur!*" I shout and gently nudge the man's shoulder. He doesn't respond.

THE IMPACT *of a* SINGLE EVENT

"*Madame! Madame!*" I yell at the woman next to him. A low moan emerges from her as I hurry to the passenger's side and crouch on one knee. Her eyelids flutter rapidly; only the whites of her eyes show. The front of her blouse is blood-stained. I struggle to undo her seatbelt, and broken glass digs into my knee. Then I remember: never move an injured person. I get up and rush back to our car to call an ambulance. Sonia is already hurrying towards me, cellphone in hand.

"...and about five kilometres from the route 241 turnoff," she is saying breathlessly into the phone.

"Two people!" I tell her. "Bleeding badly. And flames. What do we do?" I feel my own blood thumping violently in my temples.

Sonia relays the information into the phone, then hurries to the passenger side. I follow. The red stain on the woman's blouse is spreading alarmingly.

"See if the man has a pulse," Sonia instructs, motioning with her chin. With one hand she holds the phone to her ear; the other rests against the woman's neck. I run to the driver's side of the car.

"Well?" Sonia calls, seconds later.

"He has a pulse!" I yell.

"Is he breathing?" she hollers.

I get as close as I can to the man's mouth and try to listen. "I can't tell...."

"I smell gas!" Sonia screams suddenly.

I smell it too. Through the shattered rear window, I see a small puddle of something reflected in our headlights.

"Get them out!" Sonia yells.

"But they're injured," I protest. "We could make things worse."

"Emergency said, because of the flames, we have to get them out now!" Sonia sounds slightly hysterical.

She unclips the woman's seatbelt. The woman falls awkwardly, headfirst, onto the roof beneath her. I worry about her neck. Will she be paralyzed? As Sonia pulls her from the wreck, I struggle to free the man. His seatbelt comes undone, but the steering wheel still pins him to his seat. Anxiously, I glance at the growing puddle of gasoline.

"*Richard!*" Sonia screams. Her voice sounds far away.

My heart races. Are the flames getting more intense? Is the fire getting bigger? Spreading? Panic-stricken, I abandon my gentleness and yank harder at the man's arm. I still can't budge him. Desperate now, I look wildly around me and spot a knob on the side of the seat. I crank it and the seat moves back. My breath comes in hard gulps as I pull the driver from the wreck and drag him towards Sonia and the unconscious woman.

At last, safely away from the car and the flames, I lay the man on his back and check his breathing again. This time I hear him; he is making sick, gurgling sounds.

Beside me, Sonia, who is starting to hyperventilate, applies pressure to the woman's chest. The woman's blouse is now soaked with blood.

"Do you need help?" I ask, as I cast anxious glances at the wreck, where the flames are now a small fire.

"There's some glass in her chest. A big piece. Do I pull it out?" Sonia is now panting.

"Yes," I say, thinking Sonia is asking me. Then I realize her question is for the person at the other end of the phone line.

"Okay. Apply pressure and wait for the ambulance." Sonia repeats the person's instructions.

"Do you need help?" I ask again, louder this time.

Sonia looks at me. "I don't feel very well."

"Breathe *with* me, Sonia," I say, and force myself to take slow, deep inhalations, exaggerating my own breathing. I want to hold her, calm her down. But I can't leave the man; I'm scared he might stop breathing. Sonia's chest expands and contracts more slowly as she gets her breathing under control, and I notice she's wearing only a bra. In my confused state, I don't understand why. Then I realize she's used her shirt to staunch the woman's bleeding. But it's not enough. The woman is bleeding profusely.

"Here, Sonia," I say as I peel off my own T-shirt and toss it to her. She quickly replaces her blood-soaked shirt with mine and presses down on the woman's chest once more.

My head jerks at the sound of a siren, and to my relief, I see red and blue lights approaching. Less than a minute later, a police car pulls in behind our vehicle.

An officer, lanky and looking no older than sixteen, takes Sonia's place beside the injured woman. He continues to apply pressure to her chest, while a second officer, a solidly built woman, uses an extinguisher to douse the fire. By some miracle, the fire hasn't grown much bigger in the minutes since we came upon the accident.

The ambulance arrives soon after. The paramedics swiftly assess the injured couple, place them on yellow spine boards, and wrap on neck collars. They make no attempt to remove the glass from the woman's chest. Apparently, if the glass has pierced the woman's heart—which they have no way of knowing—and they remove it, she will bleed to death in seconds. She will be x-rayed at the hospital. Despondently, I wonder whether with all the blood she's already lost, she will make it that far.

A fire truck arrives just as the ambulance races away, its sirens wailing. As the police set up a roadblock to divert approaching vehicles from the scene, a few firemen seal the car's ruptured gas tank and spread something over the puddle of gasoline. At the same time, another two attend to

Sonia and me, cleaning and bandaging the mainly superficial wounds caused by the glass in our knees and hands. When they have finally finished, I take in the mess around us.

A single sock lies on the tarmac. An empty compact disk case, a pair of sunglasses, a broken camera. Small bits of people's lives strewn impersonally along some anonymous road. The sight saddens me, as if a love letter has been carelessly ripped apart and tossed away.

"We should collect their things," Sonia suggests.

I feel disoriented as I watch a photo drift across the highway. Looking at the upturned car, I see the British Columbia licence plate. The couple is a long way from home.

"Richard," Sonia says, returning me to the situation as she hands me a sweatshirt. At some point, she must have fetched clothes from our car. I hadn't noticed.

We begin to fill two big plastic suitcases, broken but still serviceable. We pack T-shirts, pants, underwear, photos, and bathing suits. One of the firefighters has given us two green garbage bags, into which we put sleeping bags, cooking pots, cutlery, shoes, and a tent.

We are gathering the injured couple's possessions when I spot the reason for the accident further up the highway, about a hundred feet from the overturned car. A deer—reddish-brown and white-tailed—lies partly hidden in dense bush. Curious, I approach it. There is no blood. No visible sign of injury. Were it not for the eyes, oddly unmoving, glassy and dark, a casual passerby would simply think the doe was resting. I half expect it to scramble to its legs, leap over the nearby fence, and disappear into the field beyond.

"Sonia!" I shout to my wife, who is well down the highway.

She looks up as I point towards the bush. Pausing to pick up what looks like a wallet, she comes to me. Glancing at the lifeless animal, she frowns and shakes her head and then returns to her sad chore.

A police officer, the lanky kid who had been first on the scene after us, tells us the couple is being taken to the Centre Hospitalier de Granby: the nearest major hospital.

"What should we do with these things?" Sonia asks.

The officer thinks a moment. "Could you take them to the hospital? We may not be able to do it ourselves before tomorrow."

I nod. "Sure, no problem." The city of Granby is not far.

"Are you from around here?" he asks, perhaps wondering if he is taking us out of our way.

"Montreal," Sonia says.

"*Bien.* Not too far for you then."

My thoughts return to the injured couple. "Who are they?" I ask.

"I'm sorry, sir; I'm not allowed to give out names. Doesn't seem right after all you've done but…" His words trail away. His youth proclaims him new to the police force; evidently, he is careful about correct procedure. I am still too shaken to persist.

Sonia and I spend the next hour salvaging whatever we can find. At length, we return to our car. I am about to get inside when I spot a book under our front bumper. I pick it up and look at it in the beam of our headlights. The book is rather shabby, with a hard brown dilapidated cover. Its corners are rounded down, exposing the flaking cardboard underneath, and the spine is cracked with missing pieces at both ends. The book is untitled and very old. The accident, I think, was not the cause of damage to the book.

By the time I get in the car, Sonia is burrowed deep in her seat. Her eyes are closed, and fatigue etches her dusty face. Her hair, usually sleek and smooth, is tangled, and her pants are stained with blood. She looks as weary as I feel.

"Sonia…" I say quietly.

"Richard." She opens her eyes, gives me a dazed look, then closes her eyes again.

"I found a book. Very old by the look of it."

"Oh…" She is not interested, not at this moment.

I am about to drive off, when curiosity gets the better of me. What is this book I have found? Something about it sparks my interest.

I flick on the interior light, then open the book. My first impression is confirmed: it's very old, an antique. A pencil sketch of a woman adorns the inside front cover. A beautiful woman with full lips, a strong jaw, small ears, and hair parted in the middle. Her lips are closed and she is smiling: a friendly, peaceful smile. Below the sketch, I read a name and date: Inga, April 1867.

On the opposite page is a drawing of a little girl, her face still chubby with baby fat. She has a pert little nose and a high forehead, and she beams joyfully. Her eyes, large and bright, are her most striking feature. Her name is Astrid, and this sketch, too, was completed in April 1867.

I gaze at the drawings a few minutes, impressed with the talent of the artist, and wonder about the identities of the woman and child. Intrigued, I flip through the next few pages, all of them blank and yellowed with age. Twenty empty pages further on, I come to another date—December 15, 2003—so recent as to seem out of place in this ancient book. Below the date is clear handwriting in blue ink. Have I found a diary?

"Richard?" Sonia says, wearily.

I glance at my watch. It is after one in the morning. I close the diary, put it on the seat between us, buckle my seatbelt, and head for the Granby Hospital.

Inga
April 1867

Astrid
April 1967

Jenner Curtis Herac

December 15, 2003

How do I add a meaningful story to a book that is of near legendary significance to my family? Thinking myself wise, I agonized over ideas I thought might leave a lasting impression on those who would receive this journal after me. But it wasn't until I realized I am not wise that I found I had something to say.

Seated in my brown leather chair, I was as usual waiting. I held the wide armrest firmly and tried to push back annoying thoughts of my wife, as my patient—Brenda—sat down on an identical chair across from me. Through the nearby window, I looked east, across the slow moving traffic of Hornby Street just two floors below, to the urban jungle of stairs, waterfalls, gardens, and the open-air ice rink of Robson Square. The fog of a Vancouver winter misted the buildings only a few blocks away.

"Is the world full of completely incompetent people?" Brenda asked peremptorily, without so much as a courteous hello. A rectangular, darkly stained mahogany coffee table bearing a crystal dish of candy and a box of tissues separated us. "All I wanted was a Grande Skim Vanilla Latte. I order the same thing every time. You'd think they could get it right. So what do they do? Make it with whole milk. I wanted to throw it at them. Fifteen minutes to get the order wrong, another ten to get it right. Twenty-five minutes to get a coffee. Unbelievable! They deserve minimum wage."

Brenda's left hand held the cup of coffee with its inevitable red lipstick stain around the rim. I couldn't remember a time when she wasn't sipping incessantly, bringing the cup to her mouth seemingly without thought, even after it was empty.

Brenda was dressed immaculately, like the cover model of a fashion magazine. Black high-heeled shoes, belt, and expensive looking purse complemented a navy suit and tailored white silk blouse. A French manicure and sleekly styled shoulder-length brown hair completed the picture. She had the knack of remaining "put together" even when she was tearful, by dabbing her bottom eyelids carefully, making sure not to smear expertly applied makeup.

I wished Brenda wasn't there. I wanted nothing more than to lie down on the leather chesterfield, close my eyes, and drift into oblivion. I wondered if Brenda could smell the alcohol on my breath. Gripping the armrest more tightly, I tried to focus on my patient.

"I think I'm going to end it," she said abruptly.

She changed the subject so fast that it was a moment before I realized what she was talking about. "It" was her ten-month relationship. She had described her boyfriend as charming, good-looking, gentle, and funny. She had professed to love him. However, on a regular basis, she'd plop herself down in my office and announce she was breaking up with her boyfriend. When asked the reason, her usual response was, "He doesn't give me everything I need." She had yet to define "everything."

"What's happening?" I asked.

I reached for a container of green breath mints from the small table on my left. Shaking out two mints, I popped them in my mouth and slipped the rest into my shirt pocket. Surreptitiously, I wiped my sweaty hands on my pants, folded my hands in front of me, and hoped the mints were strong enough to cover my breath. Foolish of me to drink so much at lunch.

"He's just so…" Brenda pursed her red-painted lips. Without completing the sentence, she took a long sip from her cup, depositing another layer of lipstick along the rim.

The first time Brenda saw me, she had just accepted a partnership at the law firm where she had been working since she was called to the bar. She had achieved what she had thought was her life's goal. Yet, after the initial satisfaction, she experienced an emptiness that frightened her. She had thought she had what she wanted, but when the achievement did not fill her with the contentment she had anticipated, she began to wonder what was missing.

"He pisses me off. Doesn't do his share of the housework. Won't clean up after himself. Last week there were tomato guts on the counter even after he wiped up, toast crumbs everywhere."

"Yes, that can be—"

"What's more, and I've talked to him about this, he leaves spots all over the mirror when he washes his face or brushes his teeth…."

My mind began to wander as Brenda spoke, and my eyes strayed to the abundance of books behind her. Row upon row of unread classic novels filled eggshell-white shelves from floor to ceiling. Behind me resided a similar accumulation of psychology textbooks and reference material.

When I first opened my practice, I had an image of the psychologist's ideal office—a big window, my framed degrees on the walls, an impressive array of literature, leather furniture, and a few tasteful carvings. Except for the textbooks, most of the volumes came from a second-hand bookstore in Coquitlam. It took several trips and two thousand dollars to acquire enough books to give the shelves a full appearance. Fortunately, I had inherited the furnishings. The tenant before me had run a fraudulent investment operation and had had to leave town quickly. In the hurry of a midnight flit, he had abandoned his expensive furniture. Besides the set of leather chairs, he had left an oak desk, which I used in my adjoining office, and the mahogany coffee table. I added the bookshelves and the little table beside my analyst's chair. Two pictures, both in thick black frames on the third shelf behind my patients' chair, were the room's only personal touches. One picture was of my wife, Kimberly. The other was of my parents, Charlotte and Max.

I had taken Kimberly's photo on a recent trip to an Okanagan winery. Standing in front of a stack of oak barrels, long black hair in a ponytail, looking like a field of daisies in her ankle-length green skirt and white blouse, Kimberly held a glass of red wine. While she did so, the winemaker described how that particular wine had been aged. Kimberly was unconcerned with how the brew was made, but as I was into wine, she feigned interest for my sake.

My parents' photo had been taken on their twentieth anniversary, ten years earlier. Wearing a blue angora sweater, her greying hair pulled back into a loose ponytail, my mother had a hand on my father's arm. As she looked up at him, her wide-lipped smile made the laugh lines at the corners of her eyes more prominent. My father, his tanned skin contrasting with my mother's pale complexion, had a wide, blue paisley necktie wrapped around his forehead and hanging down the side of his head. He was trying to look serious, but the corners of his mouth were turned up in a barely suppressed smile that reminded me of the Mona Lisa.

When Brenda paused, I waited a second before commenting; I didn't want another interruption. "I can understand your irritation," I began then. "Housework is a common issue between people living together. What have you—"

But Brenda went on as if she didn't hear me. "You know, he still hasn't acknowledged all the work I've put into our condo. The time and money I've spent making it nice for the two of us…"

I let her ramble on. Without looking away from her, I could still see, just behind her, the picture of my parents. It was funny how I always focused on that photo, especially my father, whenever Brenda came for a session. It may have been that I worried I was more like Brenda and less like my easy-going dad.

Maximilian the Great was the moniker my friends gave him. I was thirteen when two of my buddies and I stole a dozen beers from Jeff's dad. On the pretext of a sleepover, we drank them in my basement. Three or four beers each, and we were all ill. Dad came downstairs when he heard the toilet flush for the tenth time in so many minutes. He found me curled up on the bathroom floor. Jeff had barfed all over his pillow and sleeping bag, while Angelo, the dumb shit, had had the bright idea of lifting up the cushions of the couch and throwing up; in his inebriated state, he must have thought no one would notice his vomit hidden there.

Two hours later, Dad had washed Jeff's sleeping bag and pillow, scrubbed the couch, and cleaned up the bathroom.

The next morning we wondered what would become of us. Angelo, a first-generation Canadian born to strict Italian immigrants, feared for his life. Jeff, too, was worried. One day went by, then another. No fallout for Angelo, Jeff, or myself. Happy to have escaped retribution, I let the incident rest. From then on, Dad became Maximilian the Great, like one of the Russian czars we had learned about recently in social studies.

That summer, in the midst of a muggy August heat wave, an awful stench emanated from the basement. It grew steadily worse, festering badly. Eventually, my father determined it was coming from the chesterfield. Evidently, Angelo's puke had not been completely removed and had fermented in the heat. Dad winked at me as he asked me to help him take the old orange couch to the dump. On the way there, I apologized for wrecking the sofa and asked him why he had not punished me.

Dad gave me a one-eyed look. "You needed me to say something?" He was laughing, his head cocked to one side, like a dog listening to the howls of a distant pack of wolves. "You can figure things out for yourself," he said.

Brenda's voice rose an octave, and I emerged from my memories.

"I even went out and bought an A.Y. Jackson," she said. She had become steadily more excited. "He doesn't even know anything about Jackson and the Group of Seven. Have you any idea what it cost me? The guy is such a boor."

"Let's deal with one thing at a time," I said patiently. "Have you told him your concerns about housework?"

"No. How can I? I don't want to sound like a nag."

"You can't hide from the issues."

We spent some time discussing strategies Brenda might use to broach the subject with her boyfriend.

"It's more than the housework," she said at last. "He's not paying me enough attention. I wanted to spend the evening with him yesterday, but he made plans with his friends. He should know by now that Wednesday is our special night!" She shifted the coffee cup from her left hand to her right and then back again. Her blue eyes darted around restlessly, as if she were considering what to say next.

Some of my patients visit me twice, maybe three times. Often they need no specific direction; talking out loud is enough for them. Most people come to see me fifteen to twenty times over six months. Usually, in that time, clients recognize their unhelpful behaviour and adjust. And then there is a third group: clients I see for years, who make few changes, forever retaining beliefs that make them unhappy. Brenda belonged to the last group. I was beginning to wonder if I belonged to it too.

"Why didn't you put the spaghetti sauce in a dark container? Now this one is stained," I had said to Kimberly two nights before, as I was washing the supper dishes. Before dinner she had admitted to denting the door frame of the garage with the right-hand mirror of her car. The mirror now hung by a few wires.

"I'm sorry. I didn't think it was that big a deal. I'll buy new containers." She had sounded exasperated.

"That's not the point. Our stuff would last longer if you were careful," I said, referring more to the car and the garage than the spaghetti container.

"I'm sorry," she said again, but I saw her rolling her eyes as she turned away.

"You're always doing things like that." I was angry that she did not take my comments seriously. After all, she was forever doing other things too. Shrinking my shirts or leaving a window too wide open when it rained—she loved the smell of the rain—and the damp air would get the carpet wet and then mouldy. Small things, but they annoyed me.

"I'm sorry I don't do things the Jenner way," she said sarcastically.

"Don't be an idiot. I just want you to think!" My voice had risen; I was practically yelling. I regretted the words even though I meant them. I just wanted Kimberly to be more careful. I might even have apologized, but before I had a chance to control my emotions, she grabbed her car keys and left.

I compared myself to a good chess player, planning every step of my life—both personal and professional—many moves in advance. By being fully prepared for any contingency, I figured I could avoid irrevocable mistakes, big or small. But Kimberly differed from me. She liked to do things on a whim. She might want to climb a mountain, equipped with nothing but a soft drink and a chocolate bar, or give up a good job as she had done recently, for employment that lacked financial security. Her energy and unbridled enthusiasm had attracted me to her initially. She had energized my life, making it invigorating and refreshing. Now, after four years of marriage, I wondered if I could tolerate her disregard for possible consequences to her actions. Kimberly did not think things through the way I did. Sitting across the table from Brenda, I calculated that 42 hours had passed since I had last spoken with Kimberly.

"What is it you expect of your boyfriend?" I asked, as Brenda flicked the rim of her cup with a manicured finger.

She looked at me for so long that I had an uneasy sense that she could see through me. That she knew my life too was not without flaws. "Who are you to give advice?" I expected her to say.

"I don't know," she said at length. "I guess I want him to be more aware of my needs. We're supposed to look at engagement rings on Saturday, but I don't think I can go through with it. He's looking at such tiny rings. Totally inappropriate. I'd be willing to chip in myself for a decent two-carat diamond." She paused to straighten the creases of her pants, and then smoothed a fold on her jacket. "Why is he like that? Doesn't he know how important the ring is?"

She paused a moment, as if she'd heard the sound of her own words. For a moment she even looked slightly embarrassed. Then, she lifted her chin and went on. "Maybe you think that sounds awful. But it's what I want. It would make everything all right." There was longing in her tone as she said the last words.

"The diamond is so important to you?" I asked.

She made an angry face. The expression of someone who was accustomed to getting her own way and was frustrated because she wasn't getting it this time. Maybe she had even thought I would agree with her. A moment passed. "Oh, I don't want to talk about him anymore," she said then, in a huff. I knew that huff. Brenda expected easy solutions to her problems. When would she learn that my job is not to give answers? I hardly had answers for myself.

"What do you want to discuss?" I asked, and wondered if she sensed my impatience. Involuntarily, edginess emerged more and more frequently in our sessions together.

"I'd rather talk about work," she said.

"Okay."

"It's getting worse."

"Oh?"

"I'm hating work more and more."

"And?"

"I thought about what you said last week. Not to worry what people think of lawyers. Anyway, I don't believe that's what's really bothering me."

"Do you know what **is** bothering you?"

"I think so…after all the years of eighty-hour weeks, of making sacrifices to get where I am now, I believe I never really liked law."

"What would happen if you left?"

"I would lose everything I've worked for: my partnership, my reputation, the money! Ten years of sacrifice, all for nothing." She shook her head, almost as if she felt she had wasted her life.

"And if you stayed?"

Brenda did not answer. She did not even sip her coffee. Instead, she looked towards the window. I could not see her eyes now, but her face bore an unfamiliar expression. I wondered how she saw the street below us. The silence continued for a least a minute.

"Brenda?" I asked at last.

"I'm thinking." She took a long sip of coffee. "I'll be miserable if I go on practicing law, but at least, I'll be able to afford the things I want."

"What's more important?"

She answered without hesitation. "My happiness, of course. But I can't just give up the work. I'm stuck."

"So is everyone," I wanted to say. Almost everyone.

Looking over to the picture of Mom and Dad, I wondered how my father became unstuck. As a ten-year-old boy, he had contracted polio. He'd spent weeks at the Hospital for Sick Children, in Toronto. During his stay there, he'd become fascinated with the nurses, doctors, and physical therapists who cared for him. On his discharge, he dedicated himself to becoming a physician. Then one night, only months from completing his medical degree, he quit his studies and went into carpentry instead. He's been a carpenter ever since.

"Why are you stuck?" I asked Brenda.

"Think about it—how else can I use my law degree? I've read that people in other fields don't like to hire lawyers. They don't trust us; they don't believe our skills are transferable." Close by hung my degrees. Brenda gazed at them for what seemed a long fifteen seconds. "Maybe I should have been a psychologist, like you. You get to talk with people all day, to learn what makes them tick. Must be interesting."

I was always irritated when people considered therapy to be no more than friendly, helpful conversation. The three degrees represented nine years of schooling. I could have been a medical doctor in less time than that, and gotten more respect. But I wasn't allowed to give into my feelings and speak my mind. I had to remain disciplined and listen to my patients' problems, all because I'd managed an A in my first-year psychology course. I pictured a cold beer, tapped another mint into my hand, and popped it into my mouth.

"If you could do anything in the world, what would you choose?" I asked.

"I wanted to be a journalist when I first started university." She had mentioned this before.

"Why did you go into law?"

"Lawyers make more money."

It wasn't the only reason, I knew. Words had always been something of a fascinating dichotomy for Brenda. Her father was not a reader—I suspected he was illiterate, though Brenda had never actually said so. Her mother read only grocery store tabloids, which she hid when guests came to visit. More factors had been involved in Brenda's choice of a career than just money, but this wasn't the right time to discuss them. We had already gone off in too many directions in this session.

"What is so important about money?" I asked.

Brenda signed. "It makes life easier. You know what I mean."

I did. I knew what she earned, and I was envious. "What do you mean by 'makes life easier'?"

"I know it's not the be-all-and-end-all, but I can buy what I need."

"How much time can you buy?"

The question took her by surprise, as I had known it would.

"What?"

"Let's say you spend eighty hours a week working. How much time would you say your money buys you?"

Again there was silence. She seemed restless as she gazed once more through the window.

"I just can't start over again," she said at length, sadly.

"So then I guess being miserable is better than being poor?" An unprofessional question.

"Oh, I don't know what's wrong anymore," she said, putting down the cup and rubbing her temples. "Maybe I need to treat myself. Get some work done. I've been considering liposuction. I've never been happy with my hips."

If she only knew how others saw her—a beautiful woman with an almost-perfect body.

"We're getting off topic again," I said. "We were talking about work."

"I don't want to talk about it anymore; it's giving me a headache."

"Okay. What will cosmetic surgery do for you?"

"Maybe if I felt better about myself, everything else would be okay."

I wanted to shake her. Hard. Nothing had changed since Brenda had first started coming to me. She jumped from one topic to another, skimming the surface of her problems. She resisted digging down to discover what lurked underneath, to understand herself better. Yet who was I to say anything? I felt like a fraud. If I couldn't make myself happy, how could I help Brenda or anyone else? I knew my thoughts were irrational. I knew I could help others, but sometimes I wanted to close the door on my practice, burn my degrees, walk out, and never look back.

I badly wanted a drink.

"How will slimmer hips improve your relationship and make your job more enjoyable?"

Brenda flinched. She looked at me as if I had yelled at her. Perhaps I had. She took a candy from the crystal tray. I heard a car honking outside. I looked at my watch. A minute over Brenda's allotted time. She looked tired.

"Why is everything so difficult? Does the crap ever stop? Look at you—you're fine. How do you do it?" she asked.

I wanted to admit that I was anything but fine. "We're here to talk about you."

"But if I know how you do it, maybe I could do it that way, too," she said, hopefully.

"We all need to find our own way."

I stood to let her know her time was up. Childlike, she pouted. As she left, she checked her makeup in the mirror of a small compact and reapplied her lipstick.

Once she'd gone, I made notes on the session, put on my raincoat, and locked up the office. It was drizzling outside, a bleak, grey, cheerless rain. I longed for the bright cold of an Edmonton winter, but Kimberly loved Vancouver. Her favourite place was Stanley Park's seawall, nine kilometres of paved trail around the perimeter of a heavily treed peninsula jutting into the Burrard Inlet. On days like this, only the more intrepid joggers, those determined not to miss a day of training, would be on the seawall.

Across the street from my office, people with placards were demonstrating outside the art gallery. I couldn't quite make out the signs, something about protecting killer whales. I headed west down Robson Street, across Burrard Street and into the core of the tourist area. Here the stores were close together: fashion boutiques and stores selling T-shirts, jewellery, and souvenirs—paradise behind glass. A busker, her guitar case open on the ground in front of her, strummed away fervently, seemingly oblivious to the deepening rain. A car backfired somewhere down the street.

Walking along the slippery sidewalk, I thought about my dad's old truck, rust eating away at the door frame and wheel arches. A dark green half-ton GMC, paint flaking away to reveal sky blue underneath. I've never known if the truck was once blue or if that colour was the undercoating of 1963 GM trucks. My dad would joke that he had to top up the oil more often than the gas.

On Saturdays, when I was little, he would take me to whichever site he was working on. Carrying me on his shoulders, he would point out the latest additions to the particular structure he was working on. Moving from room to room in the skeleton of those newly framed buildings, we would both duck our heads as we passed through doorways. Dad would carry a bottle of orange pop that we would pass back and forth—a shared vice kept secret from my health-conscious mother. On the drive home, if there were few cars on the road, he would put me in his lap and let me steer. Sitting in that grey cab, gripping the big, white steering wheel, Dad's hands hovering close to mine, I used to wish the journey would never end.

I walked a few blocks past the pubs I usually visited, heading instead towards a bar on Broughton Street. It would not do for a psychologist to gain a reputation as a drinker. The place was empty except for two guys in suits sitting in a booth, watching a hockey game on one of the half dozen televisions above the long stone counter. The Canucks playing the Rangers in New York. An East Coast game—no wonder it's on at 3:30 in the afternoon here, I thought. I took the booth two down from the corporate types and ordered a pint of beer from the stick-thin waitress. I watched the game for a few minutes; the sound of the TV echoed in the room. I got my cold beer and downed half of it in a gulp. The mints had coated my tongue, giving the beer a strange taste, but it wasn't the taste I cared about.

Round water stains broke the pattern of the table's wood grain top. I tried to fit my glass into the stains, but they were either too big or too small, none just right. I was a frustrated Goldilocks. All the porridge, all the chairs, all the beds were too hot, too cold, too hard, too soft, too big, too small. Nothing ever seemed just right.

I thought about Kimberly and considered whether or not to phone her. She would still be at work right now.... I pictured her at her desk, designing a playground for a new school or perhaps a front yard for some wealthy family in West Vancouver. Her boss favoured comfortable clothes at work, insisting on professional attire only when visiting clients. She was probably wearing jeans and a loose sweater, years out of style: the polar opposite of Brenda's immaculate presentation.

In one sense, I had to agree with Brenda. If we don't try for the ideal, then what do we strive for? I had saved money to buy the right house, had looked carefully for the right car, the right clothes, and even the right wife. I was constantly creating new goals for myself. Each goal, an island of its own. I'd swim towards the place that seemed to hold the answer to my quest. When I found nothing there, I would make for a new island.

Even as a child, I lay awake at night worrying about being perfect. My grades were good, but not as good as some. I had friends, but I wasn't the most popular kid in the school. I was decent at sports but was never picked first for games at recess and never made an all-star team. Unable to sleep, I'd kneel on my bed and look out the window at the illuminated park across the road. I often wondered if my parents could hear me staring out the window. It's the kind of thought that occurs to a nine-year-old. My parents probably heard me sigh loudly or adjust my bedsheets as I tried to make myself comfortable enough to fall asleep.

Dad would appear at my door. "Jenner, can I ask you something?"

I'd nod to Dad and follow him down the hall. In the living room, he would sit down in his chair, lean forward with his elbows on his knees, and his interlocked fingers against his chin. In the kitchen, I could hear Mom stirring a warm pot of milk, the spoon hitting the metal pot, a strangely comforting sound. I knew what she was making.

Dad never started with "What's the matter?" He knew me, or perhaps he just understood people well enough to probe by not probing. The intent was not to get my opinion, although I felt as if he dearly wanted my input; he wanted to get me talking.

"I've been thinking where we might go for summer holidays," he'd say. In winter, he might ask me where we should go cross-country skiing or with which grandparents we should have Christmas dinner.

I'd take a moment to think. At that age, I sensed that a question asked in a serious tone should be given careful thought before one answered. "We should go to the lake." By which I meant Shuswap Lake in the interior of British Columbia. We went there most summers. I knew what I liked.

"I was thinking we might try a new lake."

We would discuss the pros and cons of going somewhere new. Mom would appear with a cup of warm Ovaltine, that sweet milk mix, then go back to the kitchen. She understood that two pairs of eyes, especially on an only child, might keep me from saying what bothered me. Predictably, I'd start to talk.

"You can't be perfect Jenner. No one is, and no one ever will be." Dad seldom had to explain. However, there were occasions when he would take from his desk the old family journal—the very journal I write in now—and use it to illustrate a point. For me, it was enough just to hear my Dad talk, to listen to someone I trusted.

When we had finished our Ovaltine, which had a way of lasting until we had finished talking, Dad would say how tired he was and would joke that he needed his beauty rest. He would stand up, letting me decide myself when I was ready for sleep. Usually, minutes later, I would feel drowsy and go to bed.

Outside the pub, the sidewalk was crowded with people going home from work. At the bar, the TV hollered the play-by-play action of the hockey game. The men in suits raised glasses of beer to their lips, their eyes glued to the tube. The waitress came by to ask if I wanted another beer. I said yes.

She set it in front of me. I grabbed it, meaning to down the glass quickly. Suddenly, I hesitated.

I knew I couldn't stall any longer. It might have been the wrong time to call Kimberly, but I had to start making changes now. I pulled out my cellphone and dialed the number. One ring; two. I cleared my throat as her voice mail greeting came on.

"Hi, Kimberly. It's me." I wondered again if I should wait to see her face to face and to tell her then, but I decided I had wasted enough time already.

"I've been doing lots of thinking, honey. How about we take advantage of the rain? Let's take umbrellas and walk around the seawall. Please, call me back, Kimberly."

Jenner Curtis Herac

Richard

For some time after leaving the accident site and heading towards Granby Hospital, Sonia and I drive in silence. Pictures relating to the accident appear like a string of billboard ads in my mind: The overturned car. The clothes scattered on the road. The man pinned to his seat by the steering wheel. The dead deer on the side of the road.

Ten minutes of silence pass, when Sonia finally speaks. "I wonder how they are."

I wonder this too. From the time they arrived at the accident, the paramedics had worked feverishly on the injured couple. Of the two, the woman appeared to be in more critical condition. But I had heard the man's breathing; it had sounded as if he were trying to suck the last of a milkshake through a straw, and I wondered if the steering wheel pinning him to his seat might have crushed his lungs.

"It's the first time I've ever seen such a terrible accident." Sonia's voice has a distant sound. She puts a hand to her mouth, as if trying to prevent certain words from emerging. Then, hastily, she rolls down the window, puts her head out, and retches.

"You all right? Want me to stop?" I take my foot from the gas pedal and let it hover over the brake.

Sonia shakes her head, pulls a tissue from the glove compartment, and puts her hand to her mouth again. She sits like that for a while, then leans her head against the door and lets the air coming in from outside rush over her. I am about to reach over and touch her leg, but after a moment, I decide to keep my hand on the wheel, denying a natural impulse to comfort her.

While Sonia fights to control her churning stomach, I glance over my shoulder at the two plastic suitcases, one blue and one yellow, and the two green garbage bags on the back seat. Not a single vehicle had passed us as we collected the couple's scattered possessions. The only people at the accident had been the police, the firemen, the paramedics, and the two of us.

"Lucky that we came across the accident when we did, or they might not have been found until morning," Sonia says, echoing my own thoughts.

"Yes," I answer. Lucky for the couple, I think: not lucky for us.

We had found ourselves on that deserted stretch of road after an early ending to our two-week vacation. Twelve days early, to be exact. I had never thought we would be one of those *"We-need-to-get-away-to-save-our-marriage"* couples; yet that had been the purpose of the aborted trip, though neither of us had dared speak the dangerous words aloud.

We were going to get along together and have fun, we said. Fun exploring what was figuratively our backyard—the *Cantons de l'Est* or *Estrie*: the region known in English as the Eastern Townships, an area east of Montreal and north of the borders of Maine, New Hampshire, Vermont, and New York State.

Originally settled in the 1780s by United Empire Loyalists—American colonists who remained loyal to the

British Crown by moving to Canada after the American Revolution—the Eastern Townships are considered one of the two main playgrounds for Montrealers, the other being the Laurentian Mountains, north of the city.

Although the Eastern Townships offer tourists everything from luxury resorts to historic *auberges* (inns) to cosy bed and breakfasts, the main focus of the region is the outdoors. In summer, rustic farmhouses surrounded by evenly spaced green vines on gently rolling hillsides are reminiscent of Tuscany. In fall, the covered bridges, the stone buildings, and the red, orange, and yellow leaves remind one of New England. In winter, the snow-covered mountains evoke memories of Austria. At least, that's what I have been told, for I have never been to any of those places.

Sonia and I had had a plan. We were going to stay at a few different B&Bs, drive around the countryside, along the covered bridges and over the gently rolling hills in search of antique stores, museums, and anything else that might strike our fancy.

The antique stores were for Sonia, who regularly sifts through Friday's *Gazette* and *La Presse* for information about local garage sales with, as she puts it, "potential." On Saturday mornings, while the kids amuse themselves with TV cartoons, Sonia enjoys hunting for old and interesting pieces for the house. Usually, she returns with nothing, but there have been Saturdays when she's made a discovery: an 1880s bowl with fancy feet, an 1860s ceramic water pitcher, or a mahogany dining table made in the early 1900s. Sonia had hoped she might find something even older or more unusual in the Eastern Townships. I, on the other hand, am more interested in museums. I especially wanted to visit the Musée J. Armand Bombardier in Valcourt, which features the inventor of the snowmobile, and the Musée Minéralogique et d'Histoire Minière in Asbestos.

We had planned to rent canoes and to go on a few vineyard tours. Though neither of us care much for wine, there was a time when we enjoyed sharing a cider before bed, especially after a busy day ferrying the kids to soccer games or pottery classes. We thought of these activities as nice "couple" things to do together. I had even considered parasailing over Lac Memphrémagog—though in the event, I might well have chickened out. I don't wear shorts and might have felt foolish in long pants when everyone else was wearing bathing suits.

We were, once upon a time, considered the ideal couple. The kind of partnership people point to and ask, "Why isn't our marriage like that?" Sonia and I used to relish the admiration, as well as the anecdotes that made the rounds at office Christmas parties and neighbourhood barbecues.

My favourite story occurred at a couples' evening, more than seven years ago. Eight of us were at Doug and Mary Olivers', where we were playing Pictionary, a game similar to charades, but played on paper rather than by acting out the answers. Played in teams—in this case, couples—the game required one team member to pull a card from the Pictionary deck. Without using numbers or letters, that person had to draw a picture representing the word on the card.

Sonia and I had garnered a reputation as an unbeatable team. No matter how poorly I drew, Sonia always guessed the word correctly. On this particular evening, Doug noticed that whenever I sketched, Sonia had a hand on my back or arm, and when she drew, I was touching her. We were accused of having telepathic abilities that came into force only when we touched. And so, Doug implemented a new rule: no touching between partners when they were playing the game. Of course, Sonia and I thought Doug was joking, but he was a competitive man, and he and his wife, Mary, usually came second to us. Sonia and I did not believe in telepathy, but reluctant to start a row, we agreed to a rule that seemed ridiculous.

Not surprisingly, we continued to win. Doug was the only one at the table who did not realize that Sonia had kicked off a shoe and was working her bare foot up my leg. Though I don't believe my wife's flirtatiousness influenced our success, it did make me feel lucky to be with her, not to mention a bit amorous. I'm pretty sure Aidan was conceived that night.

In the last year, however, things have changed. We've stopped holding hands; we no longer cuddle in our queen-sized bed but sleep with enough space between us to drive a car through, and no longer spend much time together. We don't converse, but communicate in as few words as necessary. We remain considerate to each other, though in a formal way, as one would behave with a stranger. Three ciders languish in the fridge, waiting for us to resume our intimate conversations. Gradually, the ciders have made their way to the rear of the fridge, where they now stand almost forgotten behind the rarely used bottle of Worcestershire sauce and the unopened jar of pickled onions.

It was Sonia who suggested the two-week vacation, and I agreed. We sent the kids to stay with my sister in Dartmouth, and drove a few hours to an Eastern Townships' bed and breakfast I had found on the Internet. In that quiet B&B, beside a slow-moving stream, we would get together again. Unfortunately, difficulties returned on the second night of our retreat.

We were going to spend the evening in our comfortable suite watching a quirky movie called *Better Off Dead*. While I microwaved a bag of sour cream and onion-flavoured popcorn, my favourite, Sonia, a large package of red liquorice at the ready, changed into a loose-fitting T-shirt and pyjama bottoms and arranged herself on the loveseat in front of the television. When my popcorn was ready, I started the DVD player and settled into an oversized chair. Almost immediately, Sonia began to weep.

"What is it?" I asked, trying to speak calmly. During our first fourteen years together, I had only seen her cry a handful of times. Lately, she had been doing so a lot, and it bothered me.

"You never want to be near me anymore," she sobbed.

I shook my head. "What are you talking about?"

But Sonia was right: I didn't want to sit beside her, though I wouldn't tell her so. I was trying hard to get along with her. I, too, wanted this trip to be a success.

"Then why aren't you sitting next to me?" A tear escaped and rolled down her cheek.

"I thought I'd give you lots of room to stretch out."

"I don't want room." She raised her voice. "I want you beside me!"

I wondered if her voice could be heard through the walls by the others at the B&B. I hoped not.

I thought quickly and said the wrong thing. "I thought I'd be more comfortable in the chair."

Sonia was upset. "So you don't want to be near me! *Why not?* You haven't hugged me once since we got here. In bed last night, you pulled away when I tried to touch you. Why do I disgust you?"

If only I had said those three words so vital to marriage, I could have salvaged the evening, perhaps the whole trip. *I love you. I love you.* The thing is, I really do love Sonia; more than anyone in my life, perhaps even more than the kids. But I couldn't bring myself to get the words past my lips. I wanted Sonia to be the one to break down the barrier between us. I wanted *her* to save our marriage. There may even have been some small part of me that wanted to punish her, because she hadn't tried hard enough to heal the wounds I'd suffered.

When I didn't answer right away, she began to cry in earnest. Normally, I would have held her in my arms—which is exactly what I wanted to do at that moment—but for some reason, I could not. I put on my shoes instead and went for a walk.

When I returned an hour later, Sonia was still very upset. It was not difficult to imagine the rest of the vacation consisting of nothing more than stretches of silence punctuated by Sonia's sobs. That being the case, it was probably best for us to go home and try to work things out in familiar surroundings.

I should have imparted this thought to Sonia gently. Instead, fool that I am, I blurted out the words, "Let's go. Being here is just a waste of time."

Sonia gasped, stared at me in shock, then began to weep fiercely once more.

Rattled by her intense distress, I acted unwisely: without another word, I opened the suitcase and started to pack. That done, I sat down, and waited. When her weeping had subsided, I asked Sonia if she wanted to stay after all. I spoke as gently as I could.

She did not deign to answer me with words: she just tugged on a pair of jeans, threw her clothes and makeup bag into the suitcase, and went outside to the car. I told the owner of the B&B that something had come up unexpectedly—a family emergency—necessitating our immediate return to Montreal. I hoped the story would explain Sonia's tears and our early departure.

Half an hour later, we came upon the accident.

Sonia shifts in her seat. Whenever she rubs her arms and neck, I know she is nervous or upset. She's doing it now.

"Should we have the kids come home?" I ask her. Nadie and Aidan have spent the first few days of their Nova Scotia vacation with my sister and her children, at the beach: making sandcastles, poking jellyfish with sticks, and playing in the waves of the cold North Atlantic Ocean.

"I don't think so. Why spoil their fun?" Sonia answers wearily.

I nod, more to myself than to Sonia. She's right, I think. Why bring them home? They'd want to know why, as would my sister. What would we tell them?

"Those poor people," Sonia says, "I can't believe what just happened." She stares forward through the front window into the night. The sky may be covered with cloud, for there is no light from the moon or the stars; our lonely headlights provide the only brightness.

"How are we going to get their stuff back to them?" I venture. I feel as if I'm talking to a stranger rather than to my wife of fifteen years. I turn my head again to see the suitcases and the green garbage bags. "I wish the police had told us their names," I add.

"Jenner and Kimberly Herac," Sonia murmurs.

I glance at her. "How do you know?"

"I overheard the paramedics. They didn't think they'd make it." Sonia's voice shakes. "They were bleeding internally. I keep hoping they'll be all right. Oh, Richard, that could have been us! If the deer had crossed the road a minute later...." Sonia reaches for more tissues. She has been strong until now, but with the passing of the crisis, she starts to weep.

I want very much to comfort her. I love Sonia, but having felt betrayed once, I do not want to be influenced by her tears.

As we reach Granby some ten minutes later, Sonia's sobbing slows, then ceases. As we pass beneath them, the street lights shine like strobe lights on the hood of the car. Light. Dark. Light. Dark. Light. Dark. All at once, Sonia notices the old book I found and picks it up.

"What is this? Where did you get it?" she asks curiously.

Did she not see me look at it before we left the accident scene, I wonder. "Found it at the accident," I say calmly.

As I look for signs that will direct me to the hospital, Sonia turns on the interior light and opens the diary to the first page. She gazes at the drawing of the woman and the little girl. "Wow!" she mutters, evidently as impressed as I was by the artist's skill.

She flips through the first twenty blank pages, before reaching the 2003 entry, which I had seen too. "Hmm," I hear her sigh softly, before she looks further through the brittle diary, doing so carefully. Thirty pages later, the written entry ends with a signature: Jenner Curtis Herac.

"Herac!" Sonia says, and we exchange a look of interest.

On the following page, a new date appears: June 23, 1975. The handwriting is in black ink and is quite different from that of the previous entry.

"Weird," Sonia pronounces. Then she adds in a conversational tone, almost as if she hadn't spent so long crying, "None of my business." She closes the diary and puts it back between us on the seat. Seconds later, we turn a corner and see the hospital.

Maximilian Curtis Herac

June 23, 1975

"*When* did you know something was wrong?" I asked
Grandpa Sean.

Elbows on the table, he brought his hands together like
a ball and socket, fist inside a cupped palm, and rubbed them
together.

"With your grandmother?"

I nodded, watching the play of expressions on his face as
he thought about the question: the frown that puckered his
forehead, the smile at some unspoken memory, the sheen of
sadness in his eyes.

"She let a pot of water boil dry," he said at last. "Then
another one. I think that was the first bit of unusual behaviour. She wasn't the forgetful type, as you know." He put a
hand to his mouth and rubbed a day's growth of whiskers.
Unconsciously, I did the same.

My mother leaned back in her chair, arms crossed, eyebrows knit slightly together. She looked at me. "Why do you
ask?"

"Curious," I said, feigning indifference.

It was late at night in the spring of 1962. The three of us sat around the dining room table, overhead light casting shadows on the wall behind us. The house was pleasantly calm at last, after Grandma's seventy-third birthday celebrations. Outside, the streets were quiet and dark; so dark that I could see my reflection in the room's lone window, almost as if it were a mirror.

At first, Grandpa had tried to handle the situation alone. He had spent his days watching her. But as Grandma's condition worsened, she needed greater supervision. Eventually, she began to get up in the middle of the night and leave the house to walk around the neighbourhood, curious about surroundings that had become new to her as she lost her memories. Inevitably, and despite his most devoted efforts, Grandpa's vigilance began to take its toll on his health. It would have taxed a young man to keep an eye on her twenty-four hours a day, let alone an eighty-year-old. Wanting to help Grandpa, Mom and Dad left Toronto for Edmonton, and I spent the night every once in a while when my studies allowed. This particular night was my night. I didn't mind helping out. I was in my final year of medicine at the University of Alberta, and I was getting used to the thirty-six-hour hospital shifts.

"Any new changes?" Mom asked. Although she visited nearly every day, it was difficult to gauge alterations in Grandma, unless she behaved uncharacteristically in one's presence.

"Not lately," said Grandpa. "Of course, today wasn't good for her. Too many people, I suspect."

Worse than you know, I thought to myself. "What was Grandma like when she was younger?" I asked aloud.

I had grown up in Toronto, but my grandparents had moved from there to Edmonton when I was only six. Although we visited them every few years, I had not had the chance to get to know my grandparents well. Even after I came to Edmonton, on starting medicine here, I'm sorry to say that my studies and social life kept me so busy that I didn't spend much time with them. It had taken Grandma's severe deterioration to persuade me to visit more often.

"What do you want to know?" Grandpa asked.

"Anything."

I realized that for most of my life, I had seen my grandmother mainly as a gardener. In my earliest memories, her face and arms are tanned brown by the sun, and she is pushing a wheelbarrow loaded with enough fertilizer and soil to make a man twice her size grunt with effort. Every few years, the family travelled to Alberta by train, where we would spend part of the summer with my grandparents. Each visit began with a tour of Grandma's garden. She loved to show us around and bring us up to date with the things she had worked on since last we'd seen her: a new bed of flowers, a stone birdbath, a recently planted seedling, perhaps, or well-placed stepping stones that made the flower-filled corners of her garden more accessible.

On another level, of course, I was also aware of her intellectual accomplishments. She was one of the first women in Canada to receive a Ph.D., and one of the earliest to attain the status of associate professor, events which occurred years ago, before she and Grandpa retired in Edmonton. Yet for some reason, to me Grandma was her garden and the garden was her, an indivisible unity, neither existing without the other. That is, until earlier that day when, in a kitchen crowded with family and friends, Grandma had motioned me to lean down so that she could whisper in my ear and ask, "Who am I?"

Who am I? The question startled me at the time. I still felt stunned, hours later. It was as if part of the foundation of my life, something I had always taken for granted, had started to crumble beneath me.

Dimly, I heard my mother talking. With an effort of will, I forced myself back to the present. "Dad, remember the time I froze my tongue to the axe?" she was asking my grandfather.

"Yes," he said, and made himself comfortable in the chair, as if in a theatre, waiting for a movie to begin.

Mom turned to me. "It happened at our place on Concord Avenue. I was four. I was outside, playing in the backyard after dinner. The snow was bright, lit by a full moon. Every chimney in the neighbourhood gave off smoke that looked like arms reaching for the sky. I saw the hatchet leaning against the shed. When I picked it up, ice crystals on the axe head sparkled in the moonlight. The crystals looked so beautiful that I had a sudden urge to taste them. Next thing I knew, my tongue was stuck to the cold metal. Sobbing and frightened, I stumbled back to the house. I tried to yell, hoping my parents would hear me and come to my aid, but no sound came, for the heavy hatchet, as long as I was tall, was pulling at my tongue. I was terrified my tongue would be pulled right out of my mouth. Mom was shocked when I burst into the kitchen, and she saw the hatchet on my tongue. But she hid her shock well. I still remember how calm she was. She scooped me up in her arms, sat me at the kitchen table, heated some water, and poured it over the axe head. When it came off, I was still sobbing. I cried and cried and cried. It's one of my earliest memories."

Mom had just finished her story, when Grandpa arched back in his chair and turned his head to the hallway. Putting a finger to his lips, he signalled us to be quiet. We listened and waited a few seconds, then Grandpa said, "I think I hear Viktoria," and got up to check on Grandma.

Grandma had gone to bed three hours earlier, but with her erratic sleep patterns, she could wake up and try to get out of the house at any time. When Grandpa left the room, I looked at the birthday cards set out on the china hutch. I recognized names of cousins, uncles, and aunts. There were also names I did not recognize; I presumed they belonged to friends. My eyes fell on one card in particular, a romantic-looking thing with entwined hearts and roses. "From an old boyfriend," it was signed.

"Mom, take a look at this," I said in surprise. "Who gave her this?" My grandparents had been married more than fifty years, and I found it impossible to imagine anyone tracking down my grandmother after so long.

My mother smiled as she looked at the card I handed her. "Ask your grandfather," she said.

The thought of asking Grandpa about Grandma's old flame made me uncomfortable. "Tell me," I said.

Mom just looked at me the way a teacher looks at a bright student, hoping he'll get the answer without help.

"Ask your Grandpa," she said again, just as Grandpa returned to the room.

"She's still down," Grandpa said, referring to Grandma.

"Good. Dad, Max has a question for you."

I gave Mom a dirty look. Her smile was without remorse. Trapped, I had no choice but to hand him the card and ask, "Grandpa, who is this from?"

As my grandfather looked at the card, I noticed that his fingers were gnarled with age and his hands marked with brown spots. Somewhat nervous, I glanced at his face, but his expression told me nothing. He looked up and gave me a wide grin. I felt dim-witted, as if I were the only person at a dinner party not laughing at a clever joke.

"You don't know?"

"No!"

"Me!" he said with a grin, and blew his nose like an out-of-tune horn.

At least I had the grace to feel abashed as it struck me how one dimensionally I had seen my grandparents until now. Two elderly people with no lives other than their present ones.

Earlier that day, when Grandma had asked, "Who am I?" I had given the first answer that came to mind: "Your name is Viktoria, and I am your grandson, Max."

She had looked at me a moment, without answering. Then she'd shuffled over to Grandpa, at whose side she remained for the rest of the day, like a child who stays close to a parent in a stranger's house. I had watched her follow my grandfather around, had noticed the odd strand of black hair on a head mostly grey, and observed the face tanned and wrinkled like an apple stripped of its peel and left too long in the open air. Never a tall woman, age had further diminished Grandma's stature.

For some reason, her question had affected me profoundly and reminded me of my own uncertainty. In a few short months, I would be a licensed physician, and yet I was having doubts about my chosen profession. I lacked passion for my work. Though I enjoyed studying chemistry, biology, and physiology, treating patients failed to provide me with the satisfaction I had expected. If someone had told me, before I started medical school, how I would feel around sick people—some of them complainers and malingerers—or that my patients would expect miracle cures rather than take proper care of themselves, I might not have gone into medicine.

In hindsight, I realize I should have been more realistic—after all, medicine is about illness, disease, and healing. It was only at that point, after years of study and work in hospital wards, that I had a clearer idea of what my career entailed. Now that I was so close to the end, I wondered if I had what it took to be a dedicated doctor. If I even cared about being a doctor. Could I have chosen a different career? Hard to know. After all, I had wanted to be a doctor for so long that I hadn't explored other careers. And what would happen if I did do something else?

"You know, leaving the pot to boil dry may have been the first bit of odd behaviour," said Grandpa, referring to our earlier conversation, "but the first time I really understood something was wrong was when your grandmother rearranged the house."

Mom laughed and looked at me. "You haven't heard this one?"

I shook my head.

A moment passed before Grandpa continued. "I left home to do some errands one afternoon. Viktoria hadn't done anything more than let a pot or two boil dry—unusual but not enough to indicate there was any real need for concern. When I got home, I found her exactly where I had left her, working with her flowers in the front yard. I went into the house. Max, it was as if I'd walked into a stranger's home. I can't explain it, other than to say that something didn't feel right. The furniture was all there. The pictures were hanging in the same spots. The dirty dishes were still in the sink. But somehow there was an emptiness. I looked around puzzled. Suddenly, it dawned on me...where were all the plants? As you know, Grandma not only loved growing flowers and trees in her garden, she also loved the greenery and vibrant colours of the flowers throughout the house."

Grandpa paused. His eyes had a distant expression, as if he had gone back in time. Then he went on. "When I realized the plants were missing, I thought maybe she had

taken them outside to repot, but when I looked outside, I
didn't see any houseplants. I was stunned that all of these
plants could just disappear. It wasn't possible. I was about to
ask your grandmother where they were, when I noticed soil,
like a cat's paw, extending from beneath the front closet. I
opened the closet. To my amazement, twenty houseplants
had been thrown in there helter-skelter. I couldn't believe it!
Since there should have been at least a hundred plants in the
house, I went from closet to closet and opened them. Sure
enough, I found the rest."

"Did you speak to Grandma about them?"

"I did. I went back outside and asked her why the plants
were in the closets. She looked at me with a straight face and
said, 'Because they were bad.'" Grandpa chuckled. "I don't
know what the plants did to piss off your grandmother, but
they never did it again."

I wondered how my grandfather could laugh. My grandmother's growing confusion and memory loss saddened me
profoundly—maybe because I knew from experience where
her path would inevitably lead. I had already completed a
stretch in a geriatric ward. The men and women there, forced
through necessity to leave their homes and spouses, lingered
in various stages of dementia. Those furthest along were
often angry, confused by their unfamiliar surroundings, or
immobile, lying in bed unwilling to move. My grandfather,
wise man that he was, must have known what to expect. Yet
even though he was losing more of his wife day by day, he
seemed able to accept the situation stoically.

"I have another childhood memory," said Mom, rubbing
her hands together as if for warmth. "Conrad and I got into a
big sack of flour in the pantry. It felt so good to dip our hands
in the soft flour. Pretty soon we started to fling handfuls all

over the kitchen. When your grandma came back from the neighbour's, the kitchen was covered in flour."

"Did you catch hell?" I asked.

"No. Your grandma walked into the kitchen, grabbed some change from her flour-covered purse and took us to a café on Bloor Street, where she treated us to milkshakes and pie. It was if she was rewarding us for what we'd done. I can still picture the tracks her shoes left as she walked across the kitchen floor. I remember thinking it looked like it had snowed in the house."

"She actually took you for milkshakes and pies?" I asked disbelievingly.

"Yes, really good pie too. Flapper pie!"

"*Why?*"

"What else could she do? She had only herself to blame, leaving two young children alone, even if it was just for a few minutes. She was a good mother."

Grandpa reached over and put his hand lovingly on Mom's arm. They shared a long look and an understanding that I was not part of.

Suddenly, I remembered a hot day in July 1949, a few weeks after my tenth birthday. I had been outside all day, playing Red Rover and tag with my friends. Before falling asleep that night, my legs felt stiff and sore. Next morning when I tried to get out of bed, I fell on the floor. I called my mother and told her to look at my legs because they were still sleeping. A flash of terror ripped across her face—the first and only time I saw her frightened. She was barely taller than me, but she lifted me in her arms, put me in the car, and took me to the Hospital for Sick Children.

I spent the next three months in the polio ward. Three times a day, the nurses would apply hot wet woollen cloths, called Sister Kenny Hot Packs, to my legs. The packs were meant to help loosen muscles, relieve pain, and enable my legs to be moved, stretched, and strengthened. After that, the nurses rubbed my legs with hot oil. Twice a day, my physical therapists encouraged me to get on a bicycle equipped with training wheels and to pedal the corridors of the ward. The rest of the time, I listened to baseball games on the radio and played with my new friends, who were in wheelchairs or on crutches like me.

I was one of the fortunate ones—I was only paralyzed from the waist down. Some of the people, many of them kids my age, could not breathe on their own and were placed in iron lungs, the "whoo-ish" sound filling the wards. Mom and Dad visited every day. Through the window separating us, I would tell them about my new friends, the nurses, the doctors, and the games we played. Like all parents, they brought gifts. The wealthier ones brought toys; the poorer ones lumps of sugar. Mom and Dad were always smiling and talkative, maybe because I was getting better, but I saw many parents with puffy, red eyes who would leave quickly as their tears flowed.

Three months later, I walked out of the hospital unaided. Before I left, I promised my favourite nurse Miss Hanham that I would be a doctor one day. From then on, every time I was asked what I wanted to be when I grew up, I said, "A doctor."

But it wasn't what I wanted anymore. The realization worried me. Again, I asked myself, what would I be if not a doctor? If I did something else, would that change me? Would I become something less if I did something less prestigious than medicine? Would I lose some part of myself? For so long, becoming a physician was part of my identity. Without a clear identity, I was disoriented, as if I'd been riding a fast-moving merry-go-round for too long. There was a haven of security in knowing who I was going to be, and that haven was vanishing.

"Your grandmother loved horses," said Grandpa, drawing me out of my reverie. "We used to borrow old Mr. Issacman's mares. He had a farm not far from our place on Concord Avenue."

"I remember him. Conrad and I used to raid his garden for peas. Threatened to shoot us, the old grouch," Mom reflected.

Grandpa laughed. "We told him to say that."

"*What?*"

"Just to see if it had any effect on you kids."

"Dad!"

"You turned out all right." He was still amused. "We rode those mares of his every Saturday before you kids came along. There's a great picture of Viktoria and me standing on them." Grandpa went looking for the photo. He was back quickly. "She's hiding that one again," he said, referring to Grandma's habit of hiding things that held strong memories for her. "But I found these." He handed me a pile of grainy black and white 5 x 7 photos.

The captions on the back of the photos identified members of Grandma's family. For the first time I saw pictures of my great-grandparents. In some of the photos they were cradling babies—Grandma and her two sisters.

"There's one of you and her in there somewhere," said Grandpa.

I flipped through the batch until I found a picture of Grandma and myself feeding a horse. It was taken in 1944, when I was five. A year later, Grandma and Grandpa would move to Edmonton.

"I remember this!" I said, too loudly, for Mom motioned me to keep my voice down. The picture evoked a memory of walking towards a barbed-wire fence where two or three horses stood. At the fence, Grandma would place a carrot in my outstretched hand so that I could offer the treat to whichever horse butted its head closest to me. I recall the tickling caress of gentle lips. I fed them one at a time. When the last carrot had been devoured, Grandma, her strength belying her shortness, would manage to balance me on a fence post. Standing there, secure in Grandma's arms, I enjoyed stroking the firm necks of the horses until they grew bored with us and wandered away in search of something more interesting.

"Here's another good one," said Grandpa.

Pictured was a group of people, all wearing white lab coats. In the foreground, Bunsen burners, beakers, graduated cylinders, filter flasks, test tubes, and a mortar and pestle crowded together on a table. Of the thirty-odd people, only one was a woman—Grandma, very young and fresh faced.

"Who are they?" I asked, intrigued.

"A bunch of Viktoria's undergrad students. See there, that's Charlie Best on her right."

"*Charles Best?*" Wide-eyed, I gaped at Grandpa. "Of Banting and Best? The men who discovered insulin?"

"The very same. Viktoria was a lecturer then. A few years later, she became an associate professor. You didn't know that, Max?"

"I knew Grandma taught university. I didn't know about Charles Best." I looked at my mother, wondering how I had missed this fascinating bit of information.

"It was long before you were born, honey. I haven't thought about it for years. My mother never was one to talk about herself."

"She was something else." Grandpa beamed. "In those days not many women went to university, let alone taught. Hell, women weren't even allowed to vote yet! A lot of men didn't believe she was capable of teaching—doing a man's work."

I had no women professors even now, I thought.

"Even when things were difficult," Grandpa said proudly, "I never saw Viktoria without a smile on her face."

I must have had an unpleasant look on mine.

Grandpa looked at me. "Burr under your saddle, Max?"

I bit my lip, unable to speak. I felt quite remote from Mom and Grandpa just then. Conscience-stricken. I had listened to them sharing their memories about Grandma, while at the same time I was keeping important information from them. I needed to come clean about Grandma's further mental deterioration.

I looked from my mother to my grandfather. "Grandma asked me today, 'Who am I?'"

Grandpa nodded. "She asks that once in a while," he said, without a trace of sadness in his voice.

"What do you tell her?"

"That she's anything she wants to be."

"Why?"

"Because it's what she believed." Seeing my bewilderment, Grandpa went on. "Didn't your mom ever tell you that you could be anything you wanted to be?"

I nodded, and Mom smiled. I had heard the words a million times. Mom and Dad hadn't pressured me to become a doctor—or anything else for that matter.

"So, why the look?" Grandpa persisted.

"Why wouldn't you remind Grandma she's your wife and a mother? Something like that?"

Grandpa yawned and stretched. "Because she's no one thing. She's much more complex than that." He gave me a probing look. "Do you understand, Max?"

"Yes," I lied.

"Good. Well, I better hit the kip. Viktoria went down early tonight." Grandpa gave my mom a hug and told me to wake him if I needed help.

I walked Mom to the door. "You okay?" she asked, as she put on her jacket.

"Yes. Just have lots of studying to get done."

"Don't work too hard." She gave me a hug, "Thanks for helping out tonight. I know you're busy." She drove away and I locked the door.

I walked quietly around the house that was becoming gradually more familiar to me. I wondered what would happen to it when Grandpa became too old to care for it. A carpenter by trade, my grandfather had built the house. "First came out here in '14," he once told me, "but we weren't ready to leave Toronto then. Wasn't a hell of a lot here at the time, but I sure loved the big open sky. It was like there was more room to breathe. And that river valley in the summer— green as an emerald. I knew then we'd come back one day." Right after the Second World War, my grandparents moved permanently to Edmonton. They found a piece of land west of the old McKernan homestead and south of the University of Alberta and built their retirement home. The little house, painted yellow with light green trim on the eaves, doors, and windows was now becoming the cosiest, most secure place I knew.

I went into the living room to sit down on the chesterfield and read. As I sat down, I felt something hard beneath one of the cushions. Reaching underneath, I pulled out a gilt-framed photo and an old book, both no doubt hidden by my grandmother. The photo was of Grandpa and Grandma standing side by side on top of three saddled horses, like a couple of trick riders in a circus. They were decked out in chaps, vests, and cowboy hats. Both were smiling and full of the joy of youth. I studied the photo, then put it on the coffee table and opened the old book. It took me a few moments to recognize it. It was the old journal.

It was years since I had seen the old wreck with its tattered corners and yellowed paper. My mother had often read it to me when I was young and told me one day I would add a story of my own to it. The stories hadn't interested me much then. At the time, I was too absorbed in tree forts and board games and the neighbours' three-legged dog to give much attention to some ratty old diary. The only part of the journal I did find intriguing was the geographic coordinates at the end of the original entry. I liked to imagine that the coordinates would lead me to buried pirate treasure. I sighed, wishing I were young and naive again.

I closed the old journal and lay down on the chesterfield to think about my situation. It seemed so simple when I was young. I knew what I wanted to be, and my teachers praised and encouraged my choice of career, solidifying my sense of self. What would those teachers think if I were to abandon medicine? What would my friends think of their former valedictorian, the boy most likely to succeed? What would my family think? Was I measured by the expectations of others?

I thought back to my first year anatomy class when our professor held up his hand and asked, "Is this my hand?" Sensing a trick, the class had remained silent until an intrepid student responded in the affirmative. "Has this always been my hand?" the professor continued. A student behind me said, "Yes." "Will this always be my hand?" This time I said, "Yes." "Consider," the professor said, "that it takes approximately seven years for every cell in your hand to be replaced. All your blood, bones, muscles, tendons, ligaments, hair, fingernails, skin, and fluids—what you now call your hand—was not a part of your hand seven years ago.

From down the hall, I heard some rustling and then a door opened. I lifted my head and saw Grandma. She wore a yellow housecoat, embroidered with delicate little blue-petalled flowers, over Grandpa's full-length, red, button-up long johns, which were rolled up at the ankles and sleeves.

I stood and said, "Hello."

"Conrad!" she said. In her state of dementia, she'd mistaken me for her son. "Did you see what Emily's boy drew today?" She scurried into the guest bedroom, returning with a sheet of orange cardboard paper, which she handed to me. It was a childish drawing of two stick characters, one smaller than the other, executed in black crayon. The smaller figure held what looked like a hammer; the larger one a saw. On one side a shining purple sun beat down on a half-built yellow house.

"Max drew it," Grandma said enthusiastically. On the back, in my mother's distinctive, bold handwriting were the words, "Max and his Grandpa building the house. October 1945." I was six when I drew it—a lifetime before polio, a lifetime before medical school.

"Emily tells me he wants to be a carpenter like his grandpa."

I searched my mind but didn't remember ever wanting to be a carpenter. "What if he wants to be something else?" I asked. My neck and shoulders ached with sudden tension.

"I suspect he will," she said matter of factly.

But it can't be that easy, can it? I asked myself. I expected no reply to the unspoken question. I felt as fragile as an origami crane, at the mercy of a slight breeze or angry hand. *Who am I? How do I find my place in the world?* I wondered.

It was as if Grandma had heard the questions in my mind. This mother, daughter, grandmother, wife, girlfriend, animal lover, chemist, and gardener reached up and took my face firmly, but gently, in her bird-like hands. Her eyes as sober as if a piece of her formal vital self had returned, she looked hard at me, then said, "Never let anyone define you."

And then the look was gone. Confusion replaced her lucidity. But that moment was enough. "Where am I going?" she asked. Without a word, I put her arm on mine and turned towards her bedroom.

Maximilian Curtis Herac

Richard

As we pull into the well-lit parking lot, I am struck by the construction of the hospital: a six-storey building of brown brick and concrete, one section being twentieth-century modern and the other nineteenth century or so.

A few windows in both hospital wings are aglow with late-night activity. Are Jenner and Kimberly Herac receiving attention in those illuminated rooms?

As Sonia and I go through the doors into emergency, I wonder how to explain our situation. To whom should we talk? What do we say? Do we tell the whole story, from arriving at the scene of the accident, to pulling the couple to safety from the partly burning car? Will we be forced to give our names? What if, in our efforts to rescue Jenner and Kimberly, we have badly injured them? Would they sue us if they were paralyzed, even though we had no choice but to act as we did? How do we get their possessions to them without incurring trouble ourselves?

"Wait," Sonia says, as the automatic doors close behind us. "I need the keys."

As she goes to the car, I look around.

To my left, a heavy-set security guard sporting gel-spiked hair lounges behind the information desk. He is reading a tattered magazine, his feet are propped up on the desk, and he looks half asleep.

To my right, nine or so people take up a quarter of the chairs in the waiting area. Some talk in hushed tones. There is a noticeable absence of laughter, coupled with a sense of tension and seriousness.

The automatic doors swing open beside me—Sonia, I think. Instead, I watch two paramedics quickly wheeling an elderly woman on a stretcher past me. The woman's skin is ashen and tissue-paper thin, and her eyes are closed. The brief glimpse reveals red marks on the bridge of her nose, and I know she usually wears ill-fitting glasses.

The smell of disinfectant in the emergency room is starting to make me feel nauseous. As I shift restlessly from one foot to the other, I consider waiting outside for Sonia. But tempted though I am, I decide to try to tough it out instead. I tell myself I'm too old to let this smell bother me any longer and wonder what would have happened if Sonia had given birth to Nadie and Aidan in a hospital. Could I have stayed by her side? I can't answer that. Thankfully, she gave birth to both kids at home with the help of a midwife.

As I wait for Sonia to return, I try to concentrate only on pleasant memories: holding Nadie for the first time, Aidan's first steps, teaching the two of them to ride a bike. Yet, despite all my efforts, the disinfectant smell continues to fill my nostrils, and long-buried memories stubbornly resurrect themselves.

"You'll be fine," the young nurse promised me before I was wheeled into surgery. I was six-years-old and already the veteran of seven operations. I knew this one would hurt.

Pleadingly, I looked at my mother, who gripped the railing of my bed, her knuckles as white as the tissue she clutched. "Do I have to?" I wished she would yank the bed away from the nurse, race down the hallway with it, bundle me into the car, and take me home.

But she only bit her lip, her face pained. "You want to be normal like other boys don't you? You'd like to kick a ball around with your friends. Play soccer, and one day, hockey?" she asked softly.

"Yes Mommy," I forced myself to say unhappily.

I was born with a club foot on my right side. The foot was turned in and smaller than my normal left foot; even after seven operations, the calf muscle was still very underdeveloped.

"Be strong," my mother said; then she let go of the bed. The nurse wheeled me through the operating-room doors as my mother waved goodbye. The last I saw of her was the tissue sticking out between her fingers, as if it were trying to squirm free of her tightening fist.

The nurse parked my bed in the middle of a holding area, a large peach-coloured room with white trim that framed the walls. I saw other people on beds, all of them lying still. I wondered if they were dead.

"Don't cry now, sweetie," the young nurse said, as she checked my chart and made notes.

I tried to be strong for my mother. I knew how important all these surgeries were to her, and I didn't want to disappoint her. I wanted to stop crying but I couldn't.

The young nurse was compassionate. "Can you count to one hundred?" she asked gently.

I nodded.

"Good for you. Aren't you a big boy. See this?" She pointed to a bottle turned upside down with fluid dripping from it. As I grew older, I would learn more about intravenous lines.

I nodded again and wiped my nose with my thin cotton robe.

"I want you to count the drops," she said. "And when you get to a hundred, start again. See how many times you can get to a hundred. All right?"

Obediently, I began to count. When the nurse was ready to take me to the operating theatre, I had reached 326, stopped crying, and was feeling a little woozy.

In the theatre, the nurse told me to start counting again while she left me alone a few seconds. The smell of disinfectant was so strong that it made me feel too sick to concentrate on counting. I tried to breathe through my mouth instead of my nose, but even then the smell didn't get any better.

All around me, staff in masks and gowns were busy opening and closing cabinets containing clear glass vials, rubber tubing, folded blankets, and metal pans. Beside my bed was a cart covered with a blue cloth. Underneath the cloth were bumps of different sizes. Someone brushed past accidentally, pulling away the cloth to reveal various knives and other instruments of torture. On the second shelf of the cart was a gadget that looked like my father's power saw.

"Nooooo!" I screamed, convinced they were going to cut my foot off.

A startled nurse turned to me.

"No! No! No!" I kept screaming over and over again as I tried to get off the bed.

"What is it? What is it?" the nurse asked soothingly.

"No! No! No! No!" I kept yelling.

She wrapped her arms around me, but I flailed and bit her shoulder in a desperate attempt to get away.

"What the hell is going on in here?" yelled a doctor, probably the surgeon.

The nurse saw the uncovered instrument cart and tried to replace the blue cloth, while still trying to restrain to me.

"Get that kid under control," ordered the doctor.

A few gowned nurses came to the scene and calmed me down.

"What's the matter, sweetie?" asked the nurse whose shoulder I had bitten. Her voice was gentle, even though I had bitten her as hard as I could.

"My foot is okay. I don't want it cut off!" I was distraught. "I just want to go home."

"Is that what you think?" she asked compassionately. "Nobody is going to cut off your foot, sweetie. We're going to fix it for you."

"The saw." I pointed at the blue cloth on the surgery cart, beneath which, I knew, lay the dreaded instrument.

The nurse laughed softly. The saw was for cutting off casts, she told me, and I didn't have one. Even if I did, the procedure wouldn't hurt.

Another masked doctor—the anaesthetist, I learned—came to my side. "We're going to put you to sleep now," he said quietly. "You won't feel a thing." He was friendlier than the impatient doctor.

As the anaesthetist put something over my nose, the friendly nurse promised not to leave me, and told me to count to ten. I remember getting as far as five....

When I opened my eyes later that day, my mother was sitting by my bed, reading a magazine. "Mommy," I said weakly.

"Darling, you're awake!" she said, jumping up. "How do you feel?"

How did I feel? Well, my head felt as if it had been stuffed with cotton, my throat hurt, and there was something heavy on my right leg. How had it got there? I tried to think back, but the last thing I remembered was the disinfectant smell, the thing on my nose, and counting to five.

Unable to feel my toes, I tried to wiggle them—but I couldn't. I reached down to touch my foot, but couldn't get to it.

"My foot is gone! I can't feel it," I exclaimed in high panic.

"No, darling. It's still there. You can't feel it because you have a cast on your leg," my mother explained.

Days passed. I ate lots of ice-cream and other food I enjoyed, and my family brought gifts and made a great fuss of me. I couldn't wait to get home. In time, of course, the cast was removed, but unfortunately, the surgery wasn't quite as successful as my mother had hoped it would be.

I am thinking of the kind nurses and the impatient surgeon as Sonia returns from the car.

"I found this at the accident," she says, and shows me a black wallet.

We open it and along with various customer loyalty cards and a bank card, we find a driver's licence in the name of Jenner Curtis Herac of Vancouver, British Columbia.

There is also a laminated card with the names of people to contact in case of emergency. The first name on the list is Kimberly Herac, with the word "wife" in brackets. The second name is Maximilian Herac, and the third is Charlotte Herac. Kimberly has a British Columbian phone number. Maximilian and Charlotte Herac's number has an Albertan area code.

Card in hand, Sonia approaches the sleepy guard at the information desk. "We're looking for Jenner and Kimberly Herac. They were brought in by ambulance about an hour ago."

The guard types the names into the computer, studies the screen, then shakes his head. "How do you spell the names?" he asks.

Sonia spells the names and explains about the car accident. Still, the guard can't locate the Heracs, and I begin to wonder if Jenner and Kimberly survived the ambulance ride. If not, there might have been no reason to enter their names into the hospital's computer system. My muscles tighten as I watch the man, and I begin to feel a little ill. Glancing at Sonia, I see my tension reflected in her face.

The guard lifts his head at length. "Sorry. Nothing." He gives a small shrug.

"They were brought here, though," Sonia says beseechingly. We have probably reached the same conclusion: Jenner and Kimberly are dead. Sonia looks on the verge of tears again.

"Perhaps they were taken immediately into surgery," the guard says hopefully.

"Where are the operating rooms?" I ask, as Sonia nervously twists her wedding band and scratches her forearm.

The guard gives us vague directions, though he says we cannot go there on our own.

We don't listen to further protests but head the way he explained, following signs as we go. We find Surgery and are all ready to explain once more; however, nobody is at the nursing station. Frustrated, we look around and understand we have no option but to wait. Sonia sits down while I begin to pace. The smell of disinfectant is even stronger here than in Emergency, and I breathe through my mouth in an attempt to quell my returning queasiness.

Sonia darts me a quizzical look, her lips pursed, her eyebrows raised. She knows how much I hate hospitals, and why. I wait for her to say something sympathetic, and for a moment she seems about to—then remains silent. Is she punishing me for cutting short our vacation? Maybe she is hurt, because she does not acknowledge my distress. I sit down a few seats away from her.

Some ten minutes go by before a nurse, wearing green

scrubs, appears. Her hairnet, filled with dark hair, resembles a tick engorged on blood.

"*Bonjour?*" she says, questioningly.

As we get to our feet, Sonia says, "*Bonjour.* We're looking for people...the name is Herac. Jenner and Kimberly Herac. They were in a car accident. We think they were brought here."

The nurse looks at us. "Are you family?"

Sonia explains our situation. The accident. Pulling Jenner and Kimberly from the car. Collecting their possessions.

Apparently satisfied with the explanation, the nurse tells us both Heracs are in surgery.

We wait tensely for her to say more. Though we are not family, all the same we are intimately involved in what has happened to the injured couple. It would be an act of charity on her part to ease our minds. Yet perhaps the prognosis is not good, for all she says is, "We'll know more tomorrow. I'm sorry."

Sonia's shoulders slump noticeably. She looks disappointed as she gives the list of emergency names and phone numbers to the nurse. "We found this at the accident."

The nurse takes a second to read the laminated card. "*Merci, Madame.* Someone will contact these people," she promises, and then leaves.

There is nothing more we can do. We will have to wait until morning to phone the hospital and find out if Jenner and Kimberly have lived through the night.

Emily Alethea Herac (née Linck)

April 25, 1948

The first time I laid eyes on Settie was in 1921. Of course, I didn't know his name then; I would only discover it years later. I was six-years-old, playing with my doll on the front steps. He was riding his adult-sized tricycle past our home on Concord Avenue in Toronto. He leaned over the front handlebars, his thin legs pumping madly, his white beard fluttering at his chin, and his long grey hair flowing back from his head. Had he weighed a hundred pounds more, he might have passed for a department store Santa Claus. As it was, his slim frame and worn clothes made him look like a derelict old man who survived by collecting deposits on empty bottles.

My brother, Conrad, and I were walking to school a few years later, when I saw Settie again. He looked no different from the first time.

"Neat bicycle," I said. I had not forgotten the tricycle with its wooden bin placed between the two rear wheels, large enough to carry my dog, Billy Bishop, in it.

"It's a tricycle, not a bicycle. It has three wheels, not two," Conrad told me. He was four years older than me and knew a lot more than I did.

"Tricycle, then. His tricycle is neat."

"He's a loon, and his tricycle is stupid," said Conrad.

I expected a punch then. Conrad had a habit of punching me—not very hard—whenever he said the word "stupid," as if the word triggered his fist to connect with the nearest thing, usually me. But for some reason, no punch appeared.

"What do you mean, he's a loon?" I asked curiously.

"He's crazy. If someone is a loon, it means they're crazy. For an eight-year-old you sure don't know much, Emily."

I was indignant. "I know lots. I know all the provinces in Canada and all the capitals of the provinces and all the prime ministers of Canada."

"Big deal," was my brother's response.

I hadn't realized yet that whatever I was learning, Conrad had mastered years before. My brother was very bright. I knew that because of all the awards he'd won. Each year the student with the highest marks for arithmetic, geography, history & civics, and composition & spelling won a Hershey's chocolate bar. There was also a Good Citizenship Award. Conrad had won all five chocolate bars that year. He'd given me two of them.

"Why is that guy crazy?" I asked.

"He just is. Everyone says so."

"Mom says a thing isn't true just because someone says it is," I told Conrad.

I had him, I thought gleefully. I was always trying to outwit my brother, but so far without success. I felt good about my chances this time.

"If that's what Mom says, she isn't necessarily correct either—in which case, everyone else might be right about him." Conrad grinned triumphantly. I didn't follow his logic, but the look on his face told me I'd been trumped.

A month later, I saw Settie again. It was lunch hour, and he was riding his tricycle past the far end of the school playground. He wore the same outfit as before. I was watching him when I overheard some boys talk about throwing stones at him. I turned around and saw my brother's friends Peter, Edwin, and Cyril.

"What are you looking at?" Peter asked aggressively. He was bald and self-conscious about it. His parents had found lice in his hair. The infestation was so bad, they had had to shave him clean.

"Nothing...."

"Thought so," he said, and bounced a fair-sized rock in his hand.

At the far end of the playground, Settie made a left turn and began to pedal towards us.

"He's coming," Peter said to the other two. Then he took a step towards me, so he could get closer to the street and his intended target. "Out of my way, or I'll sock you one," he ordered. I stepped aside quickly, more for fear of lice than a punch. Edwin and Cyril were close behind Peter.

Settie pedalled slowly towards us. Along the sidewalk, the boys lined up like a firing squad. Each one held a stone the size of a crab apple. They kept their hands at their sides, I noticed, so as not to spook their prey.

"Don't do it," I warned, as Settie got closer. I couldn't understand why anyone would want to attack this sad-looking, old man. Judging by his clothing, I couldn't help thinking he probably didn't have a warm place to sleep or enough to eat.

Peter ignored me as he eyed his victim.

"Buzz off, Coke Bottle," Edwin said.

I was called Coke Bottle because of my thick glasses. I hated the nickname.

"Buzz off, Coke Bottle," Cyril echoed.

I willed Settie to turn back or a teacher to come out of the school and see what was about to happen, but no teacher miraculously appeared, and Settie was about to be injured.

"I'll throw tomatoes at you if you hurt him," I yelled, recalling a few my father had missed in our little garden, and which now hung rotten with an early frost.

"Dry up, Coke Bottle," Peter said, as Settie, oblivious to the danger he was in, drew parallel with us.

Teeth clenched and eyes squinting, Peter cocked back his arm.

I stared helplessly, knowing I couldn't just let the old man be cruelly attacked, no matter that I was outnumbered. "Don't throw anything at him!" I screeched, in the same moment as I pushed Edwin into Peter.

Edwin stumbled, and as I'd hoped, knocked Peter off balance. But Peter recovered quickly. "Think you're so tough?" he hollered, turning on me. The stone was still clutched in his hand. He raised his arm again, as if to throw it at me.

As I ran off, I was thinking—almost hoping—the boys would chase me rather than turn their attention back to Settie. I should have known that the victim riding slowly by would be an easier, more tantalizing target than the wily one running away.

Settie had not heard the altercation between Peter and me above the louder shrieking and yelling of the children playing in the schoolyard. The three ruffians unleashed their arsenal at the unwary man. In their eagerness to hit him, they aimed badly and missed. Thwarted by his own eagerness, Peter yelled out in frustration at Settie, who had already ridden some way further, "Get out of here you old crazy!"

Settie heard Peter this time and turned around. In a rage I did not understand, Peter picked up another stone, a large one, and hurled it at the old man.

Settie twisted his handlebars quickly to the left to avoid being struck. But too late. The rock struck him hard on the arm. Instinctively, Settie jerked the handlebars even further, sending him crashing into the front tire of a Ford Model T parked on the side of the road. The collision threw him over the handlebars. As he fell, he hit his head on the front fender of the car.

"What's the matter? Can't ride a baby's bike?" Peter yelled. The boys laughed as Settie lay unmoving on the ground.

So incensed was I at the unprovoked attack on this defenceless man that I ignored the threat of lice, as well as my own basic need for self-preservation, and rushed at Peter. I tried to tackle him but failed to bring him down. There was, however, a satisfying grunted "oof" as the air left his lungs. He recovered quickly. Throwing me off, he pushed me to the ground.

"You asked for it," he yelled viciously, and jumped on top of me. My eyes closed; I thought I was done for. A moment passed, and then, abruptly, Peter's body was lifted from mine. I looked up. A teacher must have seen what was happening and hurried to my rescue. To my astonishment, I saw my brother clutching Peter's shirt and yanking him backwards.

"Leave her alone!" ordered Conrad, pulling Peter a few steps further, then swinging him around in the opposite direction.

The instant Conrad let go of Peter's shirt, Peter came back at me. Once more, my brother intervened. Getting between us, he growled "No!" His voice low and icy, a tone I had never heard before. I didn't like it.

"Coke Bottle started it," Peter began to defend himself. "The bearcat jumped...." He stopped abruptly. Conrad was staring at him, as if daring him to continue. Since Conrad was smaller than Peter, I'd have thought Peter could take him easily. Yet something told me—and Peter must have sensed it too—that Conrad's mood was dangerous; he wasn't to be trifled with that day.

As if to regain some dignity, Peter tucked his shirt back into his pants and gave me a dirty look. For a moment, I thought he meant to provoke Conrad further. But no. "Let's go," he muttered to his pals. Edwin and Cyril looked from my brother, to Peter, to each other. They moved away then, obediently following Peter.

I watched them slink off, then turned quickly towards Settie, who had been lying prone on the ground after the attack. To my relief, he was no longer lying in the street but was sitting up, brushing the dirt from his trousers, and investigating a hole in his sleeve. He didn't appear to be injured and was even able to stand. After checking his tricycle and the car and finding them both undamaged, he squinted at Conrad and me. I thought he would go into the school and report to a teacher what had happened. But he only lifted his cap—quite amazingly, it had remained on his head during the collision—bowed deeply, as if greeting royalty, got on his tricycle, and pedalled away.

As we walked home, I asked Conrad about his friends.

"They're not my friends anymore," he said grimly.

"Why not?"

"They're bullies and they're immature."

"What's immature?"

"They haven't grown up."

"Have you?" I asked, wondering if this was the reason why I hadn't been punched lately.

"Yes," he said firmly. "Anyway, I've stopped associating with immature people."

"Am I immature?" I asked, a little afraid to hear the answer.

"There's hope for you."

Conrad grinned at me, and I felt a warm surge of joy. Even then, I couldn't quite trust his answer.

"If I'm not mature yet, does that mean that you won't play with me anymore?"

"No, Emily, we can still play together. Sometimes."

"Good," I said with relief, feeling that everything was okay with my little world.

"Conrad...why did the old man bow to us?"

My brother looked thoughtful. "I don't know, Em."

About that time, Conrad and I began a new ritual. On Saturday mornings after breakfast, we'd walk the few blocks to the Dovercourt branch of the Toronto Public Library: a brown brick two-storey (if you include the basement) at the corner of Bloor Street and Gladstone Avenue, with high-arched windows and great, grey stone steps leading up to the front door. The children's section was in the basement; the upper floor housed the "adult" books and periodicals.

At the stairs we would part, and I would make my way to the well-lit corner of the basement for the highlight of my week—reading hour. Thirty or forty children usually gathered around the librarian, Mrs. Smith, as she sat beside the fireplace and read to us. My mother and father had read to me for as long as I could remember, but there was something special about sitting surrounded by shelves of books and other children, all of us oohing and aahing to the same story. It was better than a picture show. Once story hour was over, I would choose a book for the week, meet Conrad on the library steps, and then we would walk or ride our bicycles home for lunch.

This routine went on throughout the winter, spring, and summer, until one day I decided to look at the same books as my brother did. When I informed Conrad of my intention to join him upstairs after story hour, he told me I couldn't.

"Little kids are not allowed up there," he said.

"Why not?"

"They're too loud."

"I promise not to make noise," I whispered, showing him how quietly I could speak.

"At any rate, you wouldn't be interested in the books up there," he said, thereby increasing my desire all the more.

I pleaded, but with no success.

"When you're mature," Conrad intoned.

"When will that be?"

"I'll let you know. You can't rush these things."

My parents had made it clear that Conrad was "in charge" on these excursions. The instruction was only given out of concern for my safety, not because they wanted to keep me from any particular part of the library. I don't know if Conrad was aware of this or if he just liked to have power over me. In any event, though I did as I was told, I pouted during story hour and spent the time considering revolt. Later, when we met on the front steps, Conrad asked about my book for the week. In an inspired moment, I said, "I didn't find anything interesting. I think I'm too mature for children's books now."

He looked at me sideways, but only said, "Let's go then."

All that week, I wished I had something to read.

The following week I watched Conrad climb the stairs to his "mature" area of the library. Overwhelmed with curiosity, but with no particular plan in mind, I waited until he was out of sight before I followed him. At the top of the stairs, like a stone gargoyle, sat an old man behind a huge desk covered in books. He was writing in a ledger. I waited for him to scold me for being there as I was not old enough to be upstairs, but as he didn't seem to notice me, I slunk past him into one of the two big rooms that occupied the main floor. The room was filled with serious-looking people and rows of darkly stained shelves at least twice as tall as me. In the children's section, I was tall enough to see over the shelves, but here I could not reach the top shelf, even when I stood on my tippytoes.

Scared the librarian or Conrad would see me and send me back downstairs, I quickly hid behind the closest bookshelf. All the shelves were open, and where there were no books blocking my view, I could see right through to the back of the library. For once my smallness was an advantage, because I could see most of the room without having to bend down or climb onto a chair. I scanned the area for Conrad and saw him almost immediately; he was three rows down and moving to my right. Wanting to keep some distance between us, I moved to my left. When he moved to the next row, I moved a row as well. Like an experienced hunter, I tracked my quarry, never letting him know of my presence.

This "game" continued for about ten minutes until Conrad found the books he was after and sat down to read at one of the large tables in the middle of the room. Confident that he was settled, I began to scan the shelves for something I would enjoy reading. I saw titles like *European Masterpieces* and *Origin of the Species* and authors like Victor Hugo and Samuel Butler, but none of them interested me. Disappointed, I was about to slip downstairs to wait for Conrad when I heard someone mumbling to himself. A few feet away, a shabbily dressed man shook his head vigorously as if in response to some inner question. Settie! I recognized him immediately.

I'd heard quite recently that only crazy people talked to themselves and that craziness was contagious. Having already observed Settie's unusual behaviour and concerned it might infect me, I darted to the end of the row of shelves, to what I judged a safe distance.

I watched as Settie read and murmured quietly to himself. I saw him pull a slip of paper from his pocket and make a few notes in pencil, then close the book, and walk further. As he read something else a few rows away, I pulled his original choice from the shelf. Titled *The Meaning of Relativity,* it was written by a man called Albert Einstein. I didn't understand a word of it, and after a few seconds, I replaced the book and went back to watching Settie. Once again, he read a while, made some notes on his scrap of paper, and then put the book back. When he'd moved on, I saw it was called *Science and Hypothesis* and was by Henri Poincare. After he had made notes on a few more books, he left the room. Or so I thought.

Near one of the volumes he'd glanced at, *Philosophiae Naturalis Prinicipia Mathematica* by Isaac Newton, I happened to see a book called *Math Wizard*: a book of mathematical games and puzzles. Math was a subject I enjoyed. At last, something interesting! Forgetting Settie, I began to solve some of the problems in my head.

Absorbed in what I was doing, I did not hear the approach of shuffling footsteps. A tap on my shoulder had me lift my head. A pair of eerie-looking eyes stared down at me, the pink irises so narrow that black pupils seemed to fill his face. It was the first time I had actually noticed Settie's eyes.

His unexpected appearance and ghostly gaze heightened my fear of catching his craziness. Without thinking, I let out a squeal and dashed for the door.

As I ran past the librarian, still clutching the book, he called after me, "Hey there! You have to check that out."

Too unnerved by the encounter with Settie to heed the librarian's order, I flew down the stairs, ignored my bicycle, and began to run for home. I'd gone two blocks when, for some reason, I turned and saw my brother chasing after me. "Emily! Wait!" he shouted.

I slowed down and let Conrad catch up with me. "Something happened?" he asked, with obvious concern. I always felt safe around my brother.

"I came upstairs. I watched you. Then the old man came in, and I watched him. I thought he'd left, but he hadn't. He has such weird eyes, and I was scared. Oh, Conrad, I stole a book. I ran off with it. I didn't mean to, but I forgot I still had it. I'm sorry. What do I do now? Maybe they won't let me into the library anymore. *I'm sorry.*" The words came in a torrent and I began to cry.

Conrad took the book from my hand and put his arm around me. "It's okay, Emily. It's okay," he comforted again and again.

When he'd let me cry awhile, he said, "I'll return this to the library. I'll bring back your bicycle. Wait for me here, Emily."

Tears flowing more slowly now, I nodded.

He was back ten minutes later, riding his bike and guiding mine beside him. "It's okay. I talked to the librarian. Everything is okay."

"You won't tell Mom and Dad, will you?" I asked.

"No, Emily, I won't. Give me those," he said, reaching for my glasses. He cleaned the tear smudges off of the lenses with his handkerchief and handed them back to me.

"Thank you Conrad."

He nodded, and we rode our bikes home in silence.

We were putting away our bikes when Conrad asked if I'd understood the book I'd taken.

"I tried doing the puzzles in my head," I said, "but I couldn't do them all."

"You're fibbing, aren't you?"

"No."

He gave me an oddly curious look, as if he didn't know whether to believe me or not, but I didn't try to defend myself. My mind had only just caught up with the events at the library, and I couldn't help wondering why Settie, a man who was said to be a loon, had such a nice smell of soap about him.

That week, Conrad turned thirteen and was allowed to get a part-time job. He worked Saturdays, washing dishes at a café on the corner of Bloor and Delaware. His job meant the end of our Saturday morning library visits together, and Mom and Dad began to take me there instead. But it was no longer the same. I liked being around my brother, and besides, my parents stayed in the children's section while I chose my books. I guess I could have asked for permission to go upstairs, but I was still frightened of what the librarian might say to my parents or that I might meet Settie again.

After awhile, I forgot about Settie. It wasn't until I turned thirteen myself, the same year that Mom became one of the first women in the history of the University of Toronto to become an associate professor, that he came back into my life.

Like my brother before me, I was now allowed my first part-time job, and it also entailed washing dishes at a local café. That first Saturday morning, I got up early and rode my bicycle to work. While the cooks prepared the day's specials, I cleaned the last of the previous night's dishes, making sure to double-check that everything was in its proper place before the waitresses arrived to serve the first customers of the day.

At eleven o'clock, I stopped for lunch. Famished, I sat down at the counter and ordered a hamburger. Suddenly, a pleasant soapy smell wafted by. An evocative smell that awakened old memories. Looking up quickly, I saw a familiar figure sit down on the second seat from the end. Wearing the same clothes and not looking a day older than when I'd last seen him, he said a hearty, communal "Good morning." The five people seated at the counter, and the waitress behind it, responded with one voice, "Good morning, Settie."

I spent the last few minutes of my lunch break uneasily studying Settie out of the corner of my eyes. To my surprise—though by now I should have expected it—he was very clean. No grime on him anywhere; even his fingernails were neatly trimmed and dirt free. Though his grey beard and hair were very long, I saw no knots or tangles of the sort I got in my own hair sometimes. His clothes were somewhat worn, but well-mended. He didn't wear spectacles, but I noticed him hold up the menu at arm's length, as Dad did whenever he misplaced his glasses. Just in time, I glanced at the clock behind the counter, realized my break was over, and headed back to the kitchen and a new pile of dirty dishes.

I thought about Settie all the rest of that day. I knocked on my brother's door as soon as I got home.

"Come in," he shouted. He was leaning back in his chair, legs up on his desk, reading *The Brothers Karamazov*. "What's up?"

"Remember the fellow you said was a loon? The old man who rides around on a tricycle?" Having just learned Settie's name, I wanted to show off my new knowledge.

"Yes," he said with a sly grin. The kind of grin that says, I know something you don't. "Settie."

I was still treading in my brother's wake, but I kept on. "I saw him at work today. He seems nice."

"He is."

"How would you know? Have you actually spoken with him?"

"Yes, at the café. He eats lunch there most days."

"What do you talk about?" I felt briefly disappointed that Conrad had beaten me to something yet again. But my curiosity was stronger than my disappointment. I needed to learn more about this mysterious character who kept appearing at odd moments in my life.

"You wouldn't understand. You're too young," came the discouraging reply.

Not again, I thought. "No, Conrad, you have to tell me," I pleaded.

Perhaps my brother caught the frustration in my tone, for he put down his book, and looked at me. A thoughtful expression appeared on his face, almost as if he were deciding something. A few seconds passed, and then he said, "We talked about truth."

"What?" I looked at him in surprise.

"We talked about what is true and what isn't."

"What do you mean?"

"For example," he said, leaning forward and touching his desk, "is it true that this is brown?"

"Of course, it's brown," I said.

"You see, Emily, that's exactly why you wouldn't understand what we talk about."

"You could tell me...."

"It all depends on how you look at things, and I don't think you're ready for this."

"Please Conrad."

He shook his head. "If you don't mind, Emily, I want to go on reading now."

As I continued to stand there, he stood up, took my arm, led me gently to the door, and closed it between us.

The following Saturday I kept an eye out for Settie. From mid-morning onwards, I darted out of the kitchen every few minutes to see if he was at the lunch counter. When he showed up a few minutes before 11:00, I took my lunch break. I didn't want him to think I was watching him, so I chose a seat at the end of the counter, seven seats down from him.

After the familiar hearty "Good morning," he glanced briefly at the menu. When he had given the smiling waitress his order—I sensed it never varied much—he looked around at the ten or so people at the counter, as well as at the booths just behind it and asked whether there were any questions for him. Involuntarily, I thought back to the time Conrad had called him a loon.

To my surprise, someone spoke. "All right, Settie. Something I've thought about for some time. I say this seat is red. Anyone agree with me?" The questioner, a portly man, gestured towards his leather stool. People looked from his seat to their own—almost as if they were seeing it for the first time—then raised their hands in agreement.

"Good. Since we're all agreed the seat is red, I propose it is true that this here seat is red." The portly man gave a satisfied smile.

Propose the seat was red? What the heck did he mean? It was like saying the sky was blue, or the grass was green. Of course, the seat was red. For a moment, I wondered if all the people around me were loons.

Then Settie spoke: "Your statement is interesting, Bert, but I wonder if I might ask a question?" And when Bert nodded: "Are you saying your seat is absolutely, unquestionably red?"

Unhesitatingly, Bert said, "Yes."

Settie followed the question with another. "If you were to ask a man, blind since birth, the colour of the seat, what would he say?"

"A blind person couldn't tell me," answered Bert.

"Are you saying that to a blind person, the seat might not be red?"

Bert took a few seconds to think about this question. "Well...maybe the seat wouldn't be red to a blind person, but it's still red to the rest of us."

"So am I to understand that the seat is red because you say it is red?"

"Yes," said Bert. "I say it is red, and the folks here agree with me. Anyone who can see will agree with me."

"May I take it then, that your definition of truth is that you and all those around you believe the same thing?" asked Settie.

"The person must be able to see," amended Bert, who was beginning to look nervous as the discussion progressed.

"So, if someone sat down beside you—a person with sight, of course—and told you the seat was grey, what would you say?" asked Settie.

"I'd wonder what was wrong with that person because the seat is obviously red."

"To a colour-blind person, the seat might be grey," suggested Settie.

As Bert considered Settie's words, everyone in the café waited silently.

"I know what you're trying to do, Settie," Bert said at last, "but it won't work. Let me state my own definition of truth here. I say that any person with regular sight, like me, will agree it is true that this seat is red."

"Is the seat pale red or dark red?" Settie asked.

"Kind of pale red."

"And is pale red the same as red?"

It took Bert a while to respond. Near me, people began to whisper; the seat was dark red, or even dark pink now that they thought about it. From the sound of it, not everyone agreed that the seat was red, after all.

Finally, Bert spoke. "Yes, pale red is the same as red," he said.

I didn't agree with him, but I kept my opinion to myself. Once more there was silence, as everyone waited for Settie's response.

"Does that mean dark red is also the same as red?" asked Settie.

"...Yes."

"Well then, if dark red is red, and pale red is red, does it mean dark red and light red are both the same colour?"

It was obvious to me that dark red and pale red were quite different from each other. There was no way Bert could say otherwise.

I saw him squirm in his seat, all his confidence gone. "All right Settie. I take it back," he said. "Pale red is not the same as red."

"Does this mean the seat you are sitting on is not absolutely red after all?"

Bert sighed. "Maybe I should have said pale red."

Somebody was chuckling in one of the booths. "A little longer Bert, and Settie will have you thinking you're a rooster!" the chuckling man said.

Laughter filled the café.

"Shut up, Jimmy!" Bert yelled.

"You bet, Rooster!" Jimmy replied.

Settie held up his hand for silence.

Once it was quiet again, a red-faced Bert continued. "I still say any regular person would call this seat red—though maybe it's not absolutely red." His tone held a note of defeat.

Settie smiled gently. "I will grant that it makes it easier to communicate with those around you if everyone understands what you mean when you say a thing is the colour red, but that is quite different from saying that it is true that the seat on which your posterior rests is red. There may be other cultures that call this colour 'yuck' or 'tree.' 'Red' is simply a word, not the truth of what it is."

"But it *is* red," persisted Bert.

"Red is only the name you've used to describe it," Settie said, finality in his tone.

"Ah! You're crazy, Settie." Bert made a shooing motion with his hand, as if Settie were some annoying fly he was waving away.

Settie looked unruffled. "You wouldn't be the first to say so," he said cheerfully. He looked around. "Any other questions?"

No one said a word. Some stared blankly into space. Others returned to their meals. I sat staring at Settie, open-mouthed.

Looking directly at me, Settie asked, "Do you have a question, young lady?"

"No," I said, embarrassed for some reason. I bent my head, as if I were in a classroom and wanted to avoid eye contact with the teacher. Suddenly in a hurry to get away from the scene as quickly as possible, I left my meal unfinished on the counter, punched back in, and returned to my dishes.

Later that day, when I got home from work, I threw open the door to my brother's bedroom without knocking. "Who is Settie?" I asked.

"Hello to you too," he said, as he strummed his guitar.

"What does he do? Why does he ask people at the lunch counter for questions?"

"You wouldn't understand, Emily. You're too young."

I was so tired of hearing this all the time. "*I am not too young, Conrad!*" I shouted.

Conrad stopped strumming and looked at me musingly. "He used to work at the university with Mom. Why don't you ask her about him?"

I didn't want to go to Mom. Everyone went to her. People were always coming to the house, seeking guidance or advice: the neighbours, her students, other university professors. Once, when I asked Dad why so many people wanted to talk with her, he said, "Some people have knowledge and some people have wisdom. Your mother, Emily, has both."

"*You* tell me," I said to my brother, who was strumming once more. I did not know if he would answer and was relieved when he did.

"Settie's real name is Professor Alva Setarcos. He taught philosophy at the university. He retired about ten years ago."

"Why does he ask for questions?"

"Maybe he misses teaching. There's a question you can ask him," Conrad said impatiently, and went back to his guitar. I had been dismissed.

"I will," I said, and stormed away. Frustrated, I stomped into my bedroom and lay down on my bed. The next thing I knew, Dad was waking me for dinner.

The following Saturday, I poked my head out of the café's kitchen even earlier than before. At 11:00, as usual, Settie walked in. By the time I had punched out and taken a seat well down the counter from him, he was already being questioned by a grey-haired lady with heavily rouged cheeks. I recalled having seen her at the counter the last two Saturdays. Actually, I recognized many of the faces at the counter and in the booths behind me.

"You say there is no absolute truth—but what about the facts of mathematics? How can you declare that the facts of mathematics are not absolute?" She spoke as if she were addressing a favourite teacher. The ensuing silence was broken only by the sound of the cooks clanging plates in the kitchen. Everyone else was silent as they waited for Settie to respond.

"Are you referring to a specific fact, Amelia?" he asked.

"Yes—one plus one equals two."

"You are saying in all cases this is true?"

"Well, yes," Amelia said.

"Let me show you something." Settie turned to the waitress, Francine. "May I please have a pitcher and two glasses of water?"

When Francine had cheerfully agreed to his request, Settie continued. "Let's call each of these glasses one unit of water. If I pour the contents of the glasses into the empty pitcher, how many units of water will I have?"

"Two," Amelia said quickly.

"Two units?" Careful not to spill, Settie poured the water from both glasses into the pitcher. "I don't see two units. I see a single container with water in it," he said then.

"Ah, but if the pitcher was a measuring jug, and you added one cup to another, then you could see by the lines on the measuring jug that you had two cups of water," Amelia said with some pride.

Settie gave her a crooked smile. "You're going to make me work for this one, are you?"

"You enjoy it, Settie."

"Very well. This may take a moment." Settie took the saucer from beneath his coffee cup, wiped it, and held it up for all to see. "I will put a single drop of coffee on this clean, white saucer."

Using a spoon, he scooped up a small amount of coffee, and let a single drop fall on the gleaming white saucer. "You can see this is liquid," he said. Like a miner panning for gold, he moved the brown spot around on the saucer. Then he began to blow on it gently. The group around the counter waited in expectant silence. A minute went by and then the liquid was gone. Only a small faint stain remained. Settie held up the saucer once more. "Can you tell me what happened?"

"You dried up the coffee," said Amelia.

Settie shook his head. "I only sped up the process called evaporation, but yes, the liquid is gone. It's what happens naturally to liquids like coffee or water, given certain conditions."

He paused a moment to look at his audience. "Let's review our example. According to Amelia, if I pour one unit of water into the pitcher, then add another unit, I have two units of water. However, evaporation, or drying up, occurs even while I pour the water into the pitcher. This means that one unit of water plus one unit of water equals less than two units of water. Say about one and ninety-nine point nine units of water. So as you can see, one plus one is not always two."

"Are you saying the textbooks are wrong?" Amelia asked.

"No, I'm saying that numbers are merely the creation of mankind. When have you ever seen the number 'one' in nature? You see a single apple and use the term 'one' to communicate how many apples you see, but 'one' is just a term. Useful, but not absolute in all cases."

No one spoke for a few moments; all were waiting to see if Settie had finished. Finally, Amelia thanked him.

Settie looked around and asked if there were other questions. Silence. The customers went back to their individual conversations. I was left wanting more.

Throughout that summer, autumn, winter, and into the following spring, I watched and listened to Settie. Most Saturdays, one customer or another would propose a truth.

Always, Settie asked questions until everyone, me included, recognized that what the person had proposed might not be true after all. No two Saturdays were the same. Ethics, morality, science, medicine, physics, law, logic—no subject was taboo. Although I was beginning to believe that absolute truth did not exist, I wasn't entirely convinced. Not yet, at least.

It was almost a year before I asked a question myself, though I wasn't brave enough to ask it in front of others. I knew, of course, that Settie ate his lunch at the café most days, so in 1929, on the first Monday morning of summer holidays, I waited for him to finish his lunch. When he came out, I introduced myself.

"It's very nice to meet you formally, Emily," he said, taking my outstretched hand and shaking it. "Of course, I've known you a long time from the café. And even before that." His manner towards me was as friendly and courteous as it was with adults. "To what do I owe this pleasure?"

"I have a question for you," I said softly.

He smiled and leaned against the seat of his tricycle as I tried desperately to remember the words I had composed and rehearsed. It was important to me that I sound mature.

"I think I understand what you have been saying…you know, how there's no absolute truth. But still…" I hesitated briefly, then went on. "I love my parents. How can love not be absolute?" The words hadn't come out quite as I'd planned.

Settie stroked his long beard for a moment and then looked down. "Ah! Matters of the heart. A romantic, young lady you may be, but your question shows astuteness."

I knew astuteness meant intelligence. Only my mom and dad had ever said I was intelligent. The comment filled me with pride.

"Let me ask you this," he continued. "Can you tell me what love is?"

I thought for a moment. "Love is caring about someone a lot. It means you never want anything bad to happen to them," I stated firmly.

"Where does this love come from?"

I pointed to my chest. "It's a feeling you have inside."

"Are you telling me that love is a feeling?"

"Yes. I think so. What else could it be?"

"Have your parents ever given you a gift, for your birthday, perhaps, that made you feel happy?"

"They gave me a set of paints last year," I answered. I loved to sketch and paint, and Mom and Dad did their best to support my interests.

"Did you feel strongly towards your mother and father then?"

I told him I did.

"Superb." He smiled at me. "Now, perhaps you can tell me the last time your mother or father made you do something you didn't want to do."

I looked down at the gravel, trying to think. "My mom wouldn't let me stay out late last night. All my friends got to, but I had to be home by nine," I said.

"How did you feel about your mom, then?"

"I was angry," I said, adding quickly, "but I still love her."

Settie laughed quietly. "Emily, did you feel the same way towards your mother last night as you did when she gave you the paints?"

"Well, no…" And then it dawned on me. "I get it!" I shouted. "I love my mom and dad, but the love I feel is different depending on what the…on the situation I experience.

That's why it's not absolute!"

Settie grinned widely. "I knew you would understand. Viktoria always said you were exceptionally bright. You are definitely her daughter."

His few supportive words filled me with confidence. It was my turn to give him my biggest, toothiest smile.

"Yes," Settie continued thoughtfully, as if remembering some past encounter. "Your mother is the most exceptional person I've ever had the pleasure of knowing. You may not know this, Emily, but lecturers and professors at the university have urged her to run for public office. She always refused. She never wanted a special position or title. I suppose that's why people have always respected her." He paused a moment. "Viktoria influenced me greatly," he continued.

I looked at him doubtfully. "How could she influence you. You're so...." I stopped myself from saying the word "old." "You're older than her," I finished more tactfully.

He laughed. "Just because she's younger than I am doesn't mean I can't learn from her."

My mind raced with the implications of Settie's words. Could that mean that some day I really could be smarter than my brother?

"I think I'd better go," I said. I wanted to get home as quickly as possible, to tell my brother that Settie thought I was smart. I remembered my manners just as I was about to get on my bicycle. "Thank you, Professor Setarcos," I said.

"Call me Settie, young lady," was his smiling response.

I got on my bicycle and rode home as fast as I could. I found Conrad in the backyard, sunning himself on the grass and reading, while listening to the trumpet of his beloved Louis Armstrong, on the great black horn of the gramophone.

"I just spoke with Settie," I told him, raising my voice to be heard above the music.

"That's nice," Conrad said, paying me no real heed.

"He said I was bright," I said boastfully. I had never felt so self-assured in my life.

"Oh really?" Conrad put down his book.

"Yes. And I bet I understand him better than you do."

"Oh you do, do you?"

"Yes—I know now that there are no absolute truths." I put my hands on my hips and stuck out my chin.

My brother glanced around and then looked up at the clear blue sky. "Then maybe you can tell me, Miss Bright, if there are no absolutes, why do people say 'as sure as the sun rises and sets'?"

Normally, I wouldn't have been able to answer him immediately, but I recalled something Settie had said at the café months before. "The sun doesn't always rise and set. If you go to the North Pole in winter, you won't see the sun rise for a few months. And if you go there in summer, you won't see it set for a few months either."

As I repeated the gist of Settie's words, Conrad looked stunned. I realized he hadn't expected me to come up with an answer, let alone a good one. My year of listening to Settie was paying off, it seemed.

"All right then," Conrad said, his attitude slightly superior, "maybe you understand there are no absolutes, but do you know what that means?"

Looking down at the grass, I felt my short-lived victory starting to slip away. No absolutes meant that everything was.... Suddenly it came to me. "Change," I said.

"What?" he asked, his brow furrowing.

"Change," I said more loudly. "If there are no absolute truths, then everything is changing!"

My brother looked stunned once more. I was right! I could hardly believe it! My first conquest over my brother!

With my head held high, I walked triumphantly into the house, accompanied by Mr. Armstrong playing *West End Blues*, a victory song especially for me.

I didn't see Conrad again that day. He had gone out with his friends and didn't return home until late. I thought he was staying away because he was mad at me for being as smart as him. Never before had I been able to keep up with his quick mind; now that I could, at least once, I worried that he might dislike me.

Next day as I sat on my bed drawing, Conrad knocked at the open door. "Can I come in, Emily?" he asked.

"Yes," I said, worried he might be upset with me from the day before.

"I talked with Mom and Dad about you, last night when you were asleep," he said.

I grew tense. Why would Conrad discuss me with Mom and Dad? What had I done?

"I told them about yesterday. About our discussion about absolute truth and the idea of change."

I waited nervously.

"And I asked them if it was all right for me to give this to you." And then, from behind his back, Conrad produced a brown leather book, badly worn at the edges. I hadn't realized he was holding it.

"What is it?" I asked, puzzled.

"A journal. Mom got it from her Uncle Alexandre long ago, when she was much younger. He wasn't really an uncle but that's what she called him. Other people owned it before her. After yesterday, I knew you would understand it." With these words, he handed me the journal.

Conrad was about to leave my room, when he turned back. "I guess there really is hope for you, Emily," he said with a wink, and then left. That's when I realized something monumental: even though he always treated me like a little sister, in his own way, my brother respected me. It was the proudest moment of my life.

I got up from my bed and chased after him. "Wait," I called. My brother stopped at the end of the hallway, and looked at me. "I just wanted to say...." I couldn't get the words out of my mouth, so I threw my arms around his neck and hugged him instead.

Softly, so softly that I had to strain to hear him, he said, "I love you too, Em."

Emily Alethea Herac (née Linck)

Richard

Driving through the Eastern Townships on our way home to Montreal, I am extra cautious. Jenner and Kimberly's car accident has spooked me, making me nervous that at any moment a deer or other animal might leap out in front of me, causing me to swerve and lose control of the car. I have trouble shaking the memory of the overturned car and the two bleeding victims. Beside me, Sonia stares out of the window, lost in her own thoughts.

As we drive over the six-lane Champlain Bridge, which I've always considered the gateway to Montreal, and we are safely in the city, I loosen my grip on the steering wheel. It occurs to me involuntarily that approximately 196 million people must cross the bridge every year, making it the busiest bridge in Canada, and one of the busiest in the world. This kind of "useless" information—as Sonia refers to my knowledge of trivia—occurs to me all the time. She used to prod me to go on television game shows, the kind where such "crazy" knowledge can win you lots of money. "You could make a year's salary in a day," she'd say. Actually, it would probably be closer to two years' salary, for teaching history at a community college is not the golden path to wealth.

Obscure knowledge was one of the reasons I chose to do a master's degree in history. I enjoy names and dates and places and always imagined this kind of information would give me greater understanding of a confusing world. If I were to memorize enough esoteric information, perhaps one day I'd see a pattern of some sort, and everything would make sense.

"Look kids," I'd say as we drove past the Sun Life building. "See that? In World War II, Winston Churchill worried that Nazi Germany might invade Britain and take all her wealth. To prevent it happening, Churchill shipped billions of dollars worth of currency, artefacts, and even the Crown Jewels, to Canada. It was all stored on the third floor of this very building, guarded around the clock by the RCMP until the end of the war."

Or, driving by the prestigious St. Lawrence Hall Hotel, I'd say, "See that building, kids? Did you know that's where John Wilkes Booth, along with other conspirators, hatched his plan to assassinate Abraham Lincoln? No, I thought you didn't. Sometimes, though, when Booth drank too much and shared his plans with unwitting billiard players, they thought he was some edgy man in his cups."

Half the time, of course, the kids did not know what their wacky father was talking about. "What's a Nancy?" Aidan would ask, when I'd mention a Nazi. Or Nadie might say, "Who is John Will Book?" Often they'd lose interest halfway through an explanation, but I'd usually get an affectionate smile from Sonia. Not that I believe she found my information that interesting, but at least she listened. Sometimes, she even remembered a rare piece of slightly irrelevant data. To her credit, she would smile even after hearing the same information for the tenth time.

This time, however, I don't spout useless information as we drive through the dark streets of Montreal. Instead, I dwell on the memories that had surfaced while Sonia and

I were at the Granby hospital: my childhood surgeries, my mother's never-failing optimism that the *next* surgery would work, and the resulting disappointment when it didn't.

The teasing began after the final attempt—my ninth surgery—to make my club foot "normal." I don't recall the other kids making a big deal of my limp, or of the way my right foot turned inwards, when I was five, six, or even seven-years-old. At that age, I wouldn't have known there was anything wrong with me had my mother not reminded me so often that I wasn't quite normal, not exactly like other little boys. But by the time I was eight, children were quick to comment on differences, especially physical ones.

Actually, it was my right calf that was odd. My foot functioned fairly well, though I felt nothing in my big toe, and my range of motion was limited. But, the calf looked emaciated and stick-like.

Richard Broomstick was my first nickname. The first few times the kids called me that, I got into fights; skirmishes I lost because I was on the small side. Before long, kids I had once played with no longer wanted me around. Gradually, I realized I had to do something different if I wanted friends. So, instead of fighting the kids who called me Richard Broomstick, I tried laughing along with them. That tactic didn't make me any more popular, and I felt bad for not standing up for myself. Soon, my nickname evolved into Dick Stick and I became an outcast.

When I was fifteen, I began to lift weights in an attempt to build up the muscle in my right calf. Although the weights had no effect on the calf, no matter how hard I worked or how much I lifted, the rest of my body responded in all sorts of ways. My arms became bigger, my thighs stronger, and although I was only five-feet-eight, I discovered that by jumping off my left foot, I could dunk a basketball. That accomplishment, something no one else in my school—no matter how tall or athletic—could match, encouraged me to take up basketball. Soon, along with the weightlifting, I was practicing basketball skills after school every day. I'd shoot and jump and dribble through an obstacle course I set up with blue milk crates borrowed from behind a Green Gables' convenience store.

At the end of grade nine, before I was to start high school, it occurred to me that a fresh start might enable me to lead an ordinary life. Knowing my nickname would accompany me with my classmates, I convinced my parents to let me go to a different school from the other kids.

Over the summer, I continued to re-make myself. As well as practicing basketball and lifting weights, I exercised to strengthen my foot and reduce the limp. I spent hours picking up marbles with my toes, kicking a soccer ball sideways against a wall, and walking up slides.

In the end, all the hard work paid off. When school started in the fall, nobody called me Dick Stick. For the first time in many years, I was just plain Richard. And after participating in a few lunchtime games of pickup basketball—wearing jeans, of course—I became the guy who was a whiz with a basketball. At a school where sportsmanship was revered, I emerged as somewhat of a minor celebrity. Thinking about those days now, I remember my bliss.

The guys I played basketball with at noon—lunchball, we called it—encouraged me to try out for the senior basketball team. As shorts were an integral part of the team uniform, and I could not bear to be ridiculed again, I pretended I was too cool to play school sports, even though I badly wanted to do so. How wonderful it would have been to prove that, despite my deformity, I was as good as any of the others, if not better.

My new friends were mystified, especially David and Shawn who were going to try out, and who were, as they readily admitted, not nearly as good as me. David made the senior team, while Shawn played on the junior team. I was very happy to be accepted as a regular guy, though I couldn't help feeling envious whenever the stars of the basketball games were announced over the intercom and either David or Shawn was named.

My parents, meanwhile, were elated. For so long, they had agonised over my disability and the misery it caused me. The most they had allowed themselves to hope for was that I would one day function normally. And now I had friends and was respected.

In grade eleven, I finally decided to try out for the senior basketball team. Much as I enjoyed playing lunchball and being treated normally, when I saw how the girls were after David, who had made the senior team the year before, I wanted more too.

On the first day of tryouts, I changed in an isolated corner of the locker room. I put on my shorts and then pulled a pair of track pants over them, without anyone noticing. On the basketball court, while the others wore shorts and T-shirts, I kept on my track pants for the warm-up drills. When the scrimmages started, however, the coach told me to take off the pants. Now that the moment had come, I hesitated, wishing I knew a way out of my dilemma. But the coach was starting to look impatient, and I realized I had to do as he asked. Telling myself that most of these guys were my friends and that my skill on the court was more important than my appearance, I reluctantly complied.

To my surprise, there were no comments. The other guys ran and shot and dribbled as if their lives depended on their prowess; after all, they were trying out for the team and had more to think about than my skinny calf. At the end of the practice, I quickly put my track pants back on.

Walking home with David and Shawn, all we talked about was how hard the tryout had been and who was most likely to make the team. By the time I had left David at his house and walked the rest of the way home, I felt pretty good. My friends had said nothing about my leg. If they had noticed the deformity, they had taken it in their stride. I felt I'd played well and was optimistic I would make the senior basketball team and be really popular.

At school the next day, I got the odd sensation that everyone was looking at me. A weird and discomforting feeling. Whenever I'd catch someone staring, they'd look away from me quickly. As I walked down the halls between classes and at lunch, I noticed that conversations stopped as I passed. I could have sworn I heard people whisper, "Arr matey," and "Shiver me timbers," a couple of times behind my back. What was more, I didn't see David or Shawn, even though our lockers were together outside Mrs. Klemky's English 20 classroom. I tried to convince myself that I was imagining things, but after school, when I walked into the change room to get ready for the tryouts, the day's unusual events became clear.

"Hey, Long John Silver," said James, one of the grade 12's who had played on the senior team the year before, "where's your parrot?" A few of the guys laughed: fellows I recognized, as they had also played on the team previously.

In that second, I felt as if I might throw up. The room started to spin. My legs felt wobbly. Perspiration formed on my upper lip.

"I bet you got to be careful of woodpeckers, eh?" James said, to more laughter.

I wished I had a clever response. If only I had stood up to James right away, I might have salvaged the situation. But I had spent my childhood and teenage years being told I was different—not normal—and I lacked the confidence to stick up for myself. All I could do was stand there and think about how stupid I had been to believe I could bare my leg without ridicule. I reproached myself for wanting too much, when I should have left well enough alone and foregone the tryouts. I should have been content with being treated like a regular guy, even if it meant doing without the accolades that came with excelling at sports.

"Hey, Moby Dick, I'm talking to you," James said.

"Moby Dick was the whale, you idiot," corrected someone behind James. "Ahab was the one with the peg leg."

I scanned the group of guys behind James, hoping to see who had spoken. Maybe David or Shawn had tried to stand up for me.

"Whatever," James yapped.

I kept looking around for a friendly face, hoping at least for empathy from David or Shawn. I didn't see either of them and wondered where they were. They should also have been in the change room by then.

"Your leg is pretty freaky looking. There's like no calf, just bone, man. How the heck do you manage to jump?" James asked.

Now all those behind him seemed to be laughing and pointing—at me, I felt sure.

I simply did not have the confidence to fight back. Even though weightlifting had made me quite strong, and I could probably have bettered James in a fist fight, I made no attempt to stop his cruel taunts. Nor could I laugh with my tormentors. Besides, even in elementary school, laughter had never stopped the kids mocking me. My only option, as I saw it, was to go to the secluded corner where I had changed the day before. It made me angry to go back there as an outcast, a status I thought I had left behind. But at least this time, I wouldn't be alone. Although I felt unable to defend myself, I didn't feel as hopeless about my life as I had when I was younger. I had two good friends now, and their companionship would ease the pain of being a pariah.

I turned around and suddenly I saw where the others had been pointing—not at me, as I had thought, but at David and Shawn. They had been behind me all the time, pretending to bounce around on pogo sticks, with their tongues stuck out at me. They didn't stop what they were doing, even when I looked straight at them.

Sick at heart, I left the locker room with James calling out, "Arrr matey." I was almost certain I heard David and Shawn call the words too.

I did not attend the tryouts that afternoon, nor did I play lunchball again. And for the rest of high school, I could hardly look at David and Shawn. They just reminded me of how different I was.

When Sonia and I finally arrive at our narrow, two-storey brownstone at three in the morning, she goes straight to our room without saying a word. I bring in our suitcases and put them by the bedroom door. Briefly, I consider joining Sonia in bed, but since I realize the uncomfortable situation between us will keep me from sleeping, I decide I might as well do something useful.

I bring the suitcases and garbage bags containing the Heracs' possessions from the car and carry them down the stairs to the basement.

A single, open room with a low six-and-a-half foot ceiling and exposed water heater and furnace, the basement is divided into two. A few years ago, Sonia felt Nadie and Aidan needed a space of their own, where they could play with friends or by themselves, and so the greater part of the basement was set up for the kids. Sonia put much effort into painting the walls a bright yellow, finding soft beige area rugs to cover the cold concrete floor, and filling the room with Disney posters, beanbag chairs, a playhouse, a couple of late-forties school desks with holes for inkwells, and two huge chalkboards, which she nailed to the wall about a foot from the ground. A final touch were the green, twelve-inch-high calligraphy letters painted on the wall above the chalkboards. The calligraphy comprised the first line of Sonia's favourite poem, Robert Frost's *The Road Not Taken*. Sonia knew the whole poem by heart and would often recite it softly to the kids when they were younger, to help them fall asleep.

My office is in the other part of the basement. To the left of the water heater and furnace, and tucked into the south-west corner, stand a large, used mahogany desk and matching bookcase, which Sonia had found in an antique store in Laval. The middle of the desk contains a computer screen, an old cathode ray tube type, and an outdated computer with no connection to the Internet. The bookcase holds my reference material, including books of quotations, a thesaurus, a dictionary, and atlases, as well as authors whose writing I admire. An old swivel chair that almost matches the desk and bookshelf, but doesn't, completes what should be an ideal nook in which to write.

Unfortunately, despite all Sonia's efforts, neither area has had much use. Nadie and Aidan don't like the basement. The single, narrow window provides only limited light, and we can't rid the place of its hundred-year-old musty air, no matter how many air fresheners we use. My own excuse for not using the basement is that two young children and a full-time job leave me little time or energy for writing.

The only time the basement had been used was when Aidan drew on the chalkboards one afternoon. On an over-cast Saturday morning after the end of the good cartoons, Aidan, then five-and-a-half and full of energy, was kicking a soccer ball up and down the hallway, doing flips on the chesterfield, and sneaking up behind Nadie with a squirt gun, dousing her with water. I was trying to concentrate on the *Montreal Gazette* and gave him one of two choices—outside or downstairs. Aidan peeked through the living-room window, evidently decided he didn't like the weather, and chose the basement, instead.

A few minutes later, suspicious of the unusual silence, I peeked into the basement. Aidan was at the chalkboards, writing simple words like *aunt*, *book*, and *club*. Absorbed in what he was doing, he did not see me, and I was able to enjoy watching him unobserved. After a minute or two, I crept back up the stairs and told Sonia about our son. Incredulous that our little whirlwind was playing so calmly, she checked on him, too. She was smiling when she rejoined me and dropped an affectionate kiss on my cheek.

Some two quiet hours later, Aidan appeared for a snack. While Sonia gave him apple wedges in peanut butter, I took the opportunity to inspect what he had been doing. I half expected to see the bookshelves in disarray and the beanbag chairs gutted. But I had misjudged my son, for to my surprise, I found both chalkboards covered with what must have been every four-letter word he knew how to spell: *help, plum, kiss, dark, salt, jump*. Even the words *take, math, feet, game, left, need, race*, and a hundred more besides. The chalked words were formed in different sizes and in six different colours, making a lovely collage on the black background.

I was about to go upstairs when a separate four-letter word, on a different wall, sprang at me. Executed in lurid purple, the letters some three feet in height, was the single word: S-H-I-T. I collapsed on the floor, my hands covering my mouth, so that Aidan would not hear me laughing.

With Aidan still munching his snack, I motioned to Sonia to come with me. She had a laughing fit of her own at the sight of our son's handiwork.

"At least it wasn't the four-letter friend-getter," she sputtered, referring to the expression she liked to call "that most popular of obscenities that rhymes with 'luck.'"

As I dump the contents of the two garbage bags and spread out the things from the hastily filled suitcases on the basement floor, I swear I can still see on the wall—even though it has long been scrubbed and covered with two more coats of yellow paint—the faint outline of purple letters that amused us so much.

I begin to restore some order to the Heracs' possessions, brushing little pebbles off the camping equipment, blowing dirt off the photos, folding the clothes, and repacking the suitcases. Tidying up Jenner and Kimberly's possessions makes no real difference to anything; I know that. They may be dead. Lying in some mortuary—five-thousand miles from their home in Vancouver. Even so, I feel better doing it. As if I am contributing my own rather small share towards helping put back together two shattered lives. Perhaps by filling my time this way, I can also delay thinking about my own life.

The old diary is the last thing I pack. Although I yearn to read it, I don't. Too much of Jenner's and Kimberly's lives are already on display: to read the diary, even to open it and look at the drawings once more, would be to further invade their privacy. Placing the diary gently on top of the clothing, I shut the suitcases and leave them upstairs beside the front door.

Tired now, yet reluctant to go to our bedroom where Sonia is sleeping, I lie on the chesterfield in the living room, pull a blanket over myself, and close my eyes. I think of Sonia, about how inexcusably insensitive she had been of my feelings earlier. She knows how much I hate hospitals, how the smell makes me feel ill. I have enough trouble opening Band-Aids to put on the kids' skinned knees; the antiseptic odour affects me so badly.

I am about to go upstairs to tell Sonia what I think of her, when the memory hits me: Sonia's mother died in an automobile accident when Sonia was very young. Suddenly, I feel ashamed. Maybe *I* should go upstairs and see if *she's* all right. Yes, that's what I'll do.

At the top of the stairs, I hesitate. What if, after all, Sonia was not thinking about her mother's accident, and I were to bring it up? How would she feel then? A moment passes. Then I decide to go upstairs anyway.

The bedroom door is open; the room is in darkness. No doubt, Sonia is asleep and would not want to be disturbed. In any event, had she wanted me to join her, wouldn't she have invited me to bed? Well, maybe not in light of the abrupt way our vacation had ended. Still, at least she could have bidden me good night instead of heading straight for our room when we got home from Granby. An inner voice tells me: leaving the door open is an invitation. Lie down beside her, wrap your arms around her. But, I choose to ignore the unwelcome voice, yet again, and go back to the chesterfield. Dawn was already breaking when I fell asleep at last.

Viktoria Katharina Linck (née Kossuth)

September 28, 1919

Twelve years ago this storybook-journal came into my
hands. Like the man who possessed it before me, I find myself
forever changed by the stories it contains and by the people
who gave it to me.

With the arrival of Aunt Alethea and Uncle Alexandre at our
farm outside Weyburn, Saskatchewan, I thought my family
would be too preoccupied, if only for the weekend, to make
my future the focus of family conversations. I was wrong.

"Viktoria, have you decided yet what you'll be doing,
young lady?" my father, Gyorgy, asked as he bumped clumsily against the table, making cutlery clink against plates and
glasses slop their contents. He had a habit of lifting his short,
sturdy body out of his chair when he spoke at the dinner
table, as if to better emphasize his words. He looked, my
mother said to me one day in secret, like a jackrabbit that
had spotted a coyote in the distance and was poised to dash
for safety.

"I am still unsure, Father," I said, and looked down at my plate. Dinner had been so pleasant until then. Why did he have to do this? Especially in front of Auntie and Uncle. Let me be! I thought to myself.

"Well, I believe the bank would provide an excellent opportunity for Viktoria," my sister, Dorina, said, putting on airs. She caressed her swollen belly as proudly as if it held the next in line to the British throne. Her husband, Everett, worked for the Bank of Montreal in Pile O' Bones, as father still called Regina, and was, supposedly, making a name for himself in important circles.

"The bank is stuffy," said Vanessa. Actually, Everett was the stuffy one, but he made the bank stuffy by association. "You need a job that makes oodles of money, so you can buy me wonderful presents." She flashed her childish, aren't-I-cute smile. As the baby of the family, Vanessa was unquestionably spoiled. The family joke was that her first word was not "Ma" or "Pa," but "me."

"As long as you do something respectable, Viktoria," my mother, Cili, said as she started clearing dirty dishes. Busy though she was, her pretty skin and perfect white teeth glowed in the candlelight.

I knew, of course, what she meant by "respectable." She might just as well have said "old-fashioned." Mother had always hoped I would behave like a proper lady and raise a family. I had disappointed her frequently, by taking part in what she considered unbecoming activities. In high school, I played basketball. I remember so vividly the day I modelled the outfit I'd be wearing to games. Why, she nearly fainted. The blouse, with its high neck and long sleeves, was acceptable. The skirt, however—ending at mid-calf—now that was a different matter entirely, for the curves of my lower legs were partly revealed. I say "partly," because they were covered by stockings. Not at all ladylike in my mother's opinion.

"As a little girl, you wanted to be a teacher," my father said. "I think Normal School is the place for you."

He was right. Long ago, when I was very young, I had considered teaching school. Yet as I began to grow up, my world view widened, and I learned of other, more interesting possibilities. Though my father's world had not changed much in the past few years, mine had.

I looked down at the remains of my dinner, idly forking a few chicken bones around my plate, and only half listening as Dorina, Vanessa, and my father discussed what *they* thought I should do with my life. They spoke as if they were unaware of my presence.

I only perked up when I heard Aunt Alethea ask Uncle Alexandre what *he* thought I could do. A childless couple, Alethea and Alexandre had been given honourary titles, although we were not related. Up till now, they had tactfully refrained from stating their opinions.

Beautiful Aunt Alethea. She could so easily have been vainglorious and boastful, yet she treated everyone she met generously and compassionately. A woman of only medium height, she carried herself as if she were much taller. She kept her back straight, her chin raised, and always looked you in the eye when she spoke. Her hair, long and starting to grey, fell softly to her shoulders, and her porcelain-like skin glowed. Though she was already in her early fifties, I noticed how men watched her, always discreetly, when she passed by.

Uncle Alexandre equalled her in appearance and character. He was tall and handsome, with wide shoulders and wavy, light brown hair—grey at the temples—that had a habit of falling over his forehead. His eyes, sometimes covered by his hair, were dark brown, the colour of melting chocolate. As a little girl, I had had a crush on him—perhaps still did—and would happily have taken his advice on almost anything.

Now, though, I was seventeen, and my father tried to make me believe Uncle Alexandre's work-related advice would be ruinous. As far as I knew, he had never held the same job for more than a few years. Father used to say, only partly in jest, that Aunt Alethea and Uncle Alexandre moved to Winnipeg because Uncle had worked for "every bleeding man within a hundred-mile radius of Weyburn."

I lifted my head, and Uncle Alexandre looked at me a few seconds before he responded. "I believe," he said, turning to his wife, "I shall go see what we are having for dessert." Wincing momentarily, at the pain of what I took to be an arthritic back, he stood up, straightened, gathered some dirty dishes, and walked into the kitchen. I lowered my head again, relieved at his discretion, and taking his cue, I too grabbed a few dishes and escaped to the kitchen.

By the time Mother, Uncle Alexandre, and I returned with dessert, the topic of conversation, thankfully, had changed. Vanessa was telling Aunt Alethea all about her active social life, while Dorina and Father discussed the impending birth of the first grandchild. During and after dessert, I waited tensely for the conversation to return to my future possibilities. Mercifully, Uncle Alexandre regaled us with stories until we retired.

The following day, Father showed Uncle Alexandre all the changes he had made to the farm since their last visit, while Mother, Aunt Alethea, and my sisters went into town. They expected me to accompany them, but I feigned illness and spent a rare and glorious day home alone. As much as I loved spending time with my aunt, I could not pass up the delicious chance of being alone and enjoying my own company for a few hours. In the evening, my luck held out too—we played cards from dinner until bed, without anyone asking me anything other than perfunctory questions about whether I was feeling better.

Awakening on Sunday morning, I felt the weight of the past months vanish. Whether Auntie and Uncle acted as catalysts of sorts, or whether the solitude of the previous day had cleared things in my mind and heart, I didn't know. What I did know was that I had reached a decision that pleased me.

That afternoon, I sat on the front porch, anxiously waiting for Father to return after taking Auntie, Uncle, and Dorina to the train station. Inside the house, Mother baked bread and Vanessa played the piano. Outside, a warm wind blew in from the west, drying out the endlessly flat, mucky prairie and causing the branches of our apple tree, the only tree within miles of us, to wave its spindly arms at me. The smell of moist soil wafted by with each gust. In the distance, I eventually saw Father, mud-spattered, steering the light driving team home along the deep ruts of the wagon trail. Pulling up at the barn, he unhitched the horses and gave them water.

"They've gone," my father said, sitting down beside me. "It's always good to see your uncle and aunt. I wish they hadn't moved so far away."

Though Father sometimes made light of Uncle Alexandre's work history, he nonetheless had great respect for him. In 1899, the year Auntie and Uncle moved to our district, typhoid fever gripped Weyburn. Dr. Mitchell, the only doctor in a fifty-mile radius from Moose Jaw to Estevan, was away when Mother, Father, and Dorina all sickened. Hearing of our plight, Uncle Alexandre and Aunt Alethea, who had only met Father once before, nursed the three of them back to health. At the same time, they cared for and fed the horses, cattle, and swine and looked after Vanessa and me.

"Yes," I agreed, "their visits always go by so quickly. But you know those words of Benjamin Franklin's that Mother often quotes, 'Fish and visitors stink after three days'?"

Father smiled. "I don't think she has ever had them in mind when she's said it." He appeared deep in thought as he gazed towards the horizon. After a while, he asked, "Do you remember when your uncle taught you kids to shoot peas out of your noses?"

"Of course, I do." Uncle Alexandre's pea-shooting lesson had been solely for me, but that detail seemed to have been lost on my father.

That lesson has always been one of my favourite memories. I can still picture our meal—Uncle Alexandre, Aunt Alethea, Mother, Father, and we girls—enjoying our first dinner in our newly built, two-storey home. The spacious house, constructed of lumber shipped in from out east, had hardwood floors, oak panelling, and an inlaid buffet. It was a castle to us after the sod shack we had lived in until then, and my sisters and I, too restless to sit at the table once dinner was finished, wanted to explore. We ran about the house, frequently returning to the adults to make sure nothing more interesting was occurring. Once I found Uncle alone at the table.

"Where is everyone?" I asked.

"Your father's collecting wood, and your mother and aunt are getting tea," he said, smiling at me affectionately. Unexpectedly, he asked, "Do you know how to shoot peas out of your nose?"

Giggling, I told him, I did not.

"That is a shame," he said gravely. "Perhaps you should learn." He picked up a pea from one of the uncleared plates. "First, you take a pea and put it in one nostril, just far enough so it will not fall out." He demonstrated. "Do not," he continued, mock seriously and with a slight nasal sound, "stick it in too far, or you will dislodge your eyeball. I mean it, this isn't a joke—be careful. Next, cover the other nostril with a finger. Like this." Another demonstration followed "And then blow as if you are blowing your nose into a handkerchief."

Then he tilted back his head and blew his nose so hard that the pea shot out of his nostril and across the room towards the fireplace, where it rolled into the cinders. My scream of delight had Mother hurrying into the room, and already I could hear my sisters running down the stairs to see what they were missing. "What's the commotion?" Mother wanted to know.

Guessing he might get into trouble, my uncle put a finger to his mouth and motioned to me to be quiet. "Just playing!" he told my mother.

Too young to hold my tongue after such an amazing performance and forgetting his warning, I jumped up and down in excitement. "Do it again!" I yelled. "Do it again!" Moments later, my sisters, my mother, and my aunt were in the room too.

"What is going on in here?" Mother asked. A little sheepishly, Uncle Alexandre explained the lesson, describing the finer details of shooting peas out of one's nose. Naturally my sisters immediately demanded a repeat performance.

Mother shook her head. "Please, don't teach them that," she said, both demanding and pleading at the same time. Without another word, she turned on her heel and returned to the kitchen to finish preparing the tea. Aunt Alethea, attempting unsuccessfully to cover a grin, followed close behind. Despite repeated requests from my sisters and me for an encore performance, Uncle refused, saying he did not want to get himself—or us—into trouble. Once my sisters understood there would be no second act, they returned upstairs to play, while I remained behind with Uncle. Just before Father came in with the firewood, Uncle looked at me, winked, and said softly, "Perhaps you and I will give it a try another day." Delighted, I went off to join my sisters.

Father and I laughed about the pea incident, after which he was silent again. His next words were the ones I used to dread. "Have you decided what you want to do?"

"Yes," I said, confidently. "I want to attend the University of Toronto. I've read about a certain lady—her name is Clara Benson—who graduated from there in physical chemistry. I want to do the same. I want to study the natural sciences."

Father's astounded expression told me he was unprepared for my answer. Admittedly, the course of study I'd just mentioned was uncommon for a woman—especially then, in 1907. "I always thought you wanted to go to Normal School and study to be a teacher!" he said, visibly appalled.

"I did once—I don't any longer." With my father's angry eyes on me, I suddenly felt less certain of myself.

"What kind of work do you think you can find with physical chemistry?" He seemed to spit out the last two words.

"I want to experiment and make new discoveries," I said, with all the enthusiasm I could muster. I literally held my breath as I waited for him to speak again.

"Have you considered," he asked at last, more calmly now, "that a teacher will always be able to find work? You could be earning your keep after only one more year of schooling. Teaching is the best choice for a young woman these days."

For a few moments he looked at me without speaking. It was a look I had known well all my life. A look that said: *I'm your father, and I know what is best for you. I won't allow you to defy me.* "I'll let you think about it," he said, and left me alone on the front porch.

I didn't need to think long. At dinner that evening, I told my family that I understood my best option was to be a teacher. They congratulated me on choosing wisely. Glancing at my father, I saw a gleam of satisfaction in his eyes.

Looking back on that moment now, I wonder why I capitulated so quickly. After all, I had agonized over my decision for months; I knew what I desired. However, a few well-chosen words, as well as the knowledge that I would be disappointing my father, had been enough to make me change my mind. I had dismissed my hopes and dreams in exchange for something that was safe and practical, a choice that would satisfy my father.

Four months later, I arrived at the Manitou Normal School in southern Manitoba, near the American border. A two-day train ride from home, I had chosen the school for its up-to-date science room, double-sized library, and reading room. I boarded with Mrs. Jaspers, a finicky lady, who rented rooms to three other girls also working towards their teaching certificates. For a time, the new people and experiences were exciting, but by the end of the first month, the newness had dulled, and I began to experience feelings that I put down to homesickness.

Homesick or not, it was impractical for me to return to Weyburn before Christmas; the trip would have been too long and expensive. Fortunately, Aunt Alethea and Uncle Alexandre who lived in Winnipeg, only a few hours away by train on the CPR line, invited me to visit them at the end of September. Although going there would not be the same as going home, I thought the familiar faces might provide some comfort; and so, on the last weekend of that first month of school, I boarded the train for a weekend excursion.

Both Aunt Alethea and Uncle Alexandre were at the station to greet me when my train arrived late Friday evening. Pulled by Uncle's favourite team of Castor and Pollux, we rode to their house in an old black four-seater democrat wagon. Nestled between them, horsehair flying onto my coat from the plodding horses, my feelings of homesickness gradually vanished. I told them all about the classes I was taking—grammar analysis, impromptu composition, modern geography, home economics, and my favourite subjects: chemistry and physiology.

As soon as we arrived at their home, Aunt Alethea showed me to my room. Telling me she could not bear to see the dark circles under my eyes—clearly, I badly needed rest—she insisted I sleep at least until noon the next day. The bed, covered with quilts handmade by my dear auntie, was so warm and comfortable that I forgot my problems and slept better than I had since leaving home.

The entire visit was uneventful, but restful. I slept late both Saturday and Sunday mornings, rising in time for a hearty breakfast of bacon, eggs, beans, and tomatoes, all cooked by Uncle. We spent the afternoons strolling along the Red River, and in the evenings, we shared a bottle of lager beer and played cards. On Sunday afternoon, after a most agreeable weekend, they hitched up the team and took me back to the CPR station.

As I boarded the Sunday afternoon train, Auntie handed me a letter. "You will visit us again soon, my dear," she said. It was a command more than a courteous goodbye. I waited only until the station was out of sight before opening the letter. Inside the envelope, I found money for a return trip fare. I cried most of the way back to school.

Before long, Normal School became a drudge. It was an effort to rise in the mornings and attend classes and studying every evening was tedious and difficult—except for chemistry and physiology, which I loved. During those endless October days, when I felt most gloomy, I would read and re-read the letters that my parents sent in reply to my own. In every letter they expressed their pride and raved about the new life that awaited me as a certified teacher. Predictably, in every post-script, Mother would remind me how lucky I was to attend Normal School when most young women did not have such an opportunity. I sensed her envy; but I do not think she sensed my growing despair.

While the letters did nothing to raise my spirits, I would remind myself that life could be much worse; that at least I was not in the midst of some terrible battle, spending my days knee-deep in muddy trenches, shivering with cold, and fearful of losing my life. Imagining one of the worst places in the world I could be was my way of coping with my unhappi-ness; of forcing myself to feel gratitude for safety and relative warmth. Though I continued to carry on at school as best I could, I often wondered whether I felt something more complicated than simple homesickness.

Towards the end of October, I was desperate for another respite from the life I had begun to loathe. Aunt Alethea and I exchanged letters. A week later, I once again boarded a Friday train for a much-needed break. As before, I slept late Saturday, waking to the smell of bacon. After a splen-did breakfast, I spent much of the afternoon perusing Uncle Alexandre's well-stocked bookshelves, the contents accu-mulated through a lifetime of reading. That evening, I was treated to a night out at the Empire Theatre, where the marquee advertised the highest class of vaudeville.

A harp soloist, a comedian, a play, and a few acrobats

made for an immensely entertaining show. The highlight of the evening was a lady by the name of Ybar, also known as the Handcuff Queen, who was to imitate some of the mystifying "miracles" of the great master magician Houdini. Young and slender, dressed in a fetching white blouse and dark pants, she was shackled hand and foot, placed in a great canvas sack, and locked in a trunk. A police officer attending the performance was called to the stage to check the chains and assert to the audience that all was legitimate.

When the officer had left the stage, a black curtain—about five feet in width—dropped from the ceiling to a spot in front of the locked trunk. The orchestra began to play, while the audience waited tensely to see what would happen. Less than a minute later, following a great puff of smoke, Ybar leaped out from behind the black curtain, brandishing the shackles in one hand and the canvas sack in the other. The audience roared their tumultuous approval. Ybar curtsied deeply, and then the other performers joined her on stage for a final bow.

I spent the remainder of the evening enjoying the company and conversation of Auntie and an unusually lethargic Uncle. By Sunday morning, however, my dreaded return to school replaced the pleasant memories of the show, and I became melancholy. Lying snug in bed, reluctant to get up, I considered feigning sickness. If I were unwell, I reasoned, perhaps I could stay here with Auntie and Uncle for days or even weeks. For a few moments, I actually warmed to the possibilities, but I knew I would only be delaying the inescapable—so I rose, ate, and caught the two o'clock train back to school.

Two weeks later, through the generosity of Aunt Alethea and Uncle Alexandre, I returned to Winnipeg for a third visit. Snow was falling in big, wet, clumpy masses the night I arrived. By the time I awakened late the next morning, the world was covered in a blanket of snow. In the kitchen, I found Aunt Alethea staring out the window.

"Good morning," I said.

"Good morning, dear," she said, then turned back to the white vista outside.

I joined her at the window, curious to see what she was looking at. When I saw Uncle Alexandre rolling a great big snowball, I burst out laughing.

"What on earth is he doing?" I asked, as he picked up the snowball and placed it on top of an even larger one.

"I believe he's building a snowman, dear," Auntie said, her tone devoid of sarcasm.

I had spent enough winters on the prairies to know *that*. My sisters and I loved the snow. We would run around in it and lie in it to make snow angels. As soon as there was enough snow, we would build a snowman, covering his head with an old hat and using stones and a carrot for his eyes and nose. But I had never seen an elderly man engage in such an activity, at least not on his own. Certainly, my father would not have considered it.

"I meant *why* is Uncle Alexandre building a snowman?"

"He's having fun, dear." Auntie said, without moving her eyes from my uncle.

I had assumed that Aunt Alethea and Uncle Alexandre were no different from my own family, or from anyone else's family, for that matter. When a guest came to visit, the host was expected to be congenial and to refrain from openly displaying disturbing emotions like angst, anger, or sadness, which trouble most of us at one time or another. One had to put a mask—a smile—on one's face regardless of one's feelings. Clearly, however, Auntie and Uncle were different. Their cheerful dispositions were genuine; they were always in good humour.

Without thinking, I blurted out, "Is he always happy?"

Just then, Uncle Alexandre noticed us watching him. Like a proud child, he smiled, waved, and embraced his snowman.

Aunt Alethea returned his wave. "Yes," she said lovingly. "He is always happy. Even when he's not well." For some reason, I sensed she might say more, but she only gazed out at her husband.

Had I not been so preoccupied with my own affairs, I might have asked her to continue with what seemed like an unfinished thought. Instead, I pressed on with another question. "How can he be happy all the time?"

She continued to gaze out. "He does what he wants to do, dear." We stood silently for a minute, and then she turned from the window. "No, that's not entirely correct. It would be more accurate to say that he listens to himself. Alexandre does what he feels he needs to do."

I could only stare at her wordlessly. Her words flared in my mind, like a brush fire blown by the wind. At that moment, I knew how Ybar must have felt when she leaped out from behind the black curtain, clutching the shackles and sack. My own bondage was not as tangible as that of someone restrained by handcuffs, but it existed nevertheless—my life was restricted by my father's expectations.

I had let Father convince me that being a teacher was my best option. I knew he loved me—but how could he know what was best for me? His advice to study something safe and secure might seem right for *him*, but that didn't make it the right choice for *me*! My misery had nothing to do with homesickness; I had ignored my needs. Suddenly, the black curtain that had obscured my vision disappeared. I had to quit Normal School. I had to strike off in a different direction.

I boarded the train that afternoon, without the trepidation I'd experienced at my previous departures. I was going back to school, yes. But I was going back to pack my possessions. I was through with Normal School. I would attend university and study exactly what I wanted.

When I returned to school, however, my resolve wavered. Seeing the classrooms and teachers, listening to the chatter of the other students, many of them now my friends, I began to question my decision to leave. It took me a full week to work up the courage to tell my teachers I was discontinuing my studies. "Why?" they all asked, obviously concerned that my decision was due to a lack of money rather than a lack of will. I told them I simply did not want to be a teacher. Some were anxious, thinking I might have decided rashly. "It's the best job a young woman can hope for," were the words I'd been hearing for so long.

I packed my two trunks, sadly said my goodbyes, and left for home. I felt like a fugitive leaving school, but I knew, deep down, it was the right thing to do.

Two days later, I arrived at my station. Naturally, nobody was there to pick me up—I had not informed my parents I was returning. I had no choice but to request that the station master leave my trunks in a safe place. I then began the arduous six-mile trek home, plodding laboriously through ankle-high snow, with the wind blowing fiercely enough to split a tree.

Shock and concern greeted my unexpected arrival. Once I'd assured my family I was in good health and that nothing untoward had occurred, I told them of my decision to leave school. Father was furious. He raved about how much it had cost to send me to school, ranted about responsibility and my lack thereof, and began a tirade about how few people were lucky enough to have the opportunity I was just throwing away. I had never heard him yell as he did that day. He concluded by loudly ordering me to leave.

Watching him, listening to him, it was hard to recognize the father I loved. Had I thought about it, I would have known my decision would disappoint him. But his utter fury, this absolute refusal to hear anything I might say in defence of my actions, was unexpected. He was like a madman as he stood by the stove, arms crossed and perspiring heavily. Mother, who had left the room when the yelling began, was hiding somewhere in the house.

Distraught and confused, I ran out of the house—forgetting to pick up my coat—and trudged into the icy, razor-sharp winds. Not knowing where else to go, I headed for town. Halfway there, I realized for the first time that I did not have my coat. In the circumstances, I couldn't go back home and returned to the station for my luggage instead.

Cold, tired, and too embarrassed to seek shelter with the families of my friends, I took a room at the Waverly Hotel with what little remained of my funds. Turned out of my own home, alone in an alien room, I hugged my knees to my chest and sobbed.

What have I done? I wondered. Perhaps I had made a terrible mistake. Perhaps my father was right. I was fortunate to have gone to school and should have borne the unhappy situation better. Father was, after all, only thinking about my best interests. Maybe I could return to school? Slowly, in the dark of the night, a plan formed in my mind. With the comforting vision of my joyously forgiving father, my chest felt less tight, and I was able at last to sleep.

Next morning, I left my luggage at the hotel and walked back home. I had decided to concede to Father the tremendous mistake I had made and to tell him I would be returning to school. Mother met me at the front door.

"You father is still furious. I think it's best he doesn't see you," she whispered nervously. She looked pale and tired, as if she too had slept little the previous night.

I tried to smile. "It's okay, Mama. I'm going back to school. I've come to tell Father."

She looked relieved. "Thank goodness! He's out back."

I found him sitting on the chopping block, hands resting on the axe handle, with the birch chunks he had hauled in from Broken Shell, some eighteen miles away, piled around him like a miniature mountain range. "I told you to leave." He spat out the words, his anger evidently unabated.

Shocked, I took an instinctive step backwards, without looking behind me, exclaiming as I bumped into the cast iron pump with its red handle. Along with a moment of pain, I experienced a strange longing to drink from the well with its familiar iron taste.

"Father," I began slowly, "I made a mistake. I'm sorry. I want to return to school."

In my imagination the previous night, I had pictured him throwing his arms around me, telling me how happy he was that I had come to my senses, reassuring me that all was forgiven. I must have been crazy, for he did nothing of the sort. He just went on sitting quietly on the chopping block, his lips pressed tightly together, his jaw muscles moving as if grinding stones.

Finally, he broke the nerve-wracking silence. "You've had this stubborn streak ever since you were little, Viktoria. I kept thinking you'd outgrow it one day. 'Give her enough rope,'

I'd tell myself, 'and she'll learn some sense.' But no, you used that rope to hang yourself."

"Father—" I began, trying to speak, hoping to get him to understand.

He lifted his hand threateningly, almost as if he would hit me, forcing me to stop. "Months ago I told your mother you'd had your last chance, and I meant it. If you didn't do the proper thing and get your teaching certificate, I said— then that was it. You said you wanted to follow some foolish dream of going to school in Toronto. I nearly told you to leave right then, but with my help, you came around and did what I knew was best for you. Now you just up and quit."

He paused. His face was red with anger. He was far from finished. "I should have done you a favour years ago and whipped that stubbornness right out of you—but I didn't. My own fault, I'm too soft. Now you come and tell me you want to go back to school. Well, that's fine by me; only this time, you'll do it on your own."

He looked at me bitterly. "You see, Viktoria, I know you—you're like your Uncle Alexandre. You'll get bored and change your mind, and do whatever you want to do next. See, you got this notion that you know what's best. Well, I've got some news for you—you don't. You can't expect to please yourself. Maybe when you see what the real world is like, maybe then you'll learn your lesson. So, I'm ordering you to leave, Viktoria. And don't come back."

His words appalled me, so that for a few moments I couldn't move. I felt paralyzed by his continuing fury.

"Leave," he commanded, coldly.

I stared at him in mute distress, but his expression did not soften. It was a few seconds before I could move again. When I did, I was able to take some steps in the direction of town. A few hundred feet from the house, on snow packed hard by horses and wagons, my mother caught up with me.

"What happened?" She looked frightened.

"I'm not wanted," I whispered over the unshed tears in my throat.

"Oh, Viktoria, what have you done?" she gasped. "Wait here!"

She ran back to the house. When she reappeared, she looked about furtively, as if guilty of a crime. "Take this," she said, handing me three one-dollar bills and a handful of nickels and pennies. "Where will you stay?"

"I don't know." I was unable to look further ahead than my next footfall. "I slept at the Waverly last night."

Mother's eyes widened in horror. "You can't stay there!" she exclaimed. "What if another blackguard starts trouble?" She was referring to an incident four years earlier, when the Idaho Kid had riddled the hotel ceiling with bullets from his Colt .45 revolver and threatened to take over the town and to shoot anyone who got in his way.

"I have nowhere else to go," I said, and walked away.

To this day, I can still see my mother standing in the middle of the road, hands covering her mouth in horror, as her apron billowed in the wind.

I returned to the hotel, hands and face numb and scarlet with cold. I took a room for another night and remained there all day with my strength seeping out of me. I felt as if I were an old horse that lies down, knowing it will never stand up again. In the afternoon, hunger drove me to the common room, where I ate for the first time in a day and a half. I chose the least expensive dish—ox beef, too highly seasoned and tough. The kind of meat, Aunt Alethea would have said, that

THE IMPACT of a SINGLE EVENT

made you sit down hungry and get up tired. Chewing laboriously, I tried to make myself as small as possible, in order to avoid attention.

I was about to return to my room when Mr. Powley, the owner of the hotel and an acquaintance of my father, sat down beside me. "I know it's none of my business, Viktoria, but why are you here?"

Taught to answer when an adult asked a question, I didn't hesitate to tell him of my circumstances, although I feared he, too, would order me out.

"So you're not in a bad way?" he asked, quite kindly.

It took a moment for me to understand what he meant. "Gracious, no!"

He looked at me thoughtfully. "I could use some help here."

"You'd give me a job? Won't my father be mad?"

"For hiring a dependable worker?" Mr. Powley asked, grimly. "If he is, then damn him. I have a business to run."

Tears filled my eyes, but I wiped them away before they fell. "Thank you, Mr. Powley," I said gratefully.

"Hold your thanks. You'll be working for your wages," he told me. And I did.

Before first light, Mr. Powley led me to a little room inside the barn behind the hotel, where I would do the laundry. The room contained dry wood, a stove to heat water, lines to hang sheets, and a wash basin. After doing the laundry, I would clean the rooms and change the linens. Once these tasks were completed, I was expected to serve customers in the common room until the end of the dinner hour. As I helped people the first night, I kept glancing at the ceiling to see the marks left by the Idaho Kid's bullets.

I stayed in a dilapidated room that shared a matchstick-thin wall with the saloon. At night, I would try to ignore the conversations of the men who spoke so colourfully that I wondered if my face would still be red in the morning. The windowless room, with its own private outside entrance, had just enough space for a small stove, a single lumpy mattress, and my two trunks. In the mornings, I would find ceiling plaster covering the trunks and floor. In the weeks that followed, the falling plaster got so bad that I actually slept with an open umbrella roped to the bedpost, to prevent the falling debris from disturbing me.

I cried myself to sleep at night, picturing the days, not so long ago, when I rose in the morning to a warm bowl of porridge and then traipsed off to school with Vanessa in tow. Outside the familiar little two-storey, stone schoolhouse, I might see Mr. Knowling exit the building, having lit the fire—for which he was paid ten cents a day. Inside, I could count on Mr. Moffat's energetic delivery of the multiplication tables, while my best friend, Patricia, and I passed notes to each other and worried about such mundane things as our hairstyles. In the evenings, the family might play cards, read by the fire, or simply discuss the management of the farm. Mother might mend a dress, father smoke his pipe, and Vanessa comb the hair of the dolls she should have outgrown years earlier. As I lay in my dreary bed, recalling those idyllic times, I heard the bawdy stories of the men in the adjoining room, and wondered if I, too, would look one day as they did, with their grey skin, decaying teeth, and haunted eyes.

I had been at the Waverly three weeks when I received an unexpected visit from my mother. Her eyes were red, her face gaunt; she looked as if she had been crying. After a stunned glance at my hair—for it looked like a bewitched barley stack, she told me later—she seized me and held me in her arms. Always at the edge of fear and loneliness, I wept quietly against her neck. For a few moments, her body was rigid against mine. She went slack, and then her shoulders shuddered. She was weeping, too.

"So much has happened, Viktoria," she said, when she could speak.

"I know, Mother," I gulped on a sob. "I'm so sorry."

Gripping my shoulders, she held me at arms' length. "You don't understand, dear. This is nothing to do with you."

Fear gripped me. If my leaving home had not caused her distress, something terrible must have occurred. Father? My sisters?

"What's wrong?" I whispered, anxiously.

She looked at me, her eyes welling with tears again. "It's your Uncle Alexandre....Oh Viktoria, he died."

She might just as well have struck me in the stomach. "I don't believe it!" I exclaimed, refusing to accept the words.

"Two days ago. Your aunt sent a telegram."

"What happened?" I asked urgently.

"Cancer. He had been sick for some time. Apparently, that's why they moved from Weyburn. Your aunt wanted Alexandre to be near his doctor in Winnipeg."

I stared helplessly at my mother. "I didn't know...they never told me...he seemed so well whenever I saw him. So happy." My voice trembled as I said the last words.

"They didn't want you to be sad. Besides, we didn't know either." Once more she hugged me. "Viktoria, your aunt wants us at the funeral. We're leaving for Winnipeg tomorrow morning. I want you to come with us."

After the unhappy weeks apart, my mother's closeness was comforting. I closed my eyes and leaned against her. Behind my eyelids, I saw Uncle Alexandre frolicking in the snow, his face mischievous as he put his arms around the snowman. He had been so happy. And all the time he had known. Aunt Alethea had known, too.

I opened my eyes and stepped back. "What about Father?"

"He can't leave the farm. Too much to do."

Quickly, I calculated my finances—which did not take long as Mr. Powley paid me so little. I wanted quite desperately to go to Winnipeg, but I knew I couldn't afford it. "I don't have money for the fare." I said quietly.

My mother surprised me. "I'll have money for your fare," she said. "Just make sure to be at the station at eight in the morning."

I was at the station by eight. Though Mr. Powley was not happy to see me go, he was a good friend of my aunt and uncle and had given me his condolences, as well as a note for Aunt Alethea. Mother and Vanessa were already at the station when I got there. Together, we boarded the Soo Line to Moose Jaw and then the CPR to Regina. Dorina joined us there for the last leg to Winnipeg.

We were halfway to Winnipeg, and my sisters were dozing in their seats across from me, when my mother leaned towards me. "Viktoria, your father thinks you may have learned your lesson," she said softly.

I caught my breath, wondering what was coming. "Oh?"

"If you promise to finish your teaching certificate and to do as he says from now on, he will consider paying for you to go back to school."

I looked at her, grateful to have been readmitted to a place where I would be safe, welcomed back by my family, to my home. "Oh, Mama," I said. "Thank you."

"You may even want to study in Winnipeg. They've built a new Normal School—did you know?—and your auntie might be happy to have your company."

I hugged her, thankful for the reprieve I'd been granted.

"Let's never speak of this ugly incident again," said my mother.

I could only nod. All that I could reasonably expect or ask for was suddenly mine again. Acceptance into my old home, the security of a safe profession, a road that led directly to a foreseeable destination. Why, I wondered, did I feel relief then, but no joy?

Aunt Alethea was at the station to meet us. As beautiful as ever, even now, she greeted us with hugs and kisses. Though I sensed her deep sadness, she did not have the appearance of the grief-stricken widow I had expected. Nor was the funeral the sombre affair I had imagined. Friends from as far away as Nova Scotia and Vermont were there to bid Uncle farewell. There were tears, but more than that, there was also laughter.

We stayed with Aunt Alethea for a week after the funeral. During that time, I desperately wanted to assist her, to offer words that might somehow help her cope with her loss. Yet, whenever I started to speak, I invariably found myself expressing my gratitude for her weekend hospitality. Consistently too, Aunt Alethea was gracious. She would say how great it had been to have me around, and how she and Uncle Alexandre had hoped they could provide me with a little break from the stress I was under. Though I was tempted to confide in her, to tell her everything that had happened to me recently, I sensed it would be selfish to talk about myself in her time of bereavement.

The day we boarded the train, Aunt Alethea thrust into my hand a hastily wrapped package. "I forgot to give this to you," she said in a whisper. "Your uncle wanted you to have it."

"What is it?" I asked, but she only smiled and shook her head.

I waited until I was alone—in the dining car, as it happened—before I opened the package. Curiously, and with a growing feeling of anticipation, I carefully removed the paper wrapping. The first thing I saw was a short note. Uncle Alexandre's handwriting—free and somehow joyous—I recognized it immediately. Looking at the date, I realized it must have been written just a few days before he died.

I looked around me and saw that I was still alone. I trembled as I began to read.

My dear Viktoria,

*Many years ago, a friend entrusted me with this journal. In my own time, and in my own way, I found the ideas inside it of great value to me. It is now my turn to find a suitable person to pass it on to. For many years, Alethea and I have observed your development, and we believe you are the right person to have the journal. In time, you will understand the thoughts contained in it, but I believe you will do so well before I did, because you have learned one of the most important things in life—always use your intuition. The difficulty does not lie in knowing what is best for you. It lies in the doing. Often your path is set out before your feet. Although the path is untrodden, **trust yourself to walk it.***

Putting the note aside, I opened the journal. A picture of a beautiful woman and a child was sketched on the inside cover, followed by many blank pages. At last, I came across a story; it was dated April 26, 1894, and was written by my uncle. The entry after his was dated 1867. At the time I didn't fully appreciate what I was reading, but I understood enough.

Trust yourself, my uncle's note had advised. Easier said than done, I mused, for I had learned already that self trust entailed a cost: being engaged in constant struggle, being looked at like a two-headed calf, being treated like a leper, and appearing abnormal to others. Was it worth it?

As we sped across the flat, white prairies, the train rocking me smoothly in my seat, I reflected on the last time I had ridden the iron rails home to Weyburn. Holding the journal and my uncle's note in my hands, I thought how strange it was that history repeated itself—for I knew, with absolute and exhilarating certainly, that I was returning, once again, to disappoint my father.

Viktoria Katharina Linck (née Kossuth)

Richard

A few hours later, I wake to the sound of Sonia's voice. She is speaking on the phone in the kitchen. I can hear her from my position on the chesterfield.

"I'm inquiring about a Jenner and Kimberly Herac. The last name is spelled H-E-R-A-C. There was a car accident, and they were brought in last night," she says.

I swing my feet to the floor and rub my eyes. I sit up, waiting tensely to find out if the couple survived surgery. The sun is shining through the front window. My watch tells me it's already nine o'clock.

"Yes, please," Sonia says. And then, half a minute later, "I'm inquiring about Jenner and Kimberly Herac. Last name is spelled—Oh, you have it—yes, that's right. Yes, an accident...*oh, really?* Yes...thank you..." Then, almost as an afterthought: "What time are visiting hours?"

Sonia's response tells me at least one of the couple is alive.

"Thank you," she says again. "Thank you very much,"

Moments later, she comes to tell me that the Heracs are both alive and in the ICU.

"Thank goodness for that," I say quietly.

As I look at her standing in the doorway of the living room, I recall how tempted I was last night to wrap my arms around her. What had stopped me was the memory of the drive home from the Granby Hospital, when both of us had avoided talking about the reason we'd come upon the accident to begin with: that we'd cut down our two-week vacation by twelve days. Now, twelve hours later, what do we do? Pretend it didn't happen?

"I've made some tea," she says then. Is her tone coolly dispassionate or just extraordinarily tired? I wish I could tell.

"Thanks," I say, and join her at the round table in the kitchen.

We sit in our usual chairs, opposite each other, in the seating arrangement that evolved when Nadie and Aidan were babies. By having the kids on either side of us, Sonia and I were both able to help when food needed spooning into small mouths, meat needed cutting, or milk had to be poured. We might have gone back to sitting side by side a few years ago, when the kids became independent eaters, but Aidan's eating habits disgusted Nadie so much that we had to keep them apart.

"Get any sleep last night?" Sonia asks, stirring her tea.

"A little. You?"

"Not really," she says quietly.

Briefly, I wonder if the sad little voice is intended to manipulate me: then I notice the pupil of her left eye moving towards her nose. When Sonia is nervous or upset, she scratches her arms and neck. When she is exhausted, her left eye sometimes wanders. I've seen it happen only a few times before today, always when she was extremely tired. I don't know if Sonia is aware of her wandering eye. Concerned that she might feel self-conscious, I've never mentioned it to her. After all, I know from experience that being too aware of a physical imperfection can be debilitating.

"So," I ask, "were you told anything else about the Heracs?"

"Only what I told you—that they're in intensive care."

I look across the table at her. One hand rests on the polished wood. It would be so easy to touch it, but I don't know how she would react to the gesture. "Want to go to the hospital?" I ask. "We could drop off the Heracs' things."

Sonia nods, "Yes, I think we should go."

The drive to the hospital takes considerably longer than did our trip from Granby the night before, with accidents and backed-up traffic forcing detours and impeding our progress. As we pass the university campus, I think about Thompson House, the graduate student centre at McGill, and the Halloween party where Sonia and I met.

Around me people were drinking and enjoying themselves, but for some reason, I couldn't join in the general conviviality. I didn't want to drink. I felt out of place and lonely. I also hated my costume. I had put a few things together in haste: a laundry basket with a hole cut in the middle, which rested on my hips; socks and fabric softener sheets pinned to my sweatshirt; an empty Sunlight detergent box, which I wore on my head, like a yellow cherry on a plain vanilla sundae.

I was thinking about leaving, when Jerry, one of the guys I'd come with—debonair in World War I flying ace goggles—urged me to stay longer.

"Don't go," he said persuasively, against my protests. "Stay. So many women—the place is a target-rich environment."

"None of them are my type."

"What? You think they're all ugly?" he asked in mock surprise.

I knew he was teasing. There were lots of attractive women, but as usual when I was sober, feelings of insecurity about my leg stopped me from approaching them. Generally, I only talked to women when they approached me. Of course, Jerry was a fairly new acquaintance. He didn't know about my leg, for I had learned to hide my limp very well by then.

"There must be at least one girl here who's your type."

"Fine. Her, with the tiara." I pointed to a woman with short, dark hair, dressed up in a long, black evening dress with a pillow above her belly to indicate she was in a family way. The sash across her front read "Miss Conception." She was easily the best-looking woman at the party.

"Right," Jerry said, and moved in her direction, careful not to spill his precious rum and coke.

I didn't need to accompany him to know what would happen. Jerry would throw out some terrible pickup line, point at me, and be politely rebuffed. Unwilling to endure the humiliation of being turned down by someone I'd never met, I deliberately turned my back on what was sure to be an awkward scene and searched the crowd for someone I could talk to instead. Not much more than a minute later, someone tapped my shoulder. In shock, I looked at Jerry accompanied by the beautiful Miss Conception. Her eyes were blue or green, I couldn't tell which. She wore no visible makeup, aside from lipstick, and dangling from her neck was a fascinating necklace of Celtic art. I had to remind myself over and over again: don't look down; she'll think you're staring at her breasts. Later, I learned that Jerry's first question to her was, "Are you single?" followed by, "Do you like guys who wear laundry baskets?" She had answered yes to both questions.

Jerry threw me a wink as the lovely woman unselfconsciously introduced herself as Sonia. Jerry vanished then, leaving me to blather out my own name.

"*Parlez-vous Français?*" she asked with a smile.

"No, not very well." "Not at all" would have been a more honest answer, for to my shame, I had picked up almost no French since moving to Montreal five years earlier.

"I don't either. Only been in Montreal a couple months. Still trying to pick up the basics," she said, which was a fib.

In time, I would learn that after her mother had died in a car accident, Sonia and her brother, Anton, had travelled the world with their father, a mining engineer who worked in many different countries. Born in Burlington, Ontario, she had lived in Brazil, Chile, Tanzania, and Australia. In addition to English, she could speak Spanish, Portuguese, and Swahili. Though she is linguistically talented, I don't remember her ever boasting about all the languages she knew.

I struggled to find something—anything—to say to this beautiful woman.

"So, ah, what are you taking?" My lips felt frozen with Novocaine. Like I had just stepped out of a dentist's chair.

"A master's in environmental engineering."

I wasn't sure if she was putting me on, for female engineers were quite rare then. I wondered if she was testing me. But no, she looked serious. "Excellent!" I said inadequately, feeling a little foolish. I was acting too excited. I needed to be cool.

"What are you taking?"

I told her about my master's in history and my goal to write.

She looked interested. "History books?"

"No. Short stories. Novels."

"Why history then?"

"I got my bachelor's in history and figured I'd just keep going." I tried hard to keep my voice even. My mouth felt dry. I wished I'd had a drink.

"Have you published anything?" she asked.

"Yes," I said, and told her enthusiastically about my latest short story, which *Quill & Quire* had accepted the month before. Once started, I was able to keep going. For a while, I talked about myself and my plans to be a writer, when I realized that I should offer this beautiful woman a drink. "I'd love something cool," she said, and agreed to keep our seats while I walked across the room and around the iron railing that separated the party area from the bar.

Standing in the drinks lineup, I kept peering back to see if she was still waiting. She returned my glances with a big grin. Emboldened, and wanting her to think I was the athletic kind—isn't that what beautiful women go for?—I figured I'd show off a little and leap the railing. Knowing I could still dunk a basketball, which necessitated a jump, clearing the three-foot high railing would not pose a problem.

Holding both drinks in my right hand, I put my left hand on the iron railing. Then, in one smooth move, I pushed off with my good left foot and swung my legs up and over. With the body control of a ballet dancer, I cleared the railing with my feet together. At the same moment, revelling in a grace I had once had, I looked across the room directly at Sonia. A fraction of a second later, when my body did not follow my feet, I realized something had gone terribly wrong. The laundry basket had caught on the railing. I knew I was in trouble—which was compounded when I tried to save the situation, twisted awkwardly, and knocked my head sideways against a table. The final indignity was that I passed out a few seconds after that.

Beautiful Sonia was the first person I saw when I came to. "Are you all right?" she asked, her lovely blue-green eyes warm with concern.

"Yes," I mumbled shyly, wishing there was some way to sink through the floor.

"Are you sure?"

I felt wretched. If only I could have put my clumsiness down to excess alcohol, but I hadn't had even one drink. I closed my eyes like a child, as if the world didn't exist if I couldn't see it. It was then that I noticed the music had stopped. *Walk away. Please walk away*, I begged her silently. Instead, I heard her laugh. I looked up to a softly sweet face.

"Well, at least you saved the drinks," she said with a smile.

By some miracle, I was still holding the two drinks, with one a little sticky from the bit that had sloshed over the rim. I stood up as gracefully as possible, handed her a drink, and felt a jolt of pleasure as she gave my back an affectionate pat. She gave me her phone number that night after I walked her home.

We began to see each other frequently after that. We went to movies, to dinner. Often we walked on Mount Royal, never tiring of each other's company. To my surprise, Sonia remained as sweet and kind as she'd been that first evening.

Perhaps it was only my inexperience with women that had made me think someone so beautiful could not have other qualities as well. Even so, it took me months to summon enough courage to tell Sonia about my leg. Somehow, I had managed to hide the disfigurement until then. When I finally allowed Sonia to see my leg, she didn't react with repugnance like previous girlfriends. She simply asked if it hurt me.

Even then, relieved as I was that the withered leg didn't seem to bother Sonia, I couldn't stop wondering whether she was being honest with me. I could not rid myself of the thought. After Sonia and I were married, there was still a part of me that wondered whether she secretly wished her husband was a "whole" man. Strange though this may be, I've never stopped thinking I'd be happier if I had normal legs. It would mean not having to worry about covering up all the time. I'd be free to wear shorts. I could swim openly with the kids.

When we finally get through the Monday morning Montreal traffic and arrive at the Granby hospital, we haul the suitcases and the garbage bags to the intensive care unit. At the nursing station, Sonia and I tell a nurse why we are there. The nurse is the one Sonia spoke to a couple of hours earlier and has been expecting us.

"I'm sorry that I can't let you see them," she says. "I forgot to mention you'd have to wait until the patients are conscious and can give permission themselves for you to visit." The nurse is just obeying protocol, as did the officer the previous night when he would not give us the Heracs' names.

"Has the family been contacted?" Sonia asks.

"As far as I know, not yet."

"Can we leave a note for Jenner and Kimberly?"

"Yes, of course. I'll make sure they get it if...when they wake up."

Sonia gets a piece of paper from the nurse and fills both sides with our get-well wishes. She includes our phone number and address, as well as an invitation for them to call if they need anything.

After the friendly nurse has said where we can leave the Heracs' possessions, we walk reluctantly away.

"Richard, I can't stand the idea that those poor people are going to wake up in a strange hospital without a familiar face by their bedsides," Sonia says as we reach the elevator.

She brightens immediately when I suggest we buy flowers: the first time I've seen her smile in two days. Briefly, my mood lightens too, especially when Sonia is enthusiastic about the idea.

We are on our way to the gift shop when we realize that flowers will not be allowed in the ICU. Instead, we purchase a few useful items—toothbrushes, toothpaste, and deodorant—which we leave at the nursing station in the hope that the Heracs will soon be able to enjoy them.

"Did you pack that old diary?" Sonia asks as we get into the car.

"Yes, I put it in one of the suitcases," I say.

"I would have liked to look at the sketches again. And I'm curious about the contents."

I am curious too.

Alexandre Gerard Arouet

April 26, 1894

$\mathscr{I}$ believe it may be of interest to future recipients of this journal to know its history. The entry that follows tells the tale of how I became the temporary custodian of the journal, and of the man who bequeathed it to me.

"Good morning young sir," Mr. Sumac addressed me, the first time I walked into his store in June of 1870.

"Good morning, sir. May I come in?"

I had been prowling about outside the store since it had opened its doors a week earlier, anxious to see the contents inside, but frightened of doing so. I had been biding my time, throwing stones at the abandoned soldiers' barracks across the road and pretending to be unaware of the newest business, located between the clock repair shop and the dentist's office, on Queen Street.

"Do please enter. May I be of service?" Mr. Sumac asked from behind his large grey moustache, so bushy it covered his lower lip. Only the movement of his jaw gave any indication that the words emanated from him.

"May I look about?" I asked, as politely as I knew how. My father owned the two-storey red brick building, which housed Mr. Sumac's business. I was uncertain whether my father had warned Mr. Sumac not to admit me, for I knew he did not approve of the contents of the store.

"Why, please do," Mr. Sumac said cheerfully, pulling his small, round spectacles off his greying head and adjusting them upon his nose.

"Thank you, sir. Thank you," I said, in the manner of a starving man who had been offered a plate of gravy and a loaf of bread with which to sop it up.

On the right side of the narrow store were various stationery products as well as tobacco, cigars, cigarettes, and pipes. At the rear, where he had his counter, Mr. Sumac was well supplied with the latest newspapers and magazines such as, among others, *Godey's Lady's Book*, *The Atlantic Monthly*, and *Harper's Magazine*. Down the centre, were displayed the most recent offerings of the business: inks, embossed writing paper, magnifying lenses, pencil boxes, pen sets, and the like. These items were placed on three-foot high tables, while larger items, such as writing desks, were set on the floor. But the real magic, the enchantment that drew me, lay along the entire left wall of the store—books of fiction—from the floor to as high as I could reach.

To my father, whimsical tales and invented stories were a waste of time. According to him, works of the imagination did not prepare one for the realities of life. He told me that even if a person were to find himself in a prosperous situation with leisure time at his disposal, works of fiction only weakened the mind, thereby limiting a person's benefit to the community.

"You will restrict your reading to school books," my father had said, snatching a borrowed copy of *David Copperfield* from my hands a year earlier. He did not threaten to beat me, but his utterance was ominous enough for me to hide the passion that had been growing in me since I had learned my letters way back in the first grade.

"Is there a particular item you are interested in?" Mr. Sumac asked, coming out from behind his counter. I stood before the wall of books, staggered by the number of volumes on the shelves. There was no public library in Fredericton.

"May I touch them?" I asked hesitantly.

"Yes," he said, doing his best to hide his amusement from my serious eleven-year-old self.

Tentatively, I reached out for *The Snow-Image and Other Twice-Told Tales* by Nathaniel Hawthorne.

"What's your name, son?"

It was the question I had been dreading and hoped he would not ask. I looked down at my feet, shifting them restlessly. I was almost sure Mr. Sumac would throw me out of the store if he knew who my father was. For a moment, I actually considered inventing a name. But I didn't. "Alexandre Arouet, sir," I said softly.

Mr. Sumac's eyes widened as he looked down at me. He was surprised; I could see that. The momentary amusement was gone, replaced by an expression that was difficult to read.

"Pierre's boy?"

It was strange to hear someone speak of my father by his given name. He was an important businessman in the town, and those who knew him treated him with awe and respect. "Mr. Arouet," they called him. I had no idea how far his commercial interests extended, what little I knew having been gleaned from oddments of conversation I happened to overhear.

Once, I heard him complaining to my mother about the incompetence of his manager at the City Bakery. On another occasion, I eavesdropped on a meeting he had with Mayor Browne. Father had an office off the kitchen, with an outside entrance through which he could enter and exit. Through a keyhole in the office door, I listened to him speak to the mayor.

"We need to run that goddamn tinsmith out of town. Three more years remain on the lease, and I have plans for that building," said my father.

The tinsmith was Mr. Napoleon LaForest, a friendly man in his waning years, whose business was located on the corner of Queen and York. I once asked Father if he was related to Napoleon in France. "Don't be a goddamn fool," he said. I interpreted this as a "no." I tried very hard not to be a goddamn fool after that.

"What are you asking me to do?" Mayor Browne asked.

"Invent a charge. Force him to leave," my father said, his voice raised.

"I cannot do that, Mr. Arouet," the mayor protested. "You know my hands are tied. Get Hopkins to help you."

Mr. Hopkins, a prosperous lawyer in town, did help my father. He found an obscure clause in the lease, which allowed my father to raise Mr. LaForest's rent by 200 percent. With no means of paying such an extortionate increase, Mr. LaForest was helpless to prevent his tools and personal possessions from being seized and sold at auction.

My father insisted I attend the auction, refusing to listen to me when I pleaded not to go. I felt so bad about what was about to happen that I tried to hide in the corner. I could not bear the idea that Mr. LaForest might see me and associate me with my father's actions. For a while I succeeded. Then, almost by accident our eyes met. Mr. LaForest looked at me sadly. Perhaps he understood that this terrible thing was none of my doing. Just watching him, I felt a deep sadness of my own. Mr. LaForest looked so terribly lost, like a child on the first day of school, uncertain of where he should stand or what he should be doing—only much worse.

Once the auction began, he hid his face in his hands, and his shoulders began to heave. For much of the auction, he sobbed quietly, pulling out his handkerchief every few minutes to wipe his face. While Mr. LaForest wept, my father smirked, as if he took some perverse satisfaction in destroying a man's living and his pride. I don't know why he forced me to accompany him that day. I can only assume it was to toughen me up or to show me the extent of his power. Whatever his reason, the whole experience made me physically ill.

"Yes sir," I said to Mr. Sumac, lifting my head for a moment. "Pierre Arouet is my father."

Now, Mr. Sumac—who must surely know about the auction—would ask me to leave the store. I looked down at the floor once more, waiting for him to issue the order.

To my surprise, he did nothing of the sort. "It's a pleasure to make your acquaintance, Alexandre. My name is Torvus Sumac," he said, extending a hand.

It was rumoured, by my mother at least, that Mr. Sumac, a widower, was once a man of great wealth who had since fallen on hard times. After a stint out west to restore his fortune, he returned east to Fredericton in search of a business opportunity. Since my father did not speak of financial matters, I assumed this was not the sort of subject a polite person could discuss openly—and, therefore, I never asked Mr. Sumac if the rumours were true.

"It's a pleasure to meet you too, Mr. Sumac," I said, astonished and relieved by the unexpected welcome.

"Call me Torvus, Alexandre."

"Yes, Mr. Sumac."

He laughed. "What is it I can help you find?"

"I only wanted to see the books, Mr. Sumac, sir."

"I'd best leave you be then. Peruse away," he said, bowing and gesturing to the wall.

For the next little while I was enraptured. After reading the first page of the Nathaniel Hawthorne book, I put it back where I had found it. I pulled out another book, *An Irish Girl in America*, read the first page, then replaced it on the shelf. I continued in this way, picking up a dozen different books at random. I felt like a poor boy mistakenly invited to an exquisite banquet; I wanted to sample everything before I was asked to leave.

Nervous that my father might catch me in the store, I decided to depart of my own volition. Before leaving, I approached Mr. Sumac. He was at the counter, glasses perched on his head again, and reading a book of his own.

"Thank you, Mr. Sumac, sir."

"You're welcome, Alexandre. Please come back again," he said cheerfully.

And I did. Frequently.

At the conclusion of school each day, I would run down Brunswick Street, which usually flooded in spring when the St. John River crested its banks. I would pass Grapelawn, the name given to Mr. Botsford's vine-covered home. After that I'd head northeast down Carleton Street, then finally northwest down Queen Street and into the bookstore. Following a pleasant exchange of greetings with Mr. Sumac, I would carefully take a book from a shelf, read the first page, and then replace it. Each day I stayed a little longer—until one day I stayed too long.

I was examining a new book when the bell over the front door jingled, and a man entered the store. *My father!* Instantly, my breath grew shallow.

"Imposing" is the word that best described my father. He was a tall man, made more so by the high hats he wore. His beard and moustache were well trimmed; he habitually wore well-tailored suits and had little time for anything but the state of his commercial interests. Always in a hurry, he was frequently to be seen pacing Fredericton, chewing on an unlit cigar and perpetually consulting his gold pocket watch.

Once, in an unusual display of fellowship—induced, I believe, by the purchase of the controlling interest in the Barker House Hotel—he said to me with a grin, "Remember, Alexandre, success breeds happiness. The more you accomplish, the happier you will be." I remember these words for two reasons: first, because he rarely spoke to me; and second, because he rarely smiled.

"Good afternoon, Mr. Sumac," my father boomed from the door. He had removed his hat and was cradling it in his hand.

I dropped to the floor in terror.

"Good afternoon, Mr. Arouet," Mr. Sumac responded serenely, moving from behind the counter in my direction. "How are you this fine day?"

"Busy. Are you settling in?" asked my father. Mercifully, he had not seen me; the middle row of wares shielded me from his sight.

"Assuredly well," Mr. Sumac said, as he bent down to help me up.

I shook my head vigorously. Evidently thinking I had accidentally fallen and hurt myself, he straightened with a look of surprise.

My father took two steps further into the store. "Something the matter, Mr. Sumac?" I winced as the floor-boards squeaked beneath his heavy footfalls.

Desperately, I stared at the bookseller, my eyes pleading with him not to report my presence. I willed him to understand.

"It appears...." Mr. Sumac's words trailed away.

My father took another creaking step into the store. "Yes? What is it?" he inquired, forcefully.

I was trembling as I shrank behind a pyramid of oil lamps set up at the end of the middle row of shelves, unable to scurry away.

Mercifully, Mr. Sumac had understood me. He recovered his wits quickly. "Why, nothing amiss, only a large spider."

My father came closer, as if to investigate—perhaps he did not believe Mr. Sumac. I heard the sound of doom in his footsteps.

Mr. Sumac bent down, as if to scoop a spider into his hand. "Ah! I have the beast," he declared. Whereupon, he walked past my father through the store and tossed the imaginary spider out the door.

From behind the stack of oil lamps, I watched my father pause midway between the door and my hiding place. He stood motionless for what seemed like eternity. At last, with an almost imperceptible shake of his head, he strode back to the door.

"Very well. Good day to you, sir." My father departed, and I took a long, deep breath of musty air.

"Good day, Mr. Arouet," Mr Sumac called to a slamming door. He watched my father stride down the street and disappear around the corner. Half a minute later, he walked back to where I still cowered behind the pyramid of oil lamps.

"Can you enlighten me, Alexandre?" he asked, offering me his hand.

I blinked hard as I looked up at him, still shaken by my close escape. Had I managed to evade my father's wrath only to incur Mr. Sumac's?

"Have you been playing truant, Alexandre?"

"No, Mr. Sumac. I've never missed school, sir," I answered, as I stood up and dusted off my pants.

"Have you been dipping girls' pigtails in your ink bottle?" I thought the question was serious until I saw him wink.

"No sir," I assured him.

"Why the ruse?"

I knew very well that if I were to be honest with Mr. Sumac, I would be exiled from paradise. I strove to think of a believable lie; however, with my state of mind still so perturbed, I found my well of ideas had run dry. Finally, I spoke. "My father does not approve of books, sir."

"The deuce, you say!"

"Yes, Mr. Sumac. He believes reading to be a waste of working hours."

The bookseller looked at me, his expression enigmatic. "This puts us in an awkward situation—does it not?"

I nodded. A gloomy darkness settled about me, and the light through the windows seemed to dim, as if a cloud were blocking the sun.

"Boys must obey their fathers. Do you not agree?"

I nodded again. I stood quite still for a moment, then reluctantly began to drag my feet to the door, each footstep as heavy as if my shoes were caked with mud. The doors of paradise were about to be shut to me.

I was almost at the door when Mr. Sumac called to me. "Alexandre!"

I turned to see him pull his spectacles from his head, fold them, and then tap his palm with them. He seemed about to speak, but the words did not come. He hesitated a few seconds. Then he nodded, almost as if he were agreeing with some inner voice. "You may come here whenever you please," he said. "I will say nothing to your father."

I was suddenly breathless. *"Mr. Sumac?"*

"No man should be deprived of the pleasure of books."

Suddenly the sun seemed to regain its strength, and the store was flooded with light again. "Thank you, sir. Oh, thank you," I said, and leaped into the dusty street.

Months later I asked why, when he was aware of my father's disapproval, Mr. Sumac had invited me to visit the store. What he told me explained a lot. As a child, he had been left-handed. On first learning his letters, he had quite naturally attempted to write with his left hand. His teachers interpreted his left-handedness as a sign of satanic influence, for according to Christian Scripture, the Last Judgement would see the righteous sit on God's right, while the wicked would sit on His left. To avoid such punishment, his teachers had tied his left arm to his side, thereby forcing him to work with the correct hand—his right hand. At night, Mr. Sumac confessed, he would defy his teachers by practicing with his left hand.

"Authority lays no claim on wisdom," he stated. Then, brushing his furry lip with his index finger, he added, "But I suppose, neither can I."

For the next six months, through the summer and well into the next school year, I visited Mr. Sumac nearly every day, his books drawing me like iron filings to a magnet. Knowing I would be allowed to enter the store whenever I pleased, I ended my practice of reading a single page from every book, instead reading an entire book before starting the next. On occasion I would randomly choose a book myself, though more often than not, Mr. Sumac would suggest one to me.

I recall the first time he made a recommendation to me. Standing before a shelf of what seemed like a hundred volumes, he passed his hand over the spines of the books, almost as if he could absorb the contents through his fingertips. Pausing now and again, his brow would furrow as if in remembrance of his own experience with the book.

At one particular book, he paused. I saw his eyes widen at the same time as the furrow vanished. Sliding the book from its place on the shelf, he presented it to me with both hands. The book was *The Whale*, its author, Herman Melville. "This one is first-rate," he said, with such persuasive enthusiasm that I began to read immediately.

I cherished the time I spent in Mr. Sumac's bookshop. I loved the distinctive, musty smell of the books, the softness of the leather in my hands. The stories challenged and stimulated me, opening my mind to possibilities I had never dreamed of before. As I began to read, I always knew I could count on being transported to exciting cities, the untamed frontiers of the West, or swashbuckling adventures with Athos, Porthos, and Aramis. It seemed appropriate that the sign over the door read, *Life is a Journey*.

A typical visit would have me greet Mr. Sumac, scan the shelves for the book I was in the process of reading, and then nestle into the corner where the wall of books met the back counter. In that spot, I was hidden from the front door by the middle row of wares, thereby enjoying a modicum of protection from my father's periodic visits.

Mr. Sumac and I would read in companionable silence, rarely talking to each other, he perched on his stool, and I seated securely in my corner. Now and then, he would retreat into the stockroom to attend to his ledger, leaving me to read by myself. Whenever he did so, he would ask me to notify him if someone entered the store.

I am afraid I was not very diligent, and certainly not wary enough with regard to my father, for often Mr. Sumac would be totalling a customer's purchase before I realized there was another presence in the store. My utter absorption in remarkable fictional adventures rendered me oblivious to something as insignificant as other people. I do not think it an exaggeration to say that only a gunshot could have broken my concentration.

When my dinner hour approached, Mr. Sumac would lean over the counter and give me a gentle nudge. "Best be off," he would say. Reluctantly, I would replace the book exactly where I had found it on the shelf, and head for home empty handed.

Although I was fortunate enough to be able to read in Mr. Sumac's store, I longed to own a book of my own, which I could read wherever and whenever I chose. Three days before my twelfth birthday, an opportunity seemed to present itself.

"Is there something special you would like for your birthday?" asked my mother one evening, as I helped her set the table for dinner.

"Yes, Mother. I want *The Whale*."

"You want a whale for your birthday, dear?"

"No, mother," I said, a little bothered that she did not understand me. "I want the book, *The Whale*, by Herman Melville. It's a story about Ahab, a one-legged whaling captain who hunts a great white whale."

She shook her head sadly. "I'm sorry, dear. I do not think that will be possible."

"But, it's what I want."

My mother's eyes were troubled. "You know your father's attitude towards reading, Alexandre. How about a toy soldier?" The question was asked with pretended enthusiasm.

Not so long ago, I had been fascinated with the toy soldiers of my friends. Perhaps I had mentioned them to my mother, which would have caused her question. What she did not know was that my interest in tin soldiers had ended with my discovery of the bookstore.

"I don't like soldiers any more."

"A new pencil box?" she asked hopefully.

"No thanks, Mother. I want a book. Mr. Sumac has *The Whale* in his store," I said, forgetting the necessity to keep secret my daily foray into the bookstore.

My mother frowned, obviously puzzled. "Alexandre, you haven't been in Mr. Sumac's business, have you?"

At that moment, we both heard a click. Mother put a quick finger to her lips before knocking softly on the locked door that led to my father's study. "Pierre, are you home?" she called. When there was no answer, she turned back to me and whispered, "Have you been harassing Mr. Sumac, Alexandre?"

I regret to say I lost patience with my mother rather quickly: a reprehensible habit I was beginning to inherit from my father, who would, without provocation, yell at my mother, calling her a fool and an imbecile. "Mr. Sumac lets me read anytime I want," I said, angrily raising my voice at the insinuation that I was a nuisance. The floorboards creaked suddenly. Small hairs stood on the back of my neck, like the hackles of a frightened dog, but I failed to heed my body's warning.

"Your father will not be pleased," my mother said, sounding frightened. "You had best cease your visits to the store."

"I will not," I said, outraged at the suggestion. For half a year now, I had been living and inhaling beautiful works of the imagination: they had become such a natural part of my existence that I felt no shame at my duplicitous behaviour. "Mr. Sumac says I can visit anytime I please. I mean to read whenever I want. And you and I, Mother, and Mr. Sumac will keep my secret." I'm ashamed to admit I was bullying my mother, treating her the way I had seen my father do on numerous occasions.

At that very moment the door of my father's study opened, so noiselessly that I was not immediately aware of it happening. Ominously red-faced with wrath, my father strode into the kitchen. "Deceitful child!" he spat out. "There will be no more clandestine visits to that place."

Trembling, my aggression instantly gone, I could only look at him wordlessly. Normally, in conversation with my father, I said no more than "Yes, sir" and "No, sir." I tried to respond this time, I really did, but in my fear and confusion, I could not find words to defend myself.

"To your room. I shall deal with you there," he ordered, pointing to the stairs.

My mother looked down at her hands. She was trembling too, I noticed, realizing there was nothing she could say or do to help me. In any event, she would find herself in as much trouble as me, for failing to know the whereabouts of her son from dawn to dusk.

For the next two days, I felt as if my world had imploded. I brooded constantly upon the injustice—a cruel strapping— my father had inflicted upon me. Still, I could bear the physical insult more easily than the irrevocable loss of my reading privileges, the latter being a far more grievous injury. My father had forbidden me to enter Mr. Sumac's store ever again.

At school, in those two days before my birthday, I kept my eyes to the floor, raising them only when I had to, so that I might follow my lessons. Such were the depths of my despair that after school I wandered the snow-covered banks of the St. John, from the Cathedral Common to Government House, instead of reporting directly to my father, even though my late arrivals would prompt further strappings. Both days I stopped at the three-storey stone Government House, the site of many formal dinners and balls, and boldly walked across the sleeping garden, where in the summer, Fredericton's social elite played croquet matches. I picked out the second-storey room that had accommodated the eighteen-year-old Prince of Wales in 1860. If I were king, I mused, I would do as I pleased. On my way home, I passed the Old Burial Ground, wishing my father were interred there.

As I walked to school on the morning of my birthday, my maudlin mood yielded to anger. I do not know what elicited this change in disposition; I attribute it to the capriciousness of youth. Regardless of the cause, I felt a surging fury at my father's unreasonable attitude towards books. Young as I was, I could understand that my chores and school work might possibly have priority over reading for pleasure. What I did not understand was, if reading did not interfere with either of those duties, why should I be denied such a reasonable pastime? And so I decided that, regardless of my father's orders, I would not be denied my desire.

All the money I had was the meagre pocket money my mother sometimes slipped me surreptitiously. I was quite aware that even if I saved for an entire year, I would not have sufficient money to purchase a book. I knew also that my friends were without adequate wealth to aid me in my endeavour. I considered trading something of value with Mr. Sumac in exchange for a book, but after taking inventory of my possessions—a broken watch, a pocket knife, an odd assortment of string, buttons, and whatnot, to name just the most "valuable"—I realized that a trade was quite improbable. The watch had never worked: I had found it in the street one day and had kept it only because my father wore a pocket watch. My pocket knife would not do either. Proud of it as

I was, it paled in comparison with the one I had seen Mr. Sumac use. Lastly, it went without saying that my assortment of oddments would not be of interest to him.

I was feeling desperate, when a new thought awakened in my mind, a thought that grew rapidly, like a weed in fertile soil. It had occurred to me that my easiest course would be to steal the book I wanted from Mr. Sumac. The moment the thought materialized, I knew it was wrong, yet I managed to convince myself otherwise. Mr. Sumac, I reasoned, had so many books—hundreds, maybe thousands!—that surely he would not miss one little adventure story. Besides, as a businessman—my father being the one I knew best—he had probably cheated my father out of rent money at some point, I reckoned. This being the case, the theft of a book would be no more than the evening of the balance sheet. Having assuaged the guilty feeling, if only briefly, I began to devise a strategy.

When Mr. Sumac retreated to the stockroom, as he unfailingly did at some point in the day, I would quietly remove my chosen book from its shelf and slide it under my armpit, between my shirt and coat. With my arm pressed tightly against my body, I could hold the book in place. When Mr. Sumac emerged from the stockroom, I would pretend to read calmly for another five or ten minutes, so as not to arouse his suspicions. Then I would bid him good day, and leave. Home at last, and safe in my room, I would enjoy the fruits of my cunning. At school all that day, I remember going over the details of my plan again and again. I recall practising the armpit manoeuvre with my notebook numerous times, only stopping when the teacher ordered me to sit still.

As I made my way to the bookstore immediately after school, my heart beat as hard as if I were running to avoid an angry, barking dog. When I entered the shop, Mr. Sumac greeted me pleasantly and asked where I had been. Evidently, my father had not confronted him yet; perhaps, he had never meant to. In the past, on the odd day when I had not gone to the shop, it was usually because I had had to run errands for my father. The lie came quickly to my mind. "I had to help my father," I said.

Mr. Sumac smiled and nodded, as if he had been expecting that very response. "I have something for you, Alexandre," he said, and disappeared into his stockroom.

Unsure if I would get another chance, I jumped at the opportunity to steal my book and started towards my intended goal, but heard Mr. Sumac returning all too quickly. As the book I sought was well out of my reach, I grabbed the one nearest my right hand. Clumsily, I pushed it under my left armpit and then straightened both arms at my sides, like a soldier on parade. Seconds later Mr. Sumac appeared before me. Not knowing if he'd seen what I'd done, I was about to confess my crime when he smiled and said, "I believe it's your birthday today, and I want to give you a present. Happy birthday, Alexandre."

With these words, he produced a book from behind his back. Squeezing my left arm hard against my body to keep the stolen book from falling, I took the proffered book with my right hand. As I held the gift dumbly in front of me, I read the title: *The Count of Monte Cristo.*

"I don't believe you've read this yet, but if you have, let me know. I have another first-rate choice."

I managed to stammer that I had not read this particular book before.

"It may be a little advanced for you, but I think you will enjoy it. I hope you will." He smiled at me, took his regular seat behind the front counter, and started to read his own book for the day.

My face burned with shame. Mr. Sumac had just given

me the one thing in the world I desired the most, and yet here I was, perpetrating a crime against him. As I look back on that day now, I realize it would have been prudent to sneak the first book back onto the shelf. At the time, however, my mind was such a turmoil of conflicting emotions—self-disgust mixed with joy—that I was unable to think clearly. All I knew was that I had two books now!

I had to escape.

With my left arm clenching the stolen book tightly against my body, and my right hand holding the gift book, I ran for the door. Terror struck as I realized I needed a free hand to undo the latch. Recovering my wits, I transferred Mr. Sumac's gift to my left hand—while still keeping that arm as straight as possible—and opened the door with my right hand. I was in the process of exiting the building, when I felt a hard tug on my coat. I stopped abruptly, expecting Mr. Sumac to haul me back into his store. After a few agonizing moments I turned, only to find that, in my haste, I had let the door, which was rigged with a metal spring, close on my coat. Through the window of the door, I saw Mr. Sumac getting up from his stool, as if to assist me. Moving fast, I opened the door and ran.

Racing down Queen Street towards home, it seemed as though all eyes were on me. I was sure everybody knew what I had done. It was as if the word "criminal" was emblazoned on my forehead, so roiling were my emotions. Breathing hard and running awkwardly, my left arm still tightly at my side, I bolted into the house, past my mother, who was preparing dinner in the kitchen, and made for the stairs. In a hurry to reach my room, I tripped on the last stair, sending the purloined book sliding along the upstairs hall. My heart jumped into my throat as I scrambled for it, then dove into my room.

Once inside, I lifted the loose floorboard beneath my bed and placed the books inside my secret hiding place.

At last, I could relax—if only somewhat. I sat down at my desk and with my forearm wiped the cold sweat from my forehead. Sure that the world knew about my crime, I expected Mr. Sumac, my mother, or worst of all, my father to burst into my room with accusing fingers pointed at me, and with the help of the local constabulary to drag me off to the barren guardhouse that my friends swore was haunted by the ghosts of soldiers past. This prospect so frightened me that I didn't dare take the books from their hiding place and look at them.

By the time my mother called me for supper an hour later, I had calmed down considerably and was starting to think I might have gotten away with my crime. I did my best to act naturally during dinner. When my mother said she had a special surprise for me, my heart skipped a beat. I looked at her expectantly as she handed me two wrapped presents, one big, the other small. Instantly, I forgot about my crime and tore into my gifts. The first was a pair of new trousers, not a thing to excite me at the tender age of twelve, though I knew enough to say thanks. The second gift was an orange, which really pleased me. I thanked my mother for the orange as well, knowing she had no doubt gone to great lengths to secure both gifts. I thanked my father, too, and shook the hand he extended.

Dessert was a sugary concoction made with sweet peaches, which my mother had put up the previous fall. With the meal finished, my father left us without a word and returned to his study to work, leaving me to help my mother with the dishes. Yearning for the ill-gotten loot in my room, I asked her if I could be excused. As it was my birthday, she permitted me to leave before my chores were complete. I took the stairs two at a time.

My room was dark. I shivered with a delicious sense of anticipation as I closed the door quietly, lit a candle, and pulled the two books from their hiding place. This was my first chance to look at them, and I found myself as excited as I had ever been in my life. The book Mr. Sumac had given me was *The Count of Monte Cristo*. It was covered in purple cloth and titled in black and gold lettering on both cover and spine.

Putting down the gift book, I turned my attention to the book I had stolen. *Stolen*—what a horrible word! So rushed had I been when I'd taken it—"taken" had a much better sound—that I was shocked to see the book was *Five Weeks in a Balloon* by Jules Verne. Not the book I had initially intended to steal...take...but had I considered a second choice, it might have been this one. Delighted with my unexpected good fortune, I began to read it immediately.

Before long, however, a disturbing unease settled in my heart, and despite my best efforts, I could not help picturing over and over, Mr. Sumac's crinkling eyes and kind face when he'd given me the gift. I began to feel awful, so much so that I closed the book and put it, along with *The Count of Monte Cristo*, back in the hiding place under my bed.

For some time I sat without moving, unremitting thoughts of Mr. Sumac tormenting my mind, eating at me like a canker. The more I thought about him, the more I felt like a scoundrel. I was repaying the generous man who had fulfilled my fondest wish, by behaving like an unprincipled lout. Painfully, I recognized that Mr. Sumac was not just the proprietor of a bookstore, but that he was also my friend. The moment I understood this, I pledged to remedy the situation. Some hours later, by the time sleep overcame me, I had concocted a new scheme.

After school the next day, I walked nervously to the bookstore, flinching when a horse snorted or whinnied as it passed. I found Mr. Sumac at his regular spot on his stool behind the counter.

He looked up with a smile when he saw me. "Are you enjoying the book?" he asked enthusiastically.

"Oh yes, it's first-rate. The best present anyone has ever given me."

"Good, it pleases me to hear that."

Without another word, he turned his eyes back to the book before him. Free to carry out my plan, I roamed the store for a few minutes, pretending I was trying to decide on a book. Twice I walked by the spot from where I had stolen the Jules Verne novel. Both times I glanced at Mr. Sumac to see if he was watching me. He appeared to be engrossed in his book. I passed the same spot again, but this time I stopped. With trembling fingers, I pulled a new book at random from the shelf and sat down, as if to read.

As on the previous day, I planned to wait until the book-seller left the front of the store, at which point I would replace the book I had stolen, and which I was presently holding under my left arm. I pretended to read as I awaited my moment.

I watched Mr. Sumac out of the corner of my eye. Aside from turning the pages now and then, he scarcely moved. As the afternoon grew late and the sun began to set, I wondered if he would ever go to the stockroom. I was resigning myself to concocting a new plan, when someone walked in. Mr. Sumac closed his book immediately and came from behind the counter to help the customer: a lady who, judging by her expensive clothes and the familiar way in which Mr. Sumac greeted her, was one of his few regular customers of means.

Mr. Sumac spent the next few minutes showing the lady a few of his more recent publications. At one point, he turned his back on me. Time to act. Leaving the book I was pretending to read, on the floor, I stood up and reached under my coat to pull out the book under my left arm. As I reached over to put the stolen book back in its rightful place, it slipped out of my sweaty hand and crashed loudly to the floor. My instinctive reaction was a yelp, somewhat like an injured dog might make. Surprised by the combined noise of the falling book and my shocked screech, Mr. Sumac's customer let out a scream of her own. As Mr. Sumac looked around, his eyes alighted on me. Unprepared for my plan to go so badly awry, the only words I could manage were, "I'm sorry, I dropped a book." Shaken by the sight of the stolen book clearly visible on the ground, I grabbed it without thinking, placed it randomly on the shelf, and walked out—thereby bringing my happy days in Mr. Sumac's bookstore to an abrupt and inauspicious end.

Immediately following the events here described, my father decided it was time for me to become an adult. At the advanced age of twelve, I was to be apprenticed to him. Under his tutelage, I would learn to work hard, prosper, and demonstrate to the world that because I could make money, I was a worthy human being. I did not altogether cease my association with Mr. Sumac, but occupied as I was with my father's expectations, our encounters were few and far between.

In the fall of 1875, nearly five years after my theft, my father evicted Mr. Sumac because he was late in paying his rent. Unlike the situation with Mr. Napoleon LaForest, the tinsmith, years before, this time there appeared to be no skulduggery on my father's part. There was no 200 percent rent increase nor were false allegations of impropriety levelled against Mr. Sumac. It was a simple case of a business that failed to flourish.

On the day Mr. Wolhaupter, the High Sheriff and a businessman himself, seized the contents of the store, I feigned illness. During the course of my apprenticeship, I had been forced to partake reluctantly in a number of such seizures. More than once, a distraught wife had accosted me or the children of a man being dispossessed of his property had threatened me. I had learned to endure these unpleasant situations in order to carry out my father's wishes; however, the thought of removing the shelves of books from Mr. Sumac's store and destroying my few happy childhood memories was more than I could bear. To say nothing of how terribly I felt for Mr. Sumac.

Never again would I nestle in that familiar corner of the store, with the shelves pressing into my back and shoulders, and a book warming me like a cosy fire on a cold day. Never again would I see Mr. Sumac glide his hands over his beloved books, his eyes lighting up when he came across a story he knew I would surely enjoy. Never again would I enter worlds that were infinitely more appealing and interesting than the one in which I lived. For even during my long absence from the store, I lived in hope of the day when I might be able to return to my cherished spot.

On the day of the auction, I pretended once more to be ill. Since that first auction so many years earlier, when I had observed Mr. LaForest sob silently into his hands, I had seen many a man weep at his losses, and I could not bear the thought of seeing Mr. Sumac in a similar state. But my father was not to be duped twice; he threatened to evict me from my home if I did not take a first-hand tally of the proceeds realized from the sale of the books, stationery, pipes, shelves, and miscellaneous equipment. Reluctantly, I found myself in attendance.

The auction was held at the Exhibition Palace, a massive edifice at the corner of Saunders and Westmorland Streets, which had been built especially for the Provincial Exhibition. Before the auction began, I spotted Mr. Sumac at the rear of the building. I tried to hide myself behind a pillar, hoping to avoid him, but he saw me and waved me over. Though I had no desire to see him overcome by emotion, as I knew was inevitable, I did not want to be rude to a man I had once considered a friend. As he came near, I steeled myself against a burst of anger—after all, he was being evicted by my father. To my astonishment, he greeted me warmly, held out his hand, and smiled.

"Quite the eye-filler, this place," said Mr. Sumac, as he looked 100 feet above us to the central dome: 86 feet in diameter and said to be the largest piece of wooden frame-work ever erected in New Brunswick.

"So it is, sir," I agreed.

I disliked the Exhibition Palace. At the front, life-sized statues representing the arts, science, agriculture, shipbuild-ing, and the four seasons, combined with Corinthian pillars to make a formidable impression. Inside, huge windows brightened the vast space beneath the dome. I regarded the structure as oppressively imposing—like my father.

"I'm pleased you're here, Alexandre," Mr. Sumac said, his voice echoing in the vast building. He had the air of a man out for a pleasant stroll, almost as if this awful event neither concerned nor touched him. "I wanted to bid you farewell, for my time in Fredericton is over."

I looked at him with concern, meeting his eye this time. "Where are you going?"

"St. John's, Newfoundland. An old friend, a cod fisherman, has work for me there." As he rubbed his hands together, I noticed how big they were, veined and supple. "I'm looking forward to it."

I believed him. Placid though he was in his bookstore, I had seen Mr. Sumac several times on Sundays, racing around the one-mile track at the York Driving Park. Despite his age, he rode his chestnut mare as fast as if he were racing the wind. Inside Mr. Sumac, an adventurer lay dormant.

"When do you leave?" I asked.

"Immediately after the auction," he said.

I told him I was glad he had somewhere to go but regretted that he had to endure such a cruel fate.

"Oh, do not worry yourself," he answered calmly. "I've enjoyed my time here and have no regrets."

I thought he was being exceptionally brave and noticed that his facial expression did not contradict his words. I wished him luck and was about to take my leave, when he asked if I would stay with him to watch the auction. Since this was almost like hearing a condemned man's last request, I acquiesced.

The books were not sold off individually, which would have taken all day, but in piles of ten. They weren't grouped in any sort of order; instead, they were placed one on top of the next on the table beside the auctioneer. As the bidding began, I stared straight ahead. I didn't want to watch Mr. Sumac's inevitable emotional collapse. Eventually, however, I glanced at him without meaning to. Where I had expected tears, I saw a smile. I was stunned.

"Why are you smiling, sir?" I asked, almost as if accusing him. "Aren't you distraught that your life is going to the highest bidder?" Words my father might have spoken.

As Mr. Sumac looked at me, his smile broadened. "My life isn't being sold, Alexandre—just my books."

I was dumbstruck. "But...but you love your books," I managed to stammer at last.

He nodded. "Yes, few things give me more pleasure than good literature. But when you think about it, books are just paper and ink."

I didn't know what to say. Here was a man who, for as long as I had known him, had been surrounded by what he loved most. He was losing his world as he knew it, yet he did not seem to care—or if he did, he did not show it. If anything, he seemed more comfortable than me. I spent the rest of the auction noting the proceeds of the sales, as my father instructed. At the same time, I watched Mr. Sumac, fascinated as he continued to smile. I took in every detail of his appearance: I could have sworn he hadn't aged since the day I'd first entered the shop.

When the auction ended, Mr. Sumac took his saddlebag, and we walked together out of the Exhibition Palace and into the cool, fall air. More confused than ever at his odd reaction to seeing his treasured books sold, I could no longer remain quiet. "I don't wish to bother you, Mr. Sumac, but I am puzzled."

"What about, Alexandre?"

"You're not sad about losing all your possessions?"

Mr. Sumac stopped walking. His smile had gone, and his eyes were thoughtful, as if he was looking deep inside himself. "I have lost much more than this and survived," he said at length. "Besides, I can do nothing to save my business now. For me to bemoan my luck would do nothing to bring back what I once had. I did what I could but the world changes, Alexandre, and plans go amiss. When that happens, there is no choice but to go on."

"Maybe...but how can you watch it all being taken from you without being angry or sad?" My chest was tight with emotion. I had lost nothing, yet I was so sad that my eyes filled with tears.

Letting his saddlebags drop to the ground, Mr. Sumac turned to face me. "A life lesson from many years of experience, Alexandre—cling to the past too tightly, and the present will slip through your fingers."

Though I didn't know it at the time, they were words that would stay with me all my life.

I waited to see if he would say anything else, but he appeared lost in thought as he looked down past Saunders Street towards the skating rink. Just when I thought I should say something to break the silence, he reached into the saddlebag at his feet and pulled out a brown, leather-bound book.

"I have just remembered something. I should very much like you to have this," he said, as he handed me the book. As I took it from him, I remembered the book he had so generously given me years before.

Feeling unworthy of his kindness, I said awkwardly, "I shouldn't take this book. You may need to sell it for food or to feed your horse."

Mr. Sumac chuckled, then said, "Don't be overly concerned. I am not entirely destitute. At any rate, this is not a book like the ones I sold. It is the personal journal of a friend of mine. It came into my possession when he died. I believe it may be of some interest to you. Moreover, it may explain things better than I am able to at present."

"I still do not understand."

"I know you don't," he said kindly. "Remember, the answers we seek are not always readily apparent to us, but I believe you will understand everything in good time." He patted my shoulder. "I will take my leave of you now. It has been a pleasure knowing you, Alexandre." He shook my hand, firmly but gently. Soon his hands would be hauling nets and fishing lines; they would be calloused and rough.

Another moment passed while I hoped quite desperately that Mr. Sumac would change his mind about going. But he picked up his saddlebag and said to me, almost under his breath, "Go west." It was a hint I would not understand for some years. Then he gave me a sly wink and strode off towards the driving park.

As he walked away, I called after him, "I stole a book from you once."

He turned around, his expression unsurprised, as if he had expected the words. "I know."

"But I returned it the next day."

"I know that, too."

"Why did you say nothing?"

"A wise man does not dwell on the past, Alexandre, but he learns from it. I knew you would learn from what you did. I knew you would return the book. You have more wisdom than you realize." He turned on his heel then and went on walking. I did not see Mr. Sumac again.

That evening at dinner, my usually taciturn father regaled my mother with the story of the auction. "As we were selling him off piece by piece," he said of Mr. Sumac, "I caught the old fool's eye—and do you know, the son of a bitch smiled at me. Here I was destroying the man's life, and he was smiling, as if I were doing him a favour."

He shook his head from side to side, before turning to me. "You were standing beside him, Alexandre. Did he speak?"

I told him the gist of what Mr. Sumac had said, about doing what he could, yet plans going amiss. I kept the rest of the conversation, as well as the gift he had given me, to myself.

"Hell!" my Father exclaimed, unnecessarily loudly. "No wonder the man wasn't a success!"

Later, after my parents had gone to bed and the house was silent, I closed my bedroom door, shut the window, drew the curtains, and lit my little oil lamp. Hunched over my desk, my arms around the journal as if protecting a precious newborn, I read and reread Mr. Sumac's gift. Slowly, very slowly, I began to understand him a little better. With the morning's light, I gently wrapped the journal in an old shirt, and hid it carefully away beneath the floorboards under my bed. One day, I resolved as I did so, I will be a success like Mr. Sumac.

Alexandre Gerard Arouet

Richard

Twice daily for the next three days, Sonia calls the Granby ICU to learn whether Jenner and Kimberly have regained consciousness. Each time we are disappointed to hear there is no change. On the fourth day, a Thursday evening, we finally hear the good news that both patients are awake and anxious to meet us.

The next morning we drive out to Granby with flowers and a fruit basket. To our shock, Jenner and Kimberly are gone. Not only are they nowhere to be found in the hospital, but their possessions are gone too.

For a few dreadful moments we stare at each other. The expression in Sonia's eyes tells me we have the same the thought: could they have died?

"No. No. They've been discharged," we are informed by a male nurse, Thomas.

"When did they go? Where to?" I ask.

"They flew out on a medevac flight early this morning." We learned that hospital policy dictates that as soon as patients are considered stable enough to be flown, they are transferred to hospitals nearer their homes.

"Thank goodness!" Sonia exclaims in relief.

"By any chance, are either of you Richard or Sonia?" Thomas asks. Apparently, all the ICU staff know how we rescued Jenner and Kimberly from the wrecked car. There have also been Sonia's twice daily calls.

"I'm Richard. This is Sonia."

"They left something for you," Thomas says. He rummages through a drawer, pulls out a thick envelope, and lays it on the top of the counter.

Sonia and I exchange a confused look. We thank Thomas and leave the hospital. Sonia can barely wait to get to the car, where she opens the envelope and pulls out a sheaf of papers. The first page reads:

> *Dear Richard and Sonia,*
>
> *Thank you for our lives. There is nothing that we can ever do to repay you for the gift you have given us. It is a pity we did not have the chance to thank you in person; however, when we are fully recovered we will do just that. In the meantime, we've had the old journal you recovered from the accident photocopied for you to read—one of the nurses very kindly did it for us. The book means a great deal to our family, and we hope you'll enjoy it. Again, we can never thank you enough. Please call us.*

The note is signed Kimberly and Jenner Herac. In the bottom corner, we see a phone number and address.

Sonia puts down the note and smiles at me. "Isn't this wonderful! I guess we get to read the diary after all." Look, Richard, right on top are the lovely sketches of the woman and the child."

On the drive home, Sonia begins to read the diary out loud to me. She starts with Jenner Herac's entry written only a few years before in December 2003, and after that,

Maximilian's entry, of 1975. When we get home, I take two bottles of cider from behind the unused Worcestershire Sauce and the pickled onions in the fridge. Side by side at the kitchen table, thighs touching, we read through the afternoon and into the evening. We stop only to eat and phone Nadie and Aidan to find out how they are and to tell them we love them.

As pleasant as it is to be close to Sonia again, reading the journal and enjoying a couple of ciders together, I can't help think about what started the year of unpleasantness. I have tried many times to let the event slip into the past, but each time I think I am over it, it plays out in my head again. It was nothing more than a slip of the tongue, uttered in a moment of intense emotion, but it was enough to change everything. It saddens me that a single event could so dramatically impact how I feel about Sonia, and, therefore, how I feel about my life. Yet if I can't trust Sonia with my secrets, then that loss of trust creates a wall between us.

I've often thought that the reason Sonia loves antiques so much, why she fills our home with hundred-year-old chairs, china cabinets and clocks is because these items give her a sense of permanence. It's as if she believes something that has been around a long time can be counted on. No doubt this need for stability stems from the loss of her mother when Sonia was a little girl; also because she moved around so much as a teenager. I think for Sonia the ideal home is one where she is firmly rooted in one place.

My own concept of home is quite different. The amateur psychologist in me says that because I grew up in just one place, with familiar streets and buildings and both my parents always around, it's not very important to me to be settled in a single location. For me, trust and acceptance are all important. For that reason, I have entrusted few people with the secret of my club foot. In my experience, most people who know about my disability see me as different. Unusual. Not quite normal. Sonia was the one person I always trusted with my secrets: she accepted me with all my imperfections. Her trust and acceptance made me feel protected. Sheltered. Anchored. The confidence I gained by having a smart, sweet, beautiful woman love me and at my side was something I had never experienced before I met her. She made me feel worthwhile and valuable. Made me feel that home was not where I hung my hat or rested my head. *Home was Sonia*.

I want to forgive Sonia for her moment of indiscretion. But I can't. And the realization makes me feel lonely and isolated—as if I'm back in grade six with no one to hang out with or talk to.

As we read and reread the journal late into the night, I wonder if Sonia and I will ever again recoup the wonderful connection we once had. I wonder what Sonia can do, if anything, to repair the rift.

Unknown Writer

March 30, 1867   Calcutta, India

My Dearest Inga,

I arrived in Calcutta yesterday and set out right away to arrange passage home. As luck would have it, the Friedrich, a steamer, is bound almost immediately for Liverpool by way of the Cape of Good Hope. From Liverpool, I am confident that I shall manage to hunt down a ship traversing the Atlantic, as the Allan and Cunard Lines cross frequently. Assuming the weather is favourable, I hope to be in Halifax four months hence.

In the course of my voyage, I shall attempt to spend much time recounting the conclusions to some of my adventures in India—many of which I have already related to you—and describing the remarkable people I have encountered along the way. As you can see, I have commenced writing midway through an empty journal. Although I know this is unusual, it is my intention upon arriving home to attach the correspondence I have previously sent you to the blank pages that precede this entry. In this way, I shall have a complete record of my journey through India to look back upon.

My love, I shall begin to write to you in earnest to-morrow. To-day, I have yet to procure necessities for my voyage and must also bid faithful travelling companions fare-thee-well, before plying the winds for home.

March 31, 1867   The Friedrich

My Dearest Inga,

As we prepare to set sail early this morning, the sky is ablaze with colour. The sun, though not yet fully risen, displays already its dazzling artistry by painting the underbellies of the distant clouds in shades of brilliant reds, oranges, and yellows. Strolling about the deck, I hear the grey-bearded deckhand declare to a young ensign that a red sky at night is a sailor's delight, but a red sky at morning is a sailor's warning. His cautionary foreboding does not dampen my spirits, for I am heading home.

Dozens of coolies, dressed only in cotton loincloths wrapped about their hips, load the last of the sugar and flour. As they hurry along the jetty, they bump against one another in passing. "Thou art a swine," one will say. "Son of a festering dog," the other will reply. More jostling evokes, "Thy mother laid with monkeys," and, "Thy father is a donkey." The invectives compete with the sky for colour and hue.

My darling, do you recollect the ship we sailed on from Liverpool to New York before Astrid's birth? We played backgammon for hours on deck with that handsome board and beautifully carved ivory men. That same trip, one of the passengers, a young man from Boston, tried to play the piano with that awful sound—nobody had ever heard anything quite like it. How we laughed when the pianist discovered the culprit of the discordant noise—a rat nesting in the piano wires.

The Friedrich is similar to that other vessel, though more seasoned and weather stained. She is a three hundred-and-forty-foot, screw-driven steamer boasting three tall masts that, when the winds are favourable, allow us to sail under canvas, thereby saving valuable coal. I have been informed that she is capable of hauling two hundred first-class passengers, four hundred emigrants, one thousand tons of cargo, and twelve hundred tons of coal. Thus loaded, she can maintain fourteen knots with the screw or sixteen-and-one-half knots under a full spread of sail.

The captain of the Friedrich is a Scotchman by the name of Hugh Ferguson. By all appearances, he is a stern man, built of the same iron as this worthy vessel. He speaks to his crew in short barks and his orders are executed promptly. Of medium height and barrel-chested, he has a bald head and deep-set eyes that perpetually squint, doubtless from a life gazing windward into the distance. It is said there are old sailors and there are careless sailors. I find it reassuring that the coolies refer to Hugh Ferguson as Old Kuberdar, Kuberdar meaning careful in Hindoostani.

When the last of the coolies disembark, Captain Ferguson orders the Friedrich to be released from her moorings. Guided by a tugboat, she sets her course along the middle of the Hooghly River and ere long succumbs to its gentle flow. Without a breeze to fill the listless sails, the captain calls for the screw to be engaged, causing the ship to shudder and churn up the already muddy waters. For a moment I wonder if I shall be able to continue writing, for the screw shakes horribly, but my mind soon eases when the engines find their rhythm and we make our way smoothly downstream towards the Indian Ocean.

Sailing along the Hooghly past Calcutta is akin to an effortless tramp through a forest of leafless trees. Ships crowd the river's edge. They stretch for miles down the eastern side of the river, and I see many different vessels: sharp-bowed clippers, square-rigged frigates, paddle-wheeled steamers, and all manner of Arab, Chinese, and fanciful native boats. High aloft the many masts, men and boys set rigging to rights, while below them, streams of men, women, and boys, load and unload the vessels. In the background, the spires and lofty towers of Calcutta give the impression of a forest extending to infinity.

In contrast to the hubbub of activity on the eastern bank, the western bank is like a garden with colourful silk-cotton trees everywhere in bloom. Large crimson flowers are luminescent against a canvas of brilliant green vegetation. The scene would be near picture perfect were it not for the broken trees that tower above the foliage, still showing the disastrous effects of the cyclone of three years ago, when some fifty thousand lives were lost.

Enjoying this spectacle with me is Torvus Sumac, who plans to return home as well. He will not say, but it is my contention that he must attend to financial matters at home. It is my sincerest wish that no calamity has befallen him. A long trip can be tedious, however, without good company, and since you are not with me, I am grateful to enjoy his excellent fellowship.

Aside from Torvus, I share the view with creatures unaware of their destination. Free of their cages, a hundred hens brought on board to provide eggs for the journey peck on the deck in search of food. Likewise assisting with the provision of fresh rations, eight sturdy cows move easily among the human passengers. Timid sheep and swine join us too, but they tend to avoid their human counterparts, as if they know that they will pay more dearly than the other animals for their passage.

With all the livestock on board, I feel more at ease about the trip. In my haste to secure passage, I failed to inquire about the diet I could expect on this line. I had been assured of a "first-rate" table; however, not knowing the shipping line's reputation, I obtained an assortment of fresh fruits and vegetables before boarding, to supplement whatever might be served. Betwixt the animals and my own provisions, I shall not want.

Torvus and I share a two-berth cabin on the portside, off the dining saloon. The cabin, satisfactorily furnished with all necessary conveniences such as desk, brass basin, barometer, and so forth, is lofty, nearly seven-feet high and generously lit with three port holes. It is finished splendidly with pearl-coloured mahogany panels and gilded mouldings. My only complaint is that the candles are too large for the candlesticks.

My darling, can you tell I write to you in better spirits? My mind, once so overwhelmed with hopelessness that I believe even my description of the wondrous Taj Mahal was melancholy, now overflows with joy. I am desirous of sharing with you my experiences, but I fear I shall be incapable of describing with sufficient eloquence my epiphany regarding the natural world. Had I the skill of a poet, capturing in words the voice of the heart, I should not fret. As it is, I hope my rude attempt at confining ethereal thoughts to ink and paper shall not be pedantic or tedious.

When last I wrote, Torvus, Francoise, William, Duncan, and I were in Bhagalpur, a city of crumbling temples where the intolerable, cloying dust settled on us like flies on a carcass. The dust covered everything in sight: houses, trees, and grasses alike. From Bhagalpur we made our way north-eastwards to the edge of the lush Bengal jungle and a city called Katiham. We planned to travel north from Katiham to Darjeeling so that we might view the great Himalayas. In Katiham, however, I found myself wearied to the point of exhaustion. Though the endless trek across India was demanding, it was the silent phantoms, those I had hoped to leave behind in Canada, which fatigued me. I had come to India hoping to find some meaning in my existence, but since I had not yet found the answers I sought, I concluded that I required solitude and rest.

Parting company from my cohorts proved difficult. Since leaving Halifax more than eight months before, my companions had become for me more like family than friends. Entertaining me with stories, card games, and whimsy, they were of great comfort during our journey to and across India, especially through the hot, dry horseback ride across the country. They, too, could not bear the idea of our being parted and pleaded with me to remain in their company. To placate them, I agreed to meet them back in Katiham five weeks later, the time I thought they would require to travel north to Darjeeling and back again. They were concerned, for they seemed to sense that a wound festered in my heart. All the same, they reluctantly headed north towards the Himalayas without me.

Equally difficult to part with were the men in my employ, for they had made my travels in this foreign land tolerable; among others, there were a *do-bash* (butler), a *gorah-wallah* (horse-keeper), a grass cutter, and two coolies. I felt that if I was to be alone, I must terminate my employment of these men—even if by doing so, I made my immediate existence more difficult. After paying them off and providing them with chits—notes describing their services and virtues—I directed Zeki, my Arabian steed, to a village called Chindah, a day's ride from Katiham. There, my *do-bash* informed me, I would find an excellent government *dak*-bungalow in which to lay my head. He himself was from Chindah, and though he had not returned there for some years, he assured me it was the finest place in all the world. Perhaps, I thought hopefully, there, I would find a reprieve from my vexing thoughts.

Chindah, I discovered upon my arrival that evening, was a sparse and hapless settlement. The surrounding walls were insubstantial, more gaping holes than solid brick or stone. Later, I would learn that the holes had been caused by the removal of the stones, which were used for the maintenance of the houses in the community. The houses themselves were sadly derelict, leaning dangerously this way and that, looking as if a stiff wind was all it would take to collapse them. The narrow streets were almost devoid of life, and the swampy surroundings seemingly drained the town of its vigour. On the whole, the village was quite a pitiable place.

Dismounting somewhat nervously, I led Zeki into the village, hoping that at least the *dak*-bungalow that the *do-bash* had spoken of in such promising terms would prove to be a bright spot in this pitiful community. I found it near the centre of Chindah. I can't say I was surprised to find the bungalow closed and in a sorry state of disrepair.

Obviously, I needed to reconsider my options. The first was to camp outside the city walls, but without a tent or adequate mosquito netting—foolishly, I had left my gear with the others in the party—the biting insects would feast on me relentlessly. The second option was to rent a room from one of the villagers, but I knew the local prejudice towards one of European descent might prove troublesome. The third option, also the most dangerous one, would be to journey back to Katiham. Although I was reasonably sure I would find a hotel there, it was already nigh on evening, which would entail travelling much of the way in the dark. I laboured under no illusion of what might happen if I were to do that. Not only would I be in danger of losing my way in this alien land, but I might well become prey to the many hunting animals that prowled about at night. Not one of these options was appealing.

Perhaps it was despair that brought back a disturbing memory of a night my cohorts and I spent travelling in the bush between Bombay and Delhi. Torvus had a *do-bash* named Raanan, whose family lived near our camp. When Raanan had completed his duties for the evening, he requested leave to visit his family. Torvus consented, and with many salaams and a "Thank you, *sahib*," Raanan set off. Next morning he was not to be found. Fearing for his safety—for some had heard a tiger prowling in the night—we began an immediate search. Suddenly, a shout came from the bush. Torvus and his *gorah-wallah* had come upon Raanan in a clearing marked by tiger tracks, not fifty yards from our camp. The clearing was surrounded by dense jungle, so we had not noticed it before. The body bore a few superficial scratches, none of which seemed ominous enough to have caused Raanan's demise. When I scrutinized the corpse, already starting to decay in the heat, the skull yielded to the pressure of my hands like a bag of crushed bones. I leaped back retching. When I forced myself to look again, I understood that the horrendous injury must have been caused by a single blow of a tiger's paw.

As I stood in front of the closed *dak*-bungalow reliving that terrible experience, a crowd of villagers began to gather around me. Gesticulating and speaking amongst themselves, doubtless they wondered why a *sahib logue* (a white gentleman) was journeying without his attendants. Since it would be foolhardy for me to travel at night, and as I was without satisfactory shelter, my only option was to find somewhere to sleep in the village, if only for one night. In my very rudimentary Hindoostani—I had only managed to learn a few words since my arrival in India—I tried to make myself understood to the assembled crowd. Using wild arm gestures to portray the shapes of houses and beds, I tried to communicate my wishes, but the attempt was futile. Fatigued, hungry, and hot, I sat down on the ground, still clutching the dry, cracked reins in my hands, and hung my head like a sheep languishing under the noon sun. The situation might not normally have plunged a seasoned traveller into an abyss of despair—such a person would expect hurdles of one kind or another in foreign lands—but my thoughts turned to you and baby, Astrid, and I was overwhelmed with loneliness.

As despondent thoughts gained ascendance in my mind, I heard a woman's voice say, "*Salaam, Sahib.*" And then, miraculously in English, "May I be of service?" The words sounded like music to me.

Glancing up quickly, I saw a diminutive Indian woman standing in front of the other gathered villagers. If I was astonished at being addressed in impeccable English, I was stunned when I actually looked at the speaker, for very few Indian women dare to speak with white men. I wondered if my brain was playing tricks on me.

Kindness filled her large brown eyes; concern lurked in the shape of her lips. Long, grey hair was drawn into braids on either side of her head and hung down in front of her bright green sari. Inexperienced though I am at assessing age, I guessed hers to be about three score and five.

"Did you address me, my kind woman?" I asked.

She cocked her head to one side and said, "Yes, *Sahib.* Indeed, I did."

Her voice, gentle and melodious, reminded me of the local proverb: *a pleasant voice brings a snake out of the hole.* My troubles temporarily forgotten, I rose from the ground, brushed the dirt from my backside, and bowed to her, saying, "Thank you, yes, I do need assistance. Is there another *dak*-bungalow or hotel nearby?"

She shook her head, grey braids swishing like ponys' tails across her lean body. "No, *Sahib*. There is no hotel, and the British have long abandoned this fort. They thought this to be an area where cholera prevailed. The nearest government *dak*-bungalow is situated in Katiham."

So Chindah had once been a fort. That explained the village wall with the missing stones. It explained, too, why nobody cared if the stones were taken: the British had lost interest in the place. At least, I had learned one thing of local interest.

But my problem still had no solution. I asked the question gloomily and with little hope, "Might other shelter be found for me and my horse in the village?"

"No, *Sahib*," she said. "However, my family has a hut, which you may use. It is a short distance away. We would be pleased to take you in, if you so desire."

Gratefully, I accepted the kind woman's invitation and accompanied her out of the village.

My love, I will bid you adieu for now, and will write again to-morrow. I think of you and Astrid frequently and with great affection. I shall see you in my dreams.

April 1, 1867   The Friedrich

My Dearest Inga,

Last evening, Torvus and I stood on deck and admired
our penultimate Indian sunset. As we watched the descent
of the sun, a great cannonball of red, I noticed what I took
to be black rocks bobbing in front of us in the midst of the
river. Usually, small craft are posted along safe channels so
that ships may know where the water shoals, for the sands of
the Hooghly shift constantly, but I saw no warning vessels.
Concerned that we were off course and in danger, I was
about to notify Captain Ferguson of the error, when I realized why the rocks appeared to bob on the water. They were
not rocks, after all.

According to Hindoo mythology, the Gunga or Ganges,
of which the Hooghly is a branch, is the living water of the
river of heaven. The river is a goddess who emerges from the
earth out of a stone shaped like the mouth of a cow. This
sacred river, which traverses much of India, is believed to have
the power to cleanse the soul, allowing the dead to pass into
a better existence. Wealthy Hindoo families cremate their kin
upon a funeral pyre, after which they toss the ashes into the
Ganges. If the family cannot afford enough firewood, they
will often cast a half-burned body into the river. The very
poor simply throw the deceased into the river without setting
fire to the body first.

As the ship made its way downriver, I saw clearly that
what I had thought were rocks were actually the bloated
corpses of natives. Naked and only partially burnt, the bodies
moved aside, as if in deference to the living and to our greater
need to pass quickly through these waters. As we proceeded,

more corpses floated by, some with flesh torn from their faces by carrion birds, others swollen and unrecognizable as man or woman. Keener eyes than mine spotted corpses that had washed up along the eastern banks of the river. In cities and at busy ports, people are employed to push the bodies back into the water, but that does not happen in less-populated areas.

Travelling along the Ganges from Benares to Patna, I saw this manner of burial often, but I lacked the courage to put ink to paper and describe these morbid scenes. To dispose of departed loved ones in this way struck me as unutterably callous. In contrast, we in the West sanitize death, dressing up corpses and making them look as if they were still alive. We even memorialize them with headstones above their final resting places.

This morning, I filled my sketchbook with scenes of the activities aboard our floating village. I have produced crude renderings of the crew cleaning the animal waste from the deck, of the third mate checking the rigging on the aft topgallant mast, and from between decks, of two excitable young Indian-born Welsh lads (emigrating to Canada!) trolling for whales with a piece of salt pork. I should like to witness their success as the scene would make a fine addition to my sketchbook. Not only would the capture of a whale lead to an exotic picture, it would also make for an almost unbelievable tale—when you consider that we are still in the shallow waters of the Hooghly River!

The sails hang lazily against the masts. Although we do not require wind to make headway down the river, it is so hot that the lack of a cooling breeze forces me into our cabin to escape the ripe noon sun. Sitting beside a quiet barometer, I now peruse yesterday's entry and attempt to recollect to the best of my ability the events that followed thereon.

As the slightly-built Indian woman and I walked to her farm a few miles outside the village of Chindah, we fell into easy conversation. I learned her name was Ritika and that her family worked the nearby paddi fields and betel nut plantation. Apart from working the land, they also owned cows and chickens, which produced enough milk and eggs to feed the immediate family and to be traded at the bazaar in the village.

"From where do you hail, *Sahib*?" she asked, her enunciation as clear as any I have heard.

"Halifax, in Canada."

"Yes?" she said, in a way that seemed to indicate she wanted me to elaborate.

"I was born in Denmark and immigrated to Canada as a boy," I told her. "My mother believed the New World held a better future for me than the old. Insofar as I improved my lot in life, she was correct." It is a testament to Ritika's comforting aura (you know how reserved I am) that I nearly went into the story of how, after Mother passed on, I hid aboard an emigrant vessel when I was just twelve-years-old and managed to escape detection during the long voyage to Halifax.

"You have family?" she asked.

I hesitated, then said sadly, "Yes, I left them behind." I hoped she would not ask probing questions about you and Astrid, for I missed you both so greatly that I was in no mood for talking.

"Why are you in Bengal?"

"A respite," I said quietly.

She nodded, almost as if she knew my thoughts.

I decided it was time to change the topic. "Your English is excellent. From whom did you learn?"

"From my father. He was the village *gurumahasay*."

This was a new word to me. "*Gurumahasay?*" I asked curiously.

She smiled. "A schoolmaster."

Incredulously, I searched her face. It seemed to me improbable that a village schoolteacher living in the jungles of Bengal sixty years ago could have understood and spoken English sufficiently well to teach it.

"Your eyes speak to me. You are doubtful," she said with an expression I could not read.

Immediately, I felt ashamed, for I had no desire to offend this kind woman, who had so graciously offered to shelter a weary traveller. I was about to beg Ritika's forgiveness when we arrived at her farm.

In the dusk, I could make out fifteen one-room cottages. Built with cane walls and thatched roofs, they formed a loose circle around a banyan tree of immense proportions, doubtless to take advantage of its prodigious shade. I took Ritika's family to be prosperous, for in this part of India, a person of some means typically builds a collection of cottages rather than a large house. Family members moved among the cottages, some chatting loudly, others preparing the evening meal. Two little girls—I judged then to be about five and six years of age—ran happily to Ritika and hugged her about the legs and waist. The epitome of youthful health, they put me in mind of our own darling little Astrid. Antelope-like eyes shone in faces of glowing brown skin. Noticing the pale stranger leading an Arabian horse—a rare sight in these parts—they tried to hide, unsuccessfully, behind Ritika's slight form.

"Come now," said Ritika in English, "greet our guest."

I expected them to bow politely. Instead, they approached me as a gentleman might do at home, offering their hands.

"Greetings," they said, in excellent English.

I knelt down, and gently shook each hand in turn. "Whom do I have the honour and pleasure of meeting?" I asked.

They only giggled in response and ran off. Ritika informed me that these delightful children were her great-granddaughters.

After Ritika had shown me where I could feed and bed my Arabian, she led me to the abode that was to be mine: a cottage I would sleep in, similar to the others—a single room of cane and thatch. As we entered the cottage, Ritika grabbed a stick and poked vigorously here and there in the thatch. When I inquired if she was performing a religious ceremony, she gravely informed me that snakes sometimes take up residence in a thatched cottage that has been unoccupied for a time. I shuddered, but said no more, unwilling to interrupt this important task. Satisfied at last that the cottage was empty of reptiles, she left me to get settled, saying she would return with a meal.

When she was gone, I took an inventory of the simple but clean room. Four mats covered the wooden floor, and to my surprise, a mosquito net hung over each mat, an uncommon luxury in any but the finest government *dak*-bungalows and hotels. A notched stick, used to prop open the window if a breeze should happen to stir, leaned against the far wall. The rest of the cottage was bare.

Although the possibility of sleeping with snakes caused me alarm—despite Ritika's energetic precautions—I knew how fortunate I had been to meet her and find this oasis. As I put down my saddlebags, I thought about her and considered what an uncommon woman she was. Unlike so many of the meek, obsequious women I had come across in my Indian travels, she spoke with a poise and strength uncommon in either sex. Women in India are often regarded as inferior beings. The birth of a son is hailed with joyous celebration, whereas the birth of a daughter is often greeted with open disappointment. In rare instances, young girls are educated, but are shy of showing their erudition. According to an Indian maxim, an educated woman will have no opportunity to use her knowledge and will become bitter for this reason. Yet I sensed no bitterness in Ritika and wondered at this.

Ere long, Ritika returned with a meal. Arranged on a plantain leaf was a glorious mess of *dal* and *chitski*, a delicious vegetable curry, served with rice. I thanked her profusely for her hospitality. She entreated me to eat, and while I did so, she informed me of my surroundings. From the door of the cottage, she pointed out where I might wash, attend to my toilet, and where I could find her. She spoke to me with warmth and kindness, like a mother might talk with a son. Before excusing herself, she gently warned me not to stray far from the cottages as predators were known to appear at night. After my experience with Raanan's crushed skull, the advice was unnecessary.

As I lay on my mat that night, glad of the mosquito netting tucked securely beneath me, a vast weariness swept over me. The unpleasant thoughts that had so nearly overwhelmed and rendered me helpless in the village found no foothold in my mind now, and I slept well and deeply.

When I wakened at sunrise the next morning, I was happily surprised to find outside my door a breakfast of *paranthas*, bread made with clarified butter, and a banana, set out on a plantain leaf. In India, a lighter fare, *choti haziri*, or early breakfast, is usually consumed at first light, with more substantial meals eaten later in the day. I ate the banana hungrily, but avoided the *paranthas*. It has been my unfortunate experience that much of the food preparation in this part of the world is not what it should be, according to our standards. I once observed a *babachee* (a cook) kneading dough with his feet. By employing the full weight of his body, he was able to avoid exerting his hands and arms. Because most people walk barefoot, the practice becomes even more distasteful. Later, I happily learned that the bread here is made only by hand and is most excellent.

The night before it had been my intention to leave Ritika and her family for Katiham or another larger city. When I was able to reflect with a well-rested mind, however, I realized that this little farm would be the ideal place for me to rest and contemplate. I inquired if I might stay longer. Ritika graciously agreed, and so I found myself satisfactorily accommodated until such time as I was to meet up once more with Torvus and the others.

With all arranged, I retraced my steps to Chindah to look over the village. In my improved state of mind, I found my initial impressions—coloured by fatigue, hunger, and fear—had been formed in error. What I had thought to be dangerously leaning buildings, turned out to be just an illusion—the stalls in the bazaar having awnings that sloped downwards at such angles as to appear as if they were leaning precipitously. Indeed, in the clear light of day, the houses, pieced together with odd-sized stones from the pillaged outer wall, looked sturdy enough to withstand an earthquake.

Up and down the narrow tree-lined streets, *bunnia* (shopkeepers) dramatically argued over the price of their wares with brightly clothed customers. Unlike the practice in the larger cities, those *bunnia* who were not then busy with customers did not press passersby to enter their shops; instead, they sat easily in the shade of their little establishments. All manner of goods were being sold: earthen pots, cooking utensils, vegetables, rice, wheat, cloth, butter, salt, eggs, and spices. Everywhere, bullocks sprawled in the road, men smoked, children played, and dogs quarrelled, while an elephant made its way carefully through the confusion. The pleasant smell of ripe fruit and sandalwood permeated the air.

Most agreeable was the indifference with which I was treated. In the cities, men looking for work often accosted me. "Who you have need for? I able cook goodly," a man wearing only a dirty loincloth would proclaim. Others salaamed at my feet, only to be stepped on by some of their countrymen forcing stacks of chits—possibly borrowed from family members—into my reluctant hands. "I have worked since many great men," the owners of the chits would assure me. Behind me, another skinny man would pat Zeki on her haunches. "I would be you *gorah-wallah*," he'd announce. "You out of station"—meaning from out of town. Or: "Gentleman's want *do-bash*. I mostly free. Much cheap," another would implore. Mercifully, in Chindah nobody approached me in this manner.

After a few hours spent roaming about, I became aware of something even more unusual about the village. In India, sacred idols, stones, and even trees are coloured red by the Hindoo priests, but I found nothing painted with red ochre anywhere in Chindah or in the surrounding area. Later, when I asked Ritika about this, she explained that the village was slowly discarding the old ways. A hundred years earlier, her grandfather, the village *gurumahasay* before her father, had taught the importance of independent thought over tradition. He had spent much of his life instructing any and all of the villagers, regardless of caste—social standing—to rigorously question established beliefs. Eventually, after many years, they began to discard the customs, rituals, and habits of their ancestors.

"To find what you need, you must first dispose of the detritus of tradition," Ritika said to me. For the rest of the day, I felt I must be in the most unique place in India.

My Love, it is evening now and a familiar fit of coughing has overtaken me. I shall retire and begin again in the morrow. I shall see you in my dreams.

April 2, 1867   The Friedrich

My Dearest Inga,

We are almost at the end of the river. Soon we shall enter the great, blue waters of the Indian Ocean. As we approach Sand's Head, the bar of sand that stretches across the mouth of the Hooghly, I see only flat land adorned with stunted trees and tall grasses. To port, on a sandy bank, an oar stands on end indicating that a villager has been carried away either by a tiger or a crocodile. The locals are always eager to share stories of a relative, an uncle or second cousin perhaps, who has mysteriously disappeared. Then, lo and behold, upon opening a crocodile's belly, the rings or bracelets of the missing person are found.

I spent last evening on deck, breathing in the salt-touched air, in the company of the animals: the cows, the hens, and the lambs, which are less skittish now. After yesterday's writing, I experienced some difficulty breathing. Our cabin, though comfortable, is not well ventilated. My coughing eases when I do not spend long periods below deck. I shall have to be more careful about my health, for as you know, my lungs are devoid of strength.

You may recall me mentioning my only complaint regarding my cabin: that my candles did not fit the candlesticks. When I had finished writing yesterday's entry, I informed a crew member of this minor predicament. An hour later, when no suitable candlesticks had been located, the crew member, an enterprising young man, informed me of an overabundance of tin spittoons on board, and said he would obtain as many as I needed. Why spittoons? you may wonder quite reasonably. Why, because the candles fit into them well enough.

Now that this minor irritant is solved, I have no excuse not to write.

I filled more pages of my sketchbook this morning. Though the endless treed sandbars remain constant, there is noise and bustle everywhere on the ship, providing me with ample scenes to capture with my pencil. On deck, a tailor mends clothes; a shoemaker repairs boots; and the ship's doctor avails himself to the passengers from between decks. Some of the poorest passengers are fragile—I know this, because I hear the familiar sounds of consumptive lungs. Thankfully, Captain Ferguson is an honourable man, who distributes provisions in accordance with the stipulations of an Act of Parliament. Weekly, every adult receives two-and-one-half pounds of bread, a pound of wheaten flour, five pounds of oatmeal, two pounds of rice, two ounces of tea, half a pound of sugar, and half a pound of molasses. As my needs are satisfactorily supplied anyway, due to my status as a first-class passenger, I decided to distribute my fresh produce to people between decks, whom I found most wanting. It breaks the heart when they try to offer their own meagre possessions in thanks. One pitiable woman offered me her tinware and bedding, the only things she owned.

Apart from the scenes on the ship, I have drawn a picture of the first time I saw you, the day I delivered lumber to your papa for his new barn. I remember it as clearly as if it were happening now: You stand in your back garden, a hoe in your hands, looking up at the few white clouds floating across the sky. Beneath your mama's wide-brimmed hat, your hair is pulled back and held in place with string. You wear an old brown skirt and a white blouse, both of which are many sizes too large for you. Flecks of dirt dot your soft, white cheeks, but they cannot detract from your loveliness. At your feet, straight rows of cabbages and cucumbers peep through the black soil. Behind you, raspberry bushes, soon to turn red, develop their youthful green bounty. I have added a few lady's slippers to the foreground—though there were none present—for I know they were your favourite flowers.

Do you recollect how you treated me that day? When I inquired after your father, you ran into the house. I feared the reason was because you knew I was poor. How little I understood. You were ashamed to be seen begrimed, but you had no need to be perturbed, for your beauty blazed through the small amount of dirt. I loved you from that moment.

Three days have gone by without so much as a breeze to fill the sleeping sails, so for now we make headway with the screw. However, the amount of coal we have on board will not support our journey all the way to England—we desperately need wind to make good speed. At noon, I observed how the ship's grey-bearded carpenter—the man who had mentioned the morning sky's red warning—cast his eyes aloft and whistled. Moments later, he repeated the action. It is a belief among sailors that whistling can wake the sleeping winds, but apparently this act may only be attempted by the oldest or youngest crew member on the ship.

A fresh-faced ensign, the colour of a boiled lobster from exposure to the sun, remarked on the carpenter's whistling, and the conversation among the crew thereupon turned to the superstitions of sailors, in general. The ensign proposed stabbing the mast with a knife, a practice believed by some to conjure a breeze. The ensign opened his clasp knife, as if to follow his words with action, when the carpenter exclaimed in agitation, "Avast! What you be doing, youngster?" Evidently, it is thought by some seamen that a knife in the mast is too powerful a summons and may produce a gale. "Just summoning a breeze, Chips," the ensign said, and with a grunt, he sunk the knife into the wood of the mizzenmast.

"You'll send us to Davy Jones's Locker. Mind you give Neptune a drink," the carpenter said, referring to yet another superstition, whereby sailors pour a shot of rum overboard to endear themselves to Neptune, thus ensuring his protection. Many of the young crew members laughed derisively, but I glimpsed Captain Ferguson at the wheel, nodding approvingly.

We have just left the Hooghly River behind us, to steam between guard ships, lighthouses, and buoys, while we head towards the ocean. Taking my last glimpse of India, I escape the blazing sun for the shelter of our cabin.

The second morning in my cottage on Ritika's farm was little different from the first. I wakened to air fresh with the smell of wet grass, and to a breakfast consisting this time of oranges and a banana decoratively placed on a plantain leaf. After eating and washing, I sat against the huge trunk of the banyan tree, from where I observed Ritika and her large family. Dependent as they were on the soil, many of the family, both men and women, worked the fields. Those not engaged in such activity prepared food, sewed clothes, or in the case of the older family members, watched over the many young children. All appeared well nourished, and even when they were working, were possessed of good humour, their laughter punctuating the sounds of the surrounding jungle.

Some time before midday an old man limped out of the jungle. Ritika stood up from her sewing and welcomed him with a warm embrace. After a short conversation, she gestured in my direction. As the man walked towards me, I could not help noticing that, despite his limp, he carried himself with dignity and stateliness. Dressed in white cotton akin to the style of the ancient Greeks, he looked as if the scorching sun had sapped his body of all but the most indispensable elements—blood, bone, and tightly-drawn skin. A few wisps of grey hair fluttered on his temples, and as he came closer, I saw that his eyes were bright green, a rarity in this part of the world.

"*Sahib*, I would like to introduce you to Abhay," said Ritika in English.

In my best Hindoostani, I greeted this venerable man and observed him even more closely. Four long, deep, evenly-spaced parallel scars etched his rib cage, as if a bear or a tiger had attacked him. In contrast to the green of his irises, his pupils were the colour of dirty milk, and a considerable portion of flesh was missing from his left ear. His teeth, however, were in excellent condition: stained yellow, to be sure, but appearing as strong and healthy as those of a man in his prime.

"Abhay is my grandfather," Ritika explained.

Astonished at meeting a man of such advanced years, I must confess that I stared at him rudely.

"Abhay has returned home after walking through the night from a neighbouring village," Ritika said, breaking the intentness of my gaze, "I am sure he is anxious to rest."

In my politest Hindoostani, eager to atone for my rudeness, I bid Abhay a pleasant day. He responded in the same language and left me standing beside the great banyan tree.

That evening I apologized to Ritika for my impolite gawking. She comforted me by explaining that neither she nor Abhay had considered me rude. On the contrary, Abhay had found me to be a polite young man. I laughed at the words "young man," for I am twenty years removed from that turn of phrase, yet I was relieved to know I had caused no offence.

In an attempt to impress Ritika with my knowledge of rural affairs, I asked if Abhay was the *patel*, or headman, of the area. Called the father of the village, a *patel* is often a respected member of the community, someone who administers justice and settles disputes. Ritika explained that the term *mandel* rather than *patel* is used in Bengal and that Abhay was not the *mandel* of the village.

"Surely, you jest," I said impolitely, forgetting myself yet again. So taken was I with Abhay's deportment that I could not imagine another person better suited to be the father of the village.

"He wanders about much and is here but a portion of each season," Ritika informed me.

During my stay at the farm, I surreptitiously observed Abhay. He would rise late in the morning, take breakfast, then seat himself under the banyan tree, where he would often sew, using touch, rather than his cloudy vision, to guide his hands. Ere long, visitors would temporarily interrupt his sewing. Greeting him deferentially, men and women of all ages would sit down across from him and converse. Some were as animated as the shopkeepers bartering in the village; others whispered. Some left with smiles, others with looks of concern or confusion. Ritika told me that many people sought Abhay's wisdom, and he would counsel any who approached him.

On particularly busy days, he remained under the banyan tree from late morning until dark. On less busy days, when he was not engaged with visitors, he would graciously bring me my noon meal, then sit beside me in silence as we both ate. After his evening meal, Abhay would often enter the dark jungle, not returning for hours, occasionally even staying away the entire night. Regardless of how late he returned, I would find him each morning under the banyan tree, sewing as he awaited his inevitable guests.

I began to think of him as a jungle *wallah*, a wild man of

the woods. As one can imagine, his strange habit of walking through the treacherous jungle at night caused me to wonder about his nocturnal activities. Initially, I thought he might be secreting his wealth in some hole in the ground, for it is common amongst Indian men with abundant savings either to adorn their wives and children with silver bangles or to bury their rupees in safe places; however, I never saw him leave or return with anything more than the white cotton robe he wore. When my curiosity finally led me to inquire of Ritika about Abhay's nightly wanderings, she informed me that he taught the ways of the night animals to the youth of the village. I could not imagine a man of 120 years, with rheumy eyes and an infirm body, stumbling about at night in the jungle with its many dangers, but Ritika was in earnest. The more I learned about Abhay, the more intriguing I found him.

These days of observation were not devoid of ennui, for I could not rid myself of the idea that my life held no meaning, the absence of which had precipitated my expedition to India. What is more, I dreamed of unpleasant events. Normally, I would not in a letter burden you with details of my disturbing dreams: however, since I will be beside you when you read this, I feel it not inappropriate to share with you my state of mind.

The dreams were always the same. Dressed in layers of white chiffon, which cover you from ankle to neck and down to your delicate wrists, you rest upon the matrimonial blanket of our iron bed. A fine lace veil adorns your face, and your hair is brushed so that it looks like a shiny brown halo. By your side, sleeps the baby. She wears a simple silk dress that is too large for her little form, for the dress runs well past her toes and the sleeves swallow her tiny hands. Her face is also veiled.

Frightened by this unnatural scene, I touch your arm, desiring to wake you, but you do not stir. Slowly, I pull aside the veil. To my horror, I see that your skin is the blue-white shade of an iceberg. I do not need to remove the baby's veil to know she no longer draws breath either. As if by magic, I find myself in possession of a bouquet of daisies and a garland of green leaves. My hands shake as I dress the baby's head with the garland and lay the bouquet upon your eternally still chest.

Intense loneliness would overwhelm me whenever I woke from the nightmare, and in that loneliness, which provided fertile ground for desperate thoughts, I would see the pointlessness of my life. If the mosquitoes were not overly bothersome, I would exit my bungalow, sit against the banyan tree, and listen to the sounds of the jungle. Though the jungle is quieter at night than by day, without the cacophonous orchestra of chattering monkeys and shrieking birds that sleep in the dark, I might hear the panic-stricken scream of an animal as a predator pounced. At the otherworldly roar of a tiger, I would go to Zeki and brush him until he calmed, for he would be scared—the ominous sound of a tiger is a noise few horses can abide.

Some nights, howling jackals, scavengers known to feed off the carcasses when the principal predator has eaten its fill, would be my unwanted companions. My *Gorah-Wallah* once explained to me how jackals speak with their howls. The lead animal will call out, "Here lies the body of a dead Hindoo-oo-oo." The pack will respond with short barks: "Where? Where? Where?" The lead animal answers with a series of quick, snapping yelps, "Here, here, here."

Mornings would find me drained of energy. However, instead of spending a portion of the day sleeping, I would pace about my cottage and attempt, through logic, to find a long-lost purpose to my life. In this constant state of agitation, I was incapable of being sociable and repeatedly turned down Ritika's invitations to dine with her family. Perversely, the isolation only increased my restless state of mind.

As my time in the cottage neared its end, and cold fingers of anxiety clutched at my heart, I found myself wanting more and more to speak with Abhay about the thoughts that plagued me. If men and women travelled from great distances to seek out his wisdom, perhaps he could provide me, too, with some sage words. If only I spoke Hindoostani.

My Love, I shall end here for the day. It is time for me to inhale the wholesome air upon deck and to stretch my aching limbs. I shall see you in my dreams to-night.

April 3, 1867   The Friedrich
                          Lat. 17° 40' Long. 86° 35'

My Dearest Inga,

A fine day to-day, yet still no sign of wind. Not surprisingly, it would appear that a knife in the mast does nothing to induce the winds to blow. One of the officers tells me that the Friedrich had a sister ship named the Himalaya. Apparently the Himalaya struck a rock in the Straits of Banca near Singapore in '57 and now lies below seventeen fathoms of water. I have spent the morning sketching how she must look in her final resting place. I am pleased with my morning's efforts.

I now sit in the dining saloon where the air is not as oppressive as in the cabin, though I must endure the sound of the poultry on the deck above. They produce a noise like the tapping of a hundred, energetic telegraph operators: tap, tap, tap, tap. It is a fine saloon, especially considering the age of the ship. The saloon is, I would guess, seventy-feet long by twenty-five feet wide. The walls are panelled in satinwood, not unlike our sitting room at home. The ceiling is elaborately carved in white pine, and the benches and chairs are covered in black leather. Two long tables run the length of the saloon, with a wide space between them for easy passage down the centre. An altogether pleasant room.

Around me are other passengers, some reading, others playing whist, or enjoying a game of backgammon. Do you recollect, my darling, the lessons you gave me in backgammon? I had arranged through devious means to be invited to the O'Connells' dinner party. A man of crude upbringing and no family connections, I was out of place amongst those people, yet you took pity on me and taught me how to play the game. If I fell in love with you the first time we met, then that was the night I knew you would be my wife. I am sorry I was not a better husband, my love; only now do I recognize I did not appreciate you enough. Alas, now I am getting sentimental, so I shall return to my story.

On my last full day in the cottage, I finally summoned enough courage to speak with Abhay. I felt that if I were to leave this place without ever doing more than greet or thank the man, I would regret it for the rest of my days. Some real communication was necessary. I approached Ritika and asked if she would translate for me, so that I could converse with her grandfather.

"You need me to translate?" she asked with an enigmatic smile.

"My Hindoostani is very poor, and I wish to speak with Abhay."

Her smile deepened. "His English, you will find, is superior to my own."

I was unable to conceal my surprise. "He speaks English? Where did he learn? Why has he not spoken before?" I had many questions.

"He learned in England. As to why he has not spoken, only he can give you the answer to that."

"Do you think your grandfather would deign to speak with me?"

Ritika raised an eyebrow. "Ask him, *Sahib*."

That morning, I waited anxiously for Abhay to be alone. When I saw no other visitors, I nervously approached the man leaning quietly against the trunk of the banyan tree. I greeted him first in Hindoostani. Turning to English, I asked if he could spare me some of his valuable time.

"Please, do join me." His English was, indeed, as fine as Ritika's.

I asked him why he had never, until this moment, spoken to me in English.

"I did not wish to intrude upon your meditation," he said simply.

I thanked him for his consideration and asked when he had last been in England.

"I have not been there for over one hundred years," he said. He spoke without reservation about his childhood. His father, an Englishman from Ipswich, worked for the East India Company. His mother was from Howrah, near Calcutta. While stationed in Calcutta, his father had met his mother and had quickly fallen in love with her. They were soon married and had four children: first two girls, then two boys, Abhay being the youngest. All had received equal portions of love and adoration.

Abhay was still an infant when the family moved to England. Raised in a culture that was unwilling to accept him as one of their own, he became an introspective boy. For comfort, he read voraciously the works of great minds of the West. At the age of thirteen, he returned with his family to India where, to his dismay, he found himself once again an outsider, unwanted by all but his family. In India, his reading tastes changed, as works of eastern minds captured his interest and became his faithful companions.

As Ritika had weeks earlier, Abhay put me at ease. So relaxed did I become that I failed to notice when discussion slowly turned to my distressing thoughts. I wonder why it is that we can talk so easily with strangers about our most intimate hopes and fears, when we cannot share those same thoughts with those who know us best. Is it because we hope a stranger may have fresh words of insight that will help us see more clearly? Could it be that if a stranger judges us, it is easier to dismiss his disparaging remarks? Maybe we are reluctant to bare our deepest feelings to a friend or loved one who will always remember the thoughts we spoke of in our lowest moments, thoughts we may later wish had remained unspoken. Whatever the answer may be, in Abhay's presence, your reserved husband became talkative.

"I used to devote my waking hours to building my commercial enterprise," I told him. "At first I was employed and laboured for my wages. Gradually, I became familiar with the business of a timber merchant. When well-forested land became available, I bought an acre whenever possible. I continued to earn wages; in the evenings I cut my own timber. By the sweat of my brow, I became the proprietor of a sawmill and expanded my business with modern machinery. In time I built a second, and then, a third sawmill. As my business prospered and my profits grew, I eventually added a large fleet of boats that would carry my lumber to wherever prices were highest. I worked very hard for more than a score of years to bring about my dreams of wealth and security; yet, despite my success, I felt no closer to achieving the vision I imagined."

I paused thoughtfully, but Abhay's unblinking green eyes encouraged me to continue.

"Despair brought me to India. I had hoped that travel and adventure would challenge, stimulate, and kindle new life in me, but I am more lost now than when I left my home!"

Just by saying these words aloud, I seemed to have stirred the mud that had clogged my mind for so long. For the first time, I found myself able to give verbal expression to the disturbing thoughts that have been plaguing me since I left you. I continued on: "I was once a babe crawling upon the ground. In time, I learned to walk and run. As quick as lightning, I found myself a husband and a father. Ere long, I shall be meat for the worms. What is more, I can find no certainties to hold onto. Whatever I touch will eventually deteriorate; whatever I see is mere chimera; and those I love will die! It seems that all about me is randomly and cruelly changing."

I will spare you the further ramblings of a desperate man. Suffice it to know that I felt myself mired in a deep pit, with a fresh shovel of dirt tossed on me each day, slowly but surely erasing any hope I had once had for happiness. Much time passed as I attempted to articulate thoughts that have taken only a few strokes of the pen to write. Throughout my confused and incoherent recriminations, Abhay listened patiently and with great attention. He said nothing, only nodding thoughtfully when I paused to collect my painfully wayward thoughts. Finally, when my heart was emptied of all but my very severest pain—a pain the sagacious Abhay surely deduced—I let out a long breath, as if exhaling poisonous air, and waited for him to speak.

"You are correct in thinking," Abhay said slowly, "that all you sense and experience is eternally changing, and that there is nothing of permanence that we can grasp. How fortunate for us that is—do you not agree?"

I stared at him, feeling dazed, stunned. I had expected to be offered a soothing word or a steadfast notion to seize, something that would save me from drowning in an ocean of emotional instability. Instead, his words were a kind of challenge.

"Why do you say this?" I asked at last.

"Are we not fortunate to have a universe that eternally creates new things for us to experience? Would life not be intolerable if we relived the same events over and over again?" Abhay spoke slowly, quietly.

"But I desire permanence. I desire solidity. I desire perfection!" I cried.

"It is not possible for you to have these things. No one can," he said mildly, "Such ideas are inconsistent with a universe that is continually changing."

I had come to this man hungry for answers. I wished to gorge myself on his wisdom. Instead, I found my spiritual emptiness even more acute than before. I felt like a famished guest invited to a sumptuous meal—only to find that the food has gone bad. "Where shall I find meaning?" I asked in despair.

Abhay leaned towards me with furrowed brow and said with great earnestness, as if to make certain I would not be confused, "There is no meaning." His words were like a dagger in my heart. He watched me, his intensity tempered by concern. "It is too much to digest all at once, I know. Take time to consider my words, for deep thought is the only path to all you seek."

With these words, I felt myself dismissed. Not forgetting my manners, I thanked him in Hindoostani. As I walked back to my cottage, I am sure my face must have worn the same confused expression I had seen on others when they left Abhay's council.

My Love, I have come to the end of another entry. I now retire with a hacking cough and an anxious eye to the falling barometer.

April 4, 1867   The Friedrich

My Dearest Inga,

I was abruptly roused in the early hours—4 a.m. to be
precise—by the loud crashing of crockery in adjacent cabins.
During the night, a ferocious storm commenced and is
presently tossing us about in our berths. I thought I would
employ my wakefulness by writing to you; however, since I
cannot keep the ink from spilling from the ink bottle, I shall
write again when the weather has turned.

April 5, 1867   The Friedrich

My Dearest Inga,

    Another dirty day. The barometer remains low, and the ocean heaves about violently, putting Torvus and me in a terrible state. The seas are so bad that even the crew are sick and remain in their berths. I have not experienced such terrible seas since rounding the Cape of Storms on our way to India. Perhaps to-morrow I shall be able to continue with my story.

April 6, 1867   The Friedrich

My Dearest Inga,

    To-day, at last, the gale has hushed to a calm. After so ter-
rible a storm, we count ourselves fortunate to have lost only
our top masts, which the crew hurries to repair, as I write.
    Torvus is also damaged. Yesterday, feeling very sick, he
chose to walk about the deck to clear his head. In the midst of
the rolling and pitching, a sudden lurching of the ship threw
him against the mizzenmast, and he returned to the cabin
drenched and bleeding from a cut to the head. Referring to
his need to clear his head, he commented wryly, "I did not
mean, literally, that I should open it up and expose it to the
sea." When I had staunched the bleeding, Torvus returned to
his bunk and remained there the rest of the day. Despite the
copious bleeding and drama, I predict his full recovery.
    The storm caused yet a third casualty. I was attempting to
write a few lines the day before yesterday—I have already told
you that. What you don't know is that my inkstand fell over,
spilling most of the ink it contained. I thought I had purchased an extra bottle of violet ink before departing Calcutta,
but now it appears I failed to do so. I am, therefore, obliged
to water down the little ink I have left. I hope it shall last until
my story is concluded. Without wasting more ink, I continue
with my tale.

I slept little during my last night at the cottage. Instead, I
spent much of the night propped against the banyan tree,
listening for signs of life. For once, however, the jungle was
eerily quiet. No breeze stirred, no animals moved in the tall
grass, no tiger roared. The air was heavy with the threat of

rain, yet none fell. I felt like a man floating on what remained of the wreckage of a sunken ship: utterly alone and without hope. The intensity of my loneliness induced me to visit my Arabian steed, Zeki. For hours I brushed his coat, eager to keep my despair at bay. At first light, I saddled him, thanked Ritika once more for her hospitality, and headed out.

I arrived in Katiham by early afternoon. My companions, already waiting for me at the hotel, were high-spirited and cheerful. Just recently returned from Darjeeling and the Himalayas, their talk was punctuated with expressions such as, "I have never seen the like!" and "What a grand view!" and "Magnificent!" I attempted to listen earnestly. I nodded and smiled whenever appropriate, but I felt no interest in their stories, and they sensed this. With my mind still focused intensely on Abhay's words, nothing penetrated the surface of my gloom.

The words Abhay had spoken would not leave me. *No meaning. No meaning.* The words echoed in my ears, my mind, my heart, my very core. It would have been easy enough to refute Abhay's words had my own thoughts not been the same as his. Yet I had hoped for something more, something that would give me cause for new reflection, new hope, new direction. In my disappointment, all I could feel, for longer than I care to recall, was a deep desolation brought on by the meaninglessness of existence.

The following day, Torvus and the others rested. Spending more time in Darjeeling than they had initially planned, they had tired themselves in hastening back to Katiham. While they rested, I paced about my room like a caged lion and drank many bottles of a most villainous sherry; neither of these actions did anything to cleanse my mental palate of the bitterness of life. I cursed Abhay and then concurred with him, in turn. One moment, I was sure his ideas must be wrong and that he was a fraud; the next moment, I agreed with him. Back and forth across the room I strode, my thoughts ebbing and flowing like waves upon the shore. Outside, melancholy birds sang their sad songs, and the rain hissed as it fell upon the scorched earth.

The night before we were due to depart for Calcutta, I awoke with a start. If all really was meaningless, why did Abhay appear such a contented man? Surely a man as wise as he did not really believe in a meaningless existence? Was it possible for him to believe such an idea and yet display such equanimity at the same time? Perhaps he had more to say. Could it be that he was testing me, to determine if I was worthy of his wisdom and knowledge?

A renewed sense of life coursed through my body, and I emerged from the darkness like a coal miner leaving the deep recesses of a mine. Strength returned to my limbs, and my desolate thoughts disappeared. Breathing calmly and deeply, I resolved to return to Abhay and proclaim to him that I was prepared to know the truth, that I was indeed worthy of his wisdom. In the morning I informed my companions of my intention to return to the farm where I had spent the last few weeks. They were rightfully concerned, as my mood seemed to have veered suddenly from anguish to ecstasy. Torvus refused to let me travel alone again and insisted on joining me. I assured my companions that I should not be gone long and that I would catch up with them on the road south to Calcutta. "Leave messages for me at the various hotels, and I shall track you down. I shall not be longer than a fortnight," I promised.

More reluctantly than before and frowning in concern, my companions departed. The moment they were out of sight, I started for Chindah. Except for the rain that fell in intermittent torrents, an uneventful trip allowed me to arrive at my destination by mid-afternoon. In great excitement, I went directly to the magnificent banyan tree, expecting to see Abhay there. When I did not find him, I searched for Ritika.

"He has departed for a neighbouring village," she said, looking surprised to see me back so soon. "He will return in a few days." Then she graciously offered me my old cottage again, where I could await Abhay's return.

In those few anxious days, I often visited the village and partook of its entertainment. With a fresh plantain leaf tucked into my cap to keep me cool, I watched various performers put on clever pieces of legerdemain, my favourite being the mango trick. The conjurer begins his act by pouring some dry earth into an empty basket. In the earth, he places a seed. Finally, murmuring an incantation, he drapes a piece of cloth over the basket. A few moments pass. At last, and with great flourish, he lifts the cloth to reveal a small, green sprout. Amazing! But wait—he has not finished. The basket is covered again. The conjurer waits a few moments more; then with more incantations, he removes the cloth to reveal the sprout now grown into a plant with branches and leaves. After covering the basket once more, he removes the cloth a third time. Lo and behold! The plant is now well over a foot tall. Most astounding of all—a mango, pink and luscious, hangs from a branch. How does he do it? Nobody knows, but all applaud the achievement.

A boy is made to disappear in another mysterious act of adroitness. In a circular space clear of spectators, perhaps fifteen feet in circumference and selected by the audience, the magician places a large, empty wicker basket. The basket has two parts, one fitting on top of the other. A boy is placed in the basket. The space is very small, and the boy has no room to move. Once the basket is clasped shut, the two perform-ers begin to communicate. The conjurer pretends the boy is irritating him. In a rage, he produces a sword and thrusts it through the basket. The caged boy lets out several heart-stopping screams, while the sword, now covered in blood, is drawn out of the basket, then plunged in again and again. The audience hardly breathes. The suspense grows. And then a few spectators, more daring than all the rest, will usually rush to the scene, anxious to intervene. With a heavy sigh, the magician "reluctantly" agrees to open the basket. The spectators lean forward. The basket is empty. *Where is the boy?* Moments later, he bounds out from the crowd, quite unhurt.

I observed these tricks for hours on end, enjoying them immensely, and always unable to guess how they were done.

In the evenings, Ritika's family invited me to eat with them. Those who could speak English did so. Many in the family were what you and I would call "characters," laughing and joking as they imitated their kith and kin. It was obvious that they enjoyed one another's company. After the evening meal, I would sit against the banyan tree and watch the tantalizing flight of the fireflies: they reminded me of tiny bits of paper ejected from a fire, glowing momentarily in the dark before vanishing. At night I slept well—nary an evil thought to hinder my rest.

The few days I spent waiting for Abhay were agreeable, for I was confident that he would share his true wisdom and understanding with me upon his return. With my faith set squarely in his hands, I no longer agonized over my sorrow. Like the sleight of hand with the mango, and the boy in the basket, I sensed that a kind of magic would soon be mine, and I felt joyful.

I accosted Abhay immediately upon his return, before he had even had an opportunity to sit down. "I know there is much yet hidden from my eyes," I said eagerly. "I beseech you to share your truth with me. I want to understand how you know the meaning of things."

Rather than upbraiding me for rushing him after so long an absence from his home, Abhay bade me follow him. Excitedly I complied.

He strode into the jungle, his limp more pronounced when he walked fast. I followed him without a word. Skilfully, he picked his way through the dense tangle of trees, ferns, and tall grasses. Behind him, I stumbled over roots buried in the mossy jungle undergrowth. Deeper and deeper into the jungle we proceeded. Sweat poured from my brow. In front of me, Abhay moved soundlessly and with enviably easy assurance.

As suddenly as we had entered the jungle, we exited. A few hundred yards away stood a fort and a small village. For a moment, I did not recognize the place. Then it came to me—we were near Chindah. We had walked there by way of a shortcut.

"What do you see?" Abhay asked, pointing to my left. I saw what I had not noticed before: twelve weathered stone statues, each about fifteen feet high, shaped like men but bearing the heads of elephants, monkeys, and tigers. The figures were clothed in the manner of wealthy Indian men: jewels festooned their necks, and slippers decorated their feet.

"I see idols," I said slowly, as I recognized them for what they were.

"Are they men or stone?" Abhay asked.

"Stone."

"Do you know what these are?" he asked, pointing to indentations, each one the size and depth of a thumbnail. Sharp edges revealed the indentations were relatively new;

unlike the statues, they had not been subjected to countless years of exposure to the elements.

"Have stones been thrown at them?" I asked, curiously.

"No. Please follow me again."

Inside the familiar village, Abhay led me to the walls of the fort that faced the idols. "Do you know about the Indian War of 1857?" he asked, as he looked over the wall toward the distant statues. "You may recollect, my dear friend, reading stories of the Sepoy Rebellion in *The Times*?"

When I nodded, he continued. "There are, of course, two conflicting versions of the rebellion. The British see the uprising as a mutiny. The Indians," he said, waving his arms to encompass the surrounding Indian countryside, "call it the War of Independence."

Abhay then told me the following story. My dear, I'll summarize it for you here as best I can:

The East India Company employed some 250,000 Sepoys—native soldiers—to help maintain their interests in India. The Sepoys were under the command of approximately 40,000 British soldiers. In 1857, rumours circulated in the Sepoy army that the cartridges for their new Enfield Rifles were being greased with cow and pig fat. This information caused outrage amongst the Hindoo and the Mohammedan Sepoys, as the Hindoos regard the cow as sacred, and the Mohammedans abhor the pig. In defiance of the indignity forced upon them—merely touching the offensive cartridges would make them social outcasts—some Sepoys refused to load their rifles, thereby receiving punishment of ten years' hard labour. If British history is to be believed, this mis-understanding caused the unfortunate affair; however, this incendiary incident only set off the powder keg of more complex issues.

For a hundred years, the East India Company, arrogantly convinced of its superiority, administered much of the country. Religious customs were banned. Indians were excluded from higher government offices. Land and treasures were forcibly seized. Brutal treatment of Indians—including torture—at the hands of British officers was rampant. Heavy taxes were levied on farmers, the money frequently being demanded before they could harvest their crops. These factors, amongst others, created a severe rift between the British rulers and their Indian subjects.

Provoked by the option of either losing their social standing or spending ten years doing hard labour, three Indian regiments broke ranks at the Meerut Cantonment. On May 10th, 1857, they attacked the cantonment at Meerut, supposedly murdering the men, women, and children stationed there. A day later, the regiments marched into Delhi, forty miles to the southwest, and proclaimed Bahadur Shah to be Emperor of Hindoostan. So began the war.

"Although it now stands abandoned, this fort housed two hundred British infantry at the time of the revolt," Abhay said. "In June of 1857, four weeks after the uprising began, rumours spread that two thousand native infantry from the area had joined the rebellion and were preparing to attack the stronghold. The British, who possessed no heavy guns, feared the prospect of facing such a superior force. For many days and nights, they kept vigil as they waited for the offensive to begin."

"Finally, in the dead of night, after weeks of little food or sleep, the soldiers on watch spotted the Indians a few hundred yards away. The garrison came alive as the sleeping British soldiers were called to arms. Shoulder to shoulder, they lined the wall, firing repeated volleys of grapeshot into the front ranks of the insurgents. Many shots rang out in the night. Smoke filled the air as the men feverishly reloaded and fired again. Confusion filled the minds of the firing troops. Why, they wondered, can we not kill or even rout these men? And, in a parody of Shakespeare: Do they not bleed? Do they not fear?"

Abhay turned to look at me, obviously expecting me to comment on his story. I acquiesced. "They mistook the statues for men," I said.

He nodded his wizened head. "Yes."

"Why do you tell me this story?" I asked, baffled.

"Because my dear friend," he said, "like the soldiers on that terrible night, you see what you want to see rather than what might really be. You see change everywhere; yet you continue to search for permanence, for meaning."

"I still do not understand," I said, as if pleading for more.

"To-night you may," he said, whereupon he led me back through the jungle.

Late that afternoon, when the red sun was dropping into the mist along the horizon, Abhay bade me follow him once more. We strode along a marked path, wide and level, that cut a swath through the jungle. In the shadow of the trees, we walked in silence for more than an hour. When the jungle eased somewhat, I found myself on the banks of the great Ganges River.

"Please observe." Abhay gestured towards a distant group of men who were carefully piling up wood for what looked like a possible bonfire.

The men worked quietly and solemnly, stacking logs to form a pyre about four feet in height and six feet in length and width. Interspersed among the logs were such combustibles as dry straw and sugar cane. A mat rested on top of the pyre. Two feet above the mat, a platform of dry wood was assembled and held aloft by a slight support. With the support in place, men poured scented oils and ghee onto the mat, while half a dozen women, working with great respect and formality, adorned the pyre with fresh flowers.

Then, from out of the jungle, emerged a procession of native musicians playing horns, small drums, and a little stringed instrument that resembled a mandolin. Behind the musicians came a man carrying in his arms the body of a small girl. And behind him followed some fifty men, women, and children, several carrying kindled torches. The musicians came to a halt beside the pyre, where they continued to play while the man carried the child to the river. A woman joined the man, and both waded waist-deep into the water. While the man held the girl, the woman lovingly washed the motionless body. Upon conclusion of the ceremonial bath, the group returned to the pyre, where the man laid the little girl gently down on the mat.

So absorbed was I in the events happening before me that I forgot Abhay's presence beside me, until he whispered, "You require a reason to persist in light of a meaningless existence, do you not?"

I nodded.

"This is why," he said.

I took a step forward, enabling me to see more clearly in the growing darkness. Quick as a cat, Abhay grabbed my wrist, with such strength that I became alarmed. Surprised at the power that still remained in this very old man, I drew back beside him, whereupon he relaxed his grip. It was then that the musicians ceased their playing, and the man who carried the child—doubtless the father—was given a burning torch. He appeared to say a silent prayer; then he stepped forward reluctantly and set the funeral pyre ablaze. The structure caught alight immediately. The flames rose higher and higher, and the air was filled with the sound of crackling wood and the odour of burning straw. As the fire burned, my horrified gaze was riveted on the father. I had a clear view of his haunted eyes and his face, haggard with grief. With a great whooshing sound, the fragile supports gave way, and flames engulfed the dead girl's body. As the fire consumed her daughter, the mother—the woman who had washed her earlier—moaned loudly, "Humara baba, humara baba," or "My child, my child."

I watched the scene, aghast. I knew about funeral pyres, but I had never witnessed the event. My legs were weak; my chest felt tight.

I started when Abhay touched my shoulder. Slowly, reluctantly, I turned to him. I sensed he had a fragment of wisdom to impart, and I was not wrong.

He spoke very quietly. "This, my friend, is the reason to persist in a meaningless universe. It is the preciousness of life. A man without legs would find walking a joy. A woman without sight would be ecstatic if she could see. Death, therefore, reminds us to venerate existence."

Abhay's words failed to reach me. Unwilling to look any longer at the eyes of the father, eyes that were as dead as his daughter, or to listen to the wailing of the distraught mother, I strode away. But I found myself unable to get away from death, as I had hoped, for when I glanced along the banks of the great Ganges, I spotted what I had not previously observed—other funeral pyres on both sides of the river. Everywhere I looked, flames illuminated the grieving; the wind carried despairing wails of sorrow and separation.

Out of the darkness, Abhay appeared. "Death is all around us. To ignore it or fear it will not benefit you."

"Why have you shown this to me?" I asked angrily, unable to push aside the mental picture of our own beloved little Astrid burning on a similar pyre.

Abhay looked hard at me. I saw the glint of his eyes in the moonlight. "I see you require a more radical lesson," he said, and without another word, he set off along the path for home. Reluctantly, I followed, hating him more with every step he took. Why did I hate him so? I asked myself. Was it because I felt myself a coward? At that moment, I wished it was me ablaze on that pyre, for no longer would I have to endure a lonely, meaningless existence.

My Love, I am once more wracked with fits of coughing and must rest. Weather permitting, I will endeavour to write again to-morrow.

April 7, 1867   The Friedrich

My Dearest Inga,

    After witnessing the funeral pyre, I was not graced with sleep that night. The father's dead eyes appeared when I closed mine; the mother's pitiful cry rang in my ears. For comfort, I sat against the banyan tree imagining you holding my hand, while our darling Astrid played before us. However, even such normally delightful thoughts could not assuage me this time; the sadness of death overwhelmed me, tugging me irresistibly downwards. Unhappiness filled my heart, my mind, pouring through and over my being in a torrent of tears.

    I returned to my cottage at dawn, desirous of remaining alone, of removing myself from the living. I lay on my mat staring at the plain cane walls of my hut. The cacophony of the world outside had resumed. Hard though I tried, I was unable to push from my consciousness the singing of the birds, the chattering of the monkeys, the barking of the dogs, and the laughter of the children. Vigorous life took place beyond my walls, and I was powerless to ignore it.

    That evening the jungle seemed to exert an irresistible pull over me. If death comes to us eventually, I thought, why then not have done with it now? Heedless of the sun's imminent setting, I thrust aside the branches of the nearest trees and plunged into the darkness. Purposeful strides carried me deep into the dense vegetation. This way and that I turned. Ere long, not surprisingly, I lost my direction, yet was still able to keep my pace. Further and further, I pushed my way through thorns and brush that scraped my arms and legs and caused small trickles of blood, but I felt no pain. With luck, I would tread on a poisonous snake or come blindly to a precipice and fall to my death. Finally, I would be through with this life and would find peace in the void.

As I made my way through the tangled jungle undergrowth, I heard monkeys making a tremendous noise somewhere ahead of me. Without thought, I advanced towards the source of the noise. I caught sight of them quickly, a troop of monkeys swinging and leaping wildly from the branches of a tree, some twenty feet above an area of dense grass. They bounded from limb to limb, screeching madly, as if in great fear. Curiously, and without care for my safety, determined only to discover what was exciting the monkeys, I took a few steps into the tall grass. I did not have to walk far: no more than four feet in front of me stood a tiger. Its enormous muzzle smeared with blood, the beast tore rapaciously into the carcass of a freshly killed deer.

Instinctively, I dropped to the ground. I had entered the jungle in search of death; yet now, having encountered its face, I hoped quite desperately that the tall grass would conceal me. It did not. My heart raced with terror as the tiger lifted its head, stared at me, and bared teeth that were as long as my fingers. Growling menacingly, the tiger withdrew a bloody paw from the innards of the mutilated deer. Expecting him to pounce—**_knowing he would_**—I closed my eyes and prepared for my inevitable end. I waited. Nothing happened. Cautiously, I opened one eye, then the other. Like me, the tiger remained motionless, but for his twitching tail. Barely audible above the excited chatter of the monkeys was his angry growl.

I tried to crawl away. Stopping when I heard a deafening roar. Moments later, the tiger's hot breath was upon me—suffocating, nauseating. I closed my eyes a second time, again waiting for the end. Once more, my fears were not realized.

Trembling, I dared to open my eyes. The tiger bared his teeth, jerked his tail back and forth, and drew his brutal claws from their velvet sheaths. My chest tightened, my breathing quickened, my vision narrowed. Fearing I would succumb to unconsciousness, I concentrated my energy on breathing steadily. My only hope was to remain calm and still.

Above me the bedlam diminished as the monkeys vacated the trees and receded into the jungle. The last rays of light faded at the same time. In the renewed silence, I became aware of a buzzing in my ear—mosquitoes, drawn by the pungent smell of fresh blood, or perhaps by the tantalizing odour of human skin. They attacked my arms and hands and swarmed about my face. I dared not brush them off, forced to remain helplessly prone, as they tormented me at will. Gradually, I felt rocks and branches pushing painfully against my body, and the agony of my cramped position increased by the second. And weighing on me infinitely more than the mosquitoes, the rocks, and the branches was the menacing presence of the tiger, his green eyes glowing fiercely in the dark. I willed him to leave the scene. *Go away. Go away.* I mouthed the words silently. Fruitlessly. In my heightened sense of alertness, I heard the distant slithering of a snake in the jungle grass. Thankfully, it did not come my way: I believe my sanity would have shattered if it had.

I cannot say how long I lay there without moving. The moon rose high in the sky and cast its light over us: the tiger, the deer, and me. The maddening whine of the mosquitoes continued as they relentlessly drew blood from every inch of my exposed body. In the moonlight, I chanced a peek at the tiger. What a massive creature he was. Even had I carried a firearm, it would have been to no avail. A specimen like this one would not be brought down by a single shot. He was at least nine feet long from his nose to the tip of his tail;

each foreleg was thick as a man's head; his paws the size of serving platters. With a single blow from one of his paws, he would crush me as effortlessly as if I were a worm underfoot in the dust. Drops of blood hung like ripe fruit from his long whiskers. His malignant green eyes glared at me menacingly. Once he rested his huge head on his paws, his heavy breathing subsided and his tail stopped jerking. I took the opportunity to move slightly, to ease the dreadful pain in my knees and elbows. But if I thought the tiger's relaxed posture meant he was tired, I was quickly proved wrong: my slight movement was provocation enough for him to lay his ears against his skull; his tail resumed its jerking movement; and from deep in his throat came a threatening growl. Terror-stricken, I lay quite still. I dared not move again.

The hours crept by, warmth left the air, and the mosquitoes departed, finally satiated. A mist crept into the jungle. The sweat on my back cooled, chilling me. With the tiger's hot breath still only feet away, the suspense had become more than I could tolerate. How much longer would the tiger glare at me? Why did he play this cruel game with me? I felt parched; my tongue, thick and sticky inside my mouth, tasted of copper. The rocks dug painfully into my flesh. As the cramping of my body became unbearable, I staved off madness by repeating, like a mantra—"I want to live. I want to live."

I had reached the limits of my physical and intellectual strength, and I could stand the strain no longer, when the morning light dawned. As if offended by the illumination, the tiger rose to its feet, let out a huge final roar, and stalked off out of the *midan* and further into the denseness of the jungle. I still lay frozen for a time, uncertain whether the beast had indeed departed, or whether he would return to finish me off. When he did not reappear, I began to bend my arms and legs, very slowly, for the pain entailed in moving my limbs was almost as intense as being immobile. At last I managed to stand though stomach cramps kept me from being fully upright. Again, I expected a striped flash of rust and black, followed by a lethal pounce, but I saw no movement nor heard any sounds other than the pleasant chirping of distant birds.

I began to retrace my steps when I heard tree branches rustling behind me. Instinctively, I dropped to the ground. The sound drew closer and closer. He has come to kill me, I thought, and closed my eyes.

And then I heard a voice—a mercifully familiar voice—exclaim, "*At last!*"

I opened my eyes to see a relieved-looking Ritika. Overwhelmed by the fear and uncertainty my tormentor had caused me, and by the dread of a death I thought assured, emotion gushed like a well from my breast. I collapsed onto the ground, put my head into my hands, and wept, thankful to be alive.

When I had collected myself, Ritika led me out of the jungle and back to the farm. There she fed me a mango and water. The fruit was the finest I had ever tasted—ripe, juicy, sweet. I licked my fingers, my palms, and my forearms, anxious that not a drop of the precious nectar escape. When I had finished eating, I closed my eyes and let the breeze caress my face. So engrossed was I in this simple pleasure that I did not notice Ritika leave my side. In time, I felt an overpowering need for slumber. I went into my cottage, lay down on a mat that felt like a feather bed, and there I slept, a smile upon my face, until the following day.

My Love. I bid you another good night. I shall write again to-morrow. Once again, I'll be sleeping with a smile on my face, for I shall be dreaming of you.

April 9, 1867   The Friedrich

My Dearest Inga,

Happy birthday, my darling! Surely, you did not think I would forget such an auspicious day as this? I ordered a bottle of champagne to toast your health, but it seems the rats have gnawed the corks and chewed the mailbags! The cats are delinquent in their duties. I wonder if Captain Ferguson will punish them!

Do you remember how you used to scold me for exhausting myself? Though no longer engaged in hardship and physical labour, as in days gone by, I have nevertheless, permitted my health to falter. I have a burning fever and am very fatigued. I shall conclude my story when I am better rested.

April 14, 1867   The Friedrich

My Dearest Inga,

The weather is very fine to-day. With a steady wind blowing, the captain lifted the screw, and the ship has gone under canvas. My health, I am happy to inform you, is much improved, and I am recovering from my weakness. To reciprocate for my nursing him after his tussle with the mizzenmast, Torvus did an admirable job restoring my vigour. I was quite without appetite and would gladly have gone without eating, yet he insisted on feeding me copious amounts of soup. Though not as fine as your mama's soup, it was nevertheless quite excellent. I have been recuperating on deck, watching the sheep and cows roam about. This morning I was awakened from slumber by the gentle nudge of a sheep's nose. They are so tame now that one of the sheep actually put its nose in my lap and rubbed against my legs like a friendly dog. When the time comes to eat these gentle creatures, I shall abstain from doing so, for I no longer have the heart for it. I am now seated in the saloon, calling to mind the events that followed my near death at the hands—or paws—of the tiger.

After an entire day of dreamless slumber, I awoke feeling the agony of my night in the jungle. My muscles ached as if I had been engaged in heavy labour for months without a break. The skin on my knees and elbows was still pitted with the marks left by a night pressed against stones. My legs, arms, and face itched from a thousand mosquito bites. Yet despite the physical discomfort, I had never in my life felt so at peace!

Through the cracks in the bamboo walls came the first rays of morning light. I could feel the warmth from these golden ribbons and closed my hands around them, as if I could actually grasp something so ethereal. Turning my head, I spotted a single speck of sand on the floor. I picked it up, gently rolled it between the pads of my fingers, set it on the nail of my thumb, and wondered if, to a creature of gigantic proportions, our world would resemble a grain of sand. I then lay back on my mat and revelled in breathing. I watched my chest rise and fall. I felt the air pass through my nose and lips. I felt the air enter my lungs. I marvelled at this simple act that brings life to our fragile forms.

At my doorstep, *paranthas*, oranges, and a melon awaited me. No breakfast, I assure you, ever tasted better. Basking in the sun's warmth, I marvelled at the beauty of a spider's web, the bumpy texture of the melon rind, and the exquisite birdsong I might never have heard again.

I thought to myself: What do I need of meaning when I fill my belly after long hunger? What do I need of meaning when I enjoy the companionship of my friends? What do I need of meaning when we are intimate? It is the joy of experience that brings me happiness. My contentment is not contingent on meaning; it results from letting go of permanence and experiencing each moment as it occurs.

At that instant, I crossed my personal Rubicon, leaving behind the company of jackdaws. I was eager to find Abhay, so that I could tell him what I had learned. Disappointed not to see him in his usual spot beside the banyan tree, I asked his whereabouts of Ritika.

"He departed yesterday for the Himalayas," she told me.

"When will he return?" I was unable to keep my disappointment from my voice.

"He will return with the rains."

The season of heavy rains, called monsoons, was not due for a few months. "But I have so much I want to share with him," I exclaimed in frustration.

"Abhay knows you have learned Novus-ere—to see like new again—and is pleased for you."

"How can he know?"

"He has seen how you smile when you sleep."

For an instant, I felt sad that the wise old owl had left without saying goodbye, but my sadness was momentary.

"He wished me to tell you that you shall forget what you have learned here. Do not be discouraged thereby. Just as the flow of a river cannot be changed easily, it will take effort for you to change the path of your own thoughts." With those words, Ritika stood and bowed to me.

My lesson was over, yet I was loth to leave. For many days, I remained on the farm assisting Ritika and her family in the rice fields. I kept watching the edge of the forest keenly, hoping Abhay would appear. I desired to see him one last time, to thank him for his patience and wisdom. After a week of waiting, I knew I must leave. My companions were expecting me, and I did not want to torture them with anxiety.

I could not thank Ritika enough. Had it not been for her generous hospitality, which I could only repay handsomely in hard currency, I would have been unable to banish my emptiness and loss. To rid myself of such misery was the reason I had escaped to India.

"You are most welcome," she said, and then handed me a letter. "This is from Abhay. To be opened when you return home."

"Please convey my deepest respects to Abhay. I owe him more than I can say."

"I shall," she said, whereupon we shook hands, and I led my Arabian in the direction of Calcutta.

With my wonder at and love of life restored, I enjoyed a week of travel. Sights and sounds that had barely penetrated my previously melancholy mind, now captivated and intrigued me. The many exotic and interesting things I saw and heard along the way fascinated me. Coolies, bearing brightly-coloured palanquins and hackaries, gently admonished slow-moving bullocks with a pat on the rump and a sociable, "Move along brother." Elephants walking with measured stride rocked their riders like ships on a friendly, rolling sea. Flowers of vivid crimson and white grew beside my path, and when it rained, they emitted a sweet and often heady odour. Fig trees provided me with shade from a sun that seemed, somehow, more brilliant, yet less blisteringly hot than before. In the towns, graceful women, gold bangles jingling around their slender wrists and ankles, caught my eye. Beside them, turbaned men dressed in silken robes and plush slippers sat and smoked. All around me the melodic Hindoostani rhythms filled my ears. India appeared a splendid extravaganza, a fantastic spectacle of sights, sounds, and smells.

At the Auckland Hotel in Calcutta, the manager informed me that a room had been reserved in my name and that my companions had left a standing reservation for dinner at seven o'clock. With a few hours until dinner, I washed, then left the hotel to stroll along the nearby wharfs. I sat for an hour, watching men load bundles and bales of jute onto outbound ships. Seabirds circled noisily overhead. Lost in thought, I failed to hear footsteps approach.

"You were always one for watching others hard at work," said a voice as familiar as my own. It was Torvus.

"How good to see you again!" I said, as if it had been years, not days since I had last seen him. I thrust out my hand.

Ignoring it, he embraced me instead. "It's good to see you too, old friend."

"How are the others?"

"Everyone is very well." He took a step backwards and looked me over. "We were becoming concerned. You are usually such a punctual fellow. If you had not arrived by to-morrow, we would have set out for that little village of yours in search of you. Let us proceed to the hotel, so that we may share our stories. Our friends are waiting."

Warm handshakes greeted me at the hotel, and for the remainder of the afternoon, we sat about while my companions regaled me with their most recent adventures. I, too, shared stories of my travels, and I sensed their relief as they listened. They had been concerned about me for so long, but the good cheer in my voice and my relaxed style of storytelling put them at ease. I told them about Ritika and her family, about my little hut, the banyan tree, the nearby village, and of course, my night with the tiger. I shared everything—everything but my conversations with Abhay.

My dearest love, you may ask why I kept silent about him. I can only respond with this answer—will people be interested in ideas that undermine the beliefs they hold so dearly? If I had said to my friends, "There may be no purpose to your life, and there may be no meaning to your existence, yet joy can thrive and contentment can flourish regardless," do you think they would have understood? I did not deem it so, and therefore, decided to keep Abhay's wondrous tutorials to myself.

No longer fearing the empty life from which I had run, I informed my companions of my desire to return home. Since

I did not insist on travelling alone, and my state of mind had obviously improved, the men felt comfortable about leaving me to my own devices. It was then that I purchased this journal and decided that if this story be shared in its entirety, it would be best shared with you.

With all my love,

Your most loving husband

April 28, 1867   The Friedrich

My Dearest Inga,

This entry will come to you by way of Torvus's hand. Whatever strength my lungs possessed until now, has failed. On the 19th of this month, after a severe fit of coughing, I observed arterial blood in my handkerchief—an undeniable indication that I am consumptive. It is apparent now, nine days later, that my illness is progressing swiftly, so that it has become doubtful that I will make it home to you. My dearest love, if I do not return, Torvus will deliver this journal to you. When he does, he will explain what I want done for our little Astrid.

As I sit resting against the headboard of my berth, I contemplate my own death. In doing so, I find my life has become strange to me. It is as if I were watching these events happen to another, yet I know it may be my own end I study. Do not be alarmed, my love, for I feel no fear whatsoever: it is as if a new field of adventure is opening up before me, and I am most interested to discover where it will take me. Know, my love, that I am at ease, if not in body, then in mind, and it is in the mind that we live.

I am to rest now, my love. My course is run. Know that you have been the greatest joy of my life. You have given me laughter and beauty, and I consider myself a most fortunate man to have been your friend, lover, and husband.

May 27, 1867   The Friedrich

My Dear Inga,

It pains me to inform you that your dear husband has passed away. His death occurred on May 22nd. I would like you to know that when he died he was at peace with himself and that his last thoughts were of you.

Never before have I observed such composure. He continued to jest until the end, even when he was racked with fits of coughing. He showed no fear at any point in his sickness, and even seemed pleased, if this can be believed, by the whole experience. "It's only another part of the journey," he said.

It was only yesterday, when I read this journal, that I understood what he was saying, and the reason why. So much is clear to me that was not before. I recall your husband's strange questions, his self-imposed isolation, and then his happy return, and our reunion in Calcutta. If I had been allowed a wish, it would have been this—to have spoken with him about his experience: I believe there is much I might have learned from such a discussion. Nevertheless, I consider myself fortunate to have read the journal, and more importantly, to have known such a fine human being.

Your husband had one last request of me. I am to deliver this journal and Abhay's letter and must arrange to leave one last treasure for Astrid to find when she is old enough to go in search of it. No matter what happens, you can be sure that I will carry out his last wish.

I have the honour to be your obedient servant,

Torvus L. Sumac

August 22, 1868

Rupert's Land,
The Dominion of Canada

51° 07' 50" N 115° 06' 30" W

Torvus L. Sumac

Richard

A week has gone by since Jenner and Kimberly regained consciousness and returned to Vancouver by medevac. They phone to thank us for our help. We tell them about the accident and our part in things. They tell us about their injuries and about the last thing they remember before waking up in the Granby hospital: the car flipping over and over again. Things were tough for a while, they say, but they are both on the mend now. They even hope to be back at work soon.

"By the way, did you read the journal we left for you?" Jenner asks.

"A few times," Sonia replies. She is on the phone in the kitchen, while I'm on the cordless extension in the living room.

"Kimberly and I wanted to visit all the places the journal entries were set in," Jenner says. "We started here, Vancouver; drove to Edmonton, where I grew up; and from there to Weyburn, Toronto, and finally Fredericton."

"Have you been to India?" Sonia asks. She's always wanted to go there.

"Next year," Jenner answers.

From the living room, I think I can hear the wheels of Sonia's brain turning in the kitchen. She'll want to go to India with the Heracs.

"There are a few things I don't understand about the journal," I say.

"Oh?" Jenner answers.

"If I understood the last journal entry correctly, the one from 1867, Torvus was supposed to give the journal to his friend's wife? Why did he end up giving it to Alexandre?"

Jenner laughs. It is a good laugh. The way Santa Claus would laugh. From the belly up. After reading his journal entry, I wouldn't have guessed he'd be so jovial. "Any other questions?" he asks.

"What was left behind for the daughter?" Sonia wants to know. "The writer, whoever he was, mentioned leaving something for his daughter."

"Did you notice the numbers at the end of the journal?" Jenner's tone is enigmatic.

"Yes. What are they?"

"Coordinates. Geographic coordinates. Find their location and you'll find the answers to your questions."

Sonia tries to question Jenner further, but he doesn't answer. No amount of coaxing and cajoling will budge him. It's not that he doesn't know the answers to the questions; he just enjoys teasing us. He only says, "It's a surprise."

Kimberly takes her turn at the phone, but she too will not give us the answers we seek. The most the Heracs will tell us is that the location referred to by the coordinates is in the Canadian Rocky Mountains, about an hour from Calgary, Alberta. Specifically at the east end of a mountain called Yamnuska.

"But I've never climbed a mountain," I say in frustration. "What's more, I've never heard the name and don't know how to get there."

"Yamnuska is easily accessible and getting up is really just a hike." I heard the smile in Jenner's voice. "If you like, I'll e-mail you directions," Jenner says.

We talk a while longer. We talk about how we met our spouses, places we've visited and lived in. A surprisingly personal conversation, considering we don't know one another, but they are easy people to talk with; people we'd enjoy having as friends or neighbours. The call lasts more than an hour. Before ending it, again I ask what we'll find at the mountain coordinates, but Jenner just laughs that Santa Claus laugh again.

After the call, Sonia and I discuss the possibility of flying to the Rockies. "The kids won't be home until Monday. Let's be spontaneous," Sonia says with more enthusiasm than she's displayed in a year. She checks the Internet and finds us a flight to Calgary. The tickets cost less than the B&B we cancelled when we cut short our Eastern Townships vacation.

At first, I am dubious about going. After all we just ended the last vacation prematurely. How will this be any different? But I am intrigued by what we might find in the Rockies. More importantly, I need to do this with Sonia. I'd rather look back on this getaway with Sonia as a failure than wonder if I should have tried one last time. In the end, I agree to go. We pay for the flights and pack for what might be our last adventure together.

The mountains, their outlines as uneven and sharp as the jagged edges of a broken bottle, begin to loom impossibly large as we approach them in our rental car. Some mountain peaks are snow covered, despite the warm July weather. I wonder if we have brought enough warm clothes.

Mount John Laurie is the official name of our destination, but most guidebooks and maps call it by the more poetic name of Mount Yamnuska or just Yamnuska, a Stoney Indian word meaning mountain with sheer cliffs, or flat-faced mountain. As we get closer, I see the name is appropriate. It is daunting to a man who has never climbed a mountain.

Six cars stand in the parking lot at the base of Yamnuska; five have Alberta license plates; the sixth is from Washington State. Before we start off, we check that we have everything we need stowed in the backpack: pocket knife, first-aid kit, toilet paper, sandwiches, water, our photocopy of the journal, as well as a small folding shovel, which Sonia considers unnecessary. "Kimberly and Jenner would have told us to bring a shovel if they'd thought we needed it," she says. In my hand is the GPS receiver, which Kimberly recommended—an undreamed of navigational aid when the journal's coordinates were mentioned, but one which will make our search easier.

The mountain air is fresh and clean, and the strong smell of pine trees reminds me of Christmas. I lock the car and sling the backpack over my shoulders. Leaving the parking lot, we immediately enter a forest of pine, fir, and elm trees, along with brush and a few delicate purple mountain flowers. After half an hour of uphill hiking, we leave the trees behind and begin to zigzag up loose rock, which Sonia's newly purchased hiking book calls scree. As we continue at a steady pace up a clearly defined path, my thoughts wander to the incident when Sonia lost my trust.

Doug and Mary Oliver, our Pictionary opponents, had three children, the youngest of whom was already in high school when Mary discovered she was pregnant again. The Olivers were positive about the unplanned event, despite the risks to a baby when a mother is more than forty. They loved their children and were excited about having one more.

Doug called us from the hospital when Mary was in labour and promised to phone again when the baby was born. When hours, then a day, went by without news, we grew concerned. Eventually, Sonia called the hospital to find out what was happening.

"Mother and baby were discharged yesterday," she was told.

Anxious to find out if all had gone well and whether the new arrival is a boy or girl, Sonia phoned the Olivers. Doug answered on the second ring.

Mary was fine, Doug answered Sonia, his tone so uncharacteristically monotone that she wondered if something was wrong. The Olivers were so gregarious that we assumed they would be especially excited with a new baby.

Sonia hesitated before asking Doug if the baby was okay.

"Yes. Fine. Everything is great," he told her, still in the same monotone.

Sensing something was wrong but not wanting to pry, Sonia told Doug to call if they needed anything, anything at all, and mentioned we had enough frozen meals to last them a week, so they'd have no need to cook for a while. Doug thanked Sonia politely, but the conversation was so strained and awkward that the call was over before Sonia realized she hadn't even learned the baby's gender.

It was two weeks before the Olivers invited us over. Carrying shopping bags filled with frozen meals, we walked the four blocks to their house.

Doug greeted us at the door. He shook my hand and, with visible reluctance, allowed Sonia to kiss his cheek. Inside the house, the curtains were closed against the hot summer sun, and I could hear the hum of the air conditioner. For some reason, I had the sense in that cool, quiet, dark house that someone had died. Uneasily, Sonia and I exchanged a look before following Doug to the living room, where Mary sat in a rocking chair by a dim lamp, holding a swathed baby. She gave us a half-hearted smile and gestured that the baby was asleep.

To our surprise, Mary didn't offer to show us her new baby. She clutched it closely to her chest. After another quick glance at each other, we sat down on the chesterfield across from her.

"Boy or girl?" Sonia asked softly.

Doug sat down in a chair beside Mary and answered for her. "Boy. His name is Keith." A small smile appeared on his face, softening his stern features. After three girls, we had thought the Olivers wanted a boy, though they had never actually said so.

"What a lovely name," Sonia said brightly.

"Thanks," they said together.

A few strained moments went by. Then Sonia asked, "Are you all right?"

"We're fine," Doug answered, a little too quickly.

Mary hadn't moved her eyes from the baby since our arrival.

"Mary?" Sonia said, and I heard tension in her voice.

Mary finally looked up. "Did I do something wrong?" she asked. Her lips quivered. She looked as if she was about to cry.

"What do you mean?" Sonia asked. At the same moment, Doug's somewhat forced smile vanished. I felt confused.

"I didn't take any medication while I was pregnant. I took my vitamins. I ate properly. What went wrong?" Mary asked, making me even more confused.

"You did nothing wrong, sweetheart," Doug said, putting a hand on Mary's knee, which had started to pump rapidly up and down, like that of a nervous child.

"Then why did this happen?" Mary asked.

"It just did sweetheart. You're not to blame. And the baby will be fine," Doug said in a quiet, reassuring voice. Then he kissed Mary and the baby.

I felt even more uncomfortable, as if I were watching something private and intimate. I wanted to leave. Whenever I found myself in an uncomfortable situation like this, I took my cues from Sonia, who always seemed to know the right thing to do. She was sitting quite still, so I sat still too.

"Keith is a beautiful baby, Mary," Doug said, his voice a little more animated. "Let's show him off to Richard and Sonia."

Mary hesitated, looking uncertain. But she gave the baby to Doug, who in turn handed him to Sonia.

He was, indeed, very cute. Round face, dimpled cheeks, pouting lips, and a head covered with fuzz as dark as his parents' hair.

"He's beautiful," Sonia said softly, in that tone she takes on when she looks at babies. I echoed the sentiment as Sonia handed Keith to me.

The baby was surprisingly heavy for a newborn, with most of the weight in the legs rather than the torso. "Solid little fellow," I said as cheerfully as I could. I hoped my tone would help Mary feel good about what seemed a healthy baby boy.

"It's the cast," Doug said. He took the baby from me and began to unwrap him. A shiver tingled along my spine, a kind of premonition, so that as Doug removed the blanket I already knew why Mary was so despondent.

She had started to rock in her chair, very quickly. "A club foot," she said, with tears in her voice. "My beautiful baby has a club foot. A deformity. He'll have trouble walking. Other children will make fun of him. It's not fair." Mary put her hands to her face and burst into tears.

Sonia, always caring and empathetic, hated to see anyone in pain, especially when that person was close to her. Quickly, she went to Mary and hugged her.

THE IMPACT *of a* SINGLE EVENT ·

Sonia's arms went around Mary, who gratefully hid her head against Sonia's shoulder. Sonia rocked her in an effort to comfort her. As Mary went on sobbing, Sonia said gently, "Everything will be fine. Your boy will turn out great. Just look at…"

I jerked upright in horror, finding it hard to believe what I was hearing. In the second before she completed her sentence, I had the urge to shout "*No!*" How could Sonia even think of blurting out the one thing I never spoke of to anyone but her? A secret I'd thought I could rely on her to keep quiet forever.

But, "…Richard," she finished.

"*What?*" Doug stared at me blankly.

"Richard has a…" Sonia began, only to stop when she realized—too late—that in trying to comfort Mary and Doug, she had betrayed me.

"Richard has a…a club foot?" Doug asked, after a charged moment.

Could I have denied it? I don't know. I do believe that had I been quicker I could have come up with a way to interrupt Doug: "What Sonia meant is—I have a cousin with a club foot. Or, I had a schoolmate with a club foot." But I didn't think fast enough. Instead, I just said, as nonchalantly as I could, "I was born with a club foot."

Mary stopped crying as she lifted her head from Sonia's shoulder. Doug looked stunned. Sonia had her hand to her mouth, and her eyes opened wide in alarm. She knew instantly that she had made a mistake.

At that point, of course, my only option was to be upfront and honest. "Take a look," I said, as I began to take the sock off my right foot and rolled up my pant leg. Outwardly I was calm; inside I was seething. *How could you do this to me, Sonia?* I raged internally.

The Olivers behaved as I expected they would, as everyone else had ever done when they saw my deformed leg. They gaped. As a boy, I had found it difficult to listen to the cruel taunts and the name-calling, but the stares, often blatant and unashamed, had been worse. Sometimes those stares had made me feel less than human, like a curiosity in a circus sideshow.

"I know—there are lots of scars," I said, trying to meet the Olivers' looks head-on. "Most of my surgeries were performed forty years ago. Operating techniques have improved a lot since then."

"Does it hurt?" Mary asked curiously. Doug was still silent. Sonia had taken her hand from her mouth, but her eyes were still wide.

"No," I lied, for it hurt quite a lot if I stood for too long. But that was not what Mary needed to hear right then. "Sometimes it aches, but a hot bath almost always does the trick," I reassured her.

"I had no idea," Mary said wonderingly. "Neither of us knew—did we Doug?"

We talked for the next hour about what I had experienced and the information the doctors had given them. The baby had metatarsus varus, a less severe type of club foot than the talipes equinovarus that I was born with. More than anything, Mary needed assurance that everything would be all right for their baby boy, so I told them only the good things. I had never had problems walking and running and had even dunked a basketball when I was in grade nine. By the time we left the Olivers, Mary was smiling.

"I'm so sorry, honey. I didn't mean to say anything, but with Mary so upset, I spoke without thinking." Sonia was contrite as we walked home.

"It's okay," I said. Really, I was very angry. Angry and hurt. I didn't want Sonia near me. If I were to be honest with myself, I would say I actually hated her at that moment.

Though she apologized, the uncertainty of whether or not I could trust her made me wary. Deep down I knew I was overly sensitive about my club foot, but Sonia betrayed my trust in her. Regardless of how insignificant my condition may seem to others, the bigger concern was that I didn't feel secure confiding in Sonia anymore. What else had she let slip when I wasn't around?

Normally I would fall asleep holding Sonia, but not that night. When Sonia tried to snuggle up to me, I pulled away.

"What's wrong?" she asked.

"Just not comfortable," I told her.

"Anything I can do?" she asked amorously.

"No. I might go watch some television." A moment later I got up and didn't return until she fell asleep.

For the next few days, if she tried to hold my hand, I told her I was too sweaty. If she tried to kiss me on the lips, I turned to give her my cheek. In the evenings, after we had put the kids to bed, I pretended to write in the basement late into the night. When she asked if anything was wrong, I told her I was "thinking about all the work I had to do." Soon she stopped grabbing my hand or attempting intimacy.

One evening, a few weeks after the incident, Sonia cornered me in the basement.

"I want to know why you're being so distant...is this about what happened at Doug and Mary's?" Sonia's forearms were red and raw. So was her neck. She had been scratching. A lot. A sure sign she was upset.

"No," I said. I had recently begun to get some perspective about my feelings. As far as I knew, Sonia had kept my confidences since I met her at McGill. Although still a little shaken, I was beginning to forgive her.

"Because if it is, I told you I was sorry." She didn't seem sorry. Actually, she was very worked up. More than I had ever seen her. Her eyes narrowed, her lips curled back, and her hands balled into fists like she was ready to hit me. Had my aloofness made her this irate or had something else happened?

I probably should have been honest with her, but she didn't seem to be in a mood to talk. Uncharacteristically, she looked like she was itching for a fight. "I told you I'm fine," I said defensively.

"Then what's the matter?" she snapped.

"I just have a lot on my mind."

"Don't we all!" she said angrily, and began to scratch her arm.

"What's the matter with you?"

"I think you're still mad because of what happened at Doug and Mary's, and you're being ridiculous," she said, raising her voice.

Ridiculous? Ridiculous because I wouldn't talk with her or ridiculous to let her indiscretion affect me so much? She hadn't grown up as an outcast! Her parents never told her she was different! Beautiful Sonia had never been friendless, much less ridiculed, for something she couldn't control. How dare she!

I couldn't look at her. I was more upset than I had been at the Olivers. "Excuse me," I said furiously, behind clenched teeth.

I stormed out of the house and drove aimlessly around Montreal for a while, then made my way up Mount Royal. Parking near *Lac Aux Castors*, I walked the dark trails of the park. After an hour my anger subsided. At the belvedere in front of *Le Chalet*, I stared down on the illuminated city and self-pity descended. The one person who I had thought understood me, understood nothing. I felt alone. I knew I should call Sonia to tell her of my whereabouts, but I did not. I didn't want to hear her voice. After a few hours I got tired and returned to my car, where I fell into a troubled sleep in the back seat.

When I returned home next morning, a gulf stretched between Sonia and me. I believed it was Sonia's responsibility to bridge that chasm. No doubt she felt it was my job, as neither of us did much to mend our faltering relationship. In time, the gap between us grew bigger and more palpable.

Now, as I climb the loose rock on the front face of Yamnuska, I think about the past year and wish it was only a bad dream. Although I feel a little closer to Sonia since we came together to rescue Jenner and Kimberly, I long for a return to my old life, when Sonia and I had been so happy together.

I glance at the GPS device. We are making progress. Before long, we are up the slope and at the face of the sheer cliff. The cliff towers a thousand feet above us, extending approximately half a kilometre on either side. The wall of rock is immense, like a giant movie screen. A path runs parallel to the sheer cliff. Heeding Jenner and Kimberly's instructions, we choose the eastern path.

On the GPS, the latitudinal and longitudinal coordinates are quickly approaching the coordinates in the journal. Excitement mounts as we realize we must be nearing our destination. I wonder how the person who mapped out the original coordinates did so without a GPS. Did they use sextants a hundred-and-forty years ago? And how did the journal writer think others would find the location so many years later?

We reach the eastern end of the cliff wall. If the GPS is correct, this is it! We've reached our destination.

I turn to Sonia. "We made it! We're here!"

She laughs as she looks around. "*What now, Richard?*"

I am as puzzled as she is. What now, indeed? We begin to search the ground for markings, for some indication that we really are in the right spot. As we hunt, my imagination runs wild.

The writer of the original entry must have been well off to be able to travel so extensively in 1867. He may have had his friend bury money or some other form of wealth. It was also possible that the original author brought back treasures from his travels overseas. It was not unusual in those days for an adventurer to bring home a rare artefact: what today would be considered stealing a national treasure, would have been common practice back then. I try to rein in my thoughts: after all, Jenner and Kimberly have been here, as have, I would guess, the other journal authors.

Twenty minutes of wandering around yields nothing. I'm beginning to think either Jenner and Kimberly are having a joke at our expense, or whatever was once here has been removed. Disappointed, Sonia and I round the eastern edge of the cliff. All we want now is to get out of the wind, which chills our sweaty backs, and to find a place to eat our lunch.

Suddenly, I see it. It practically jumps out at me. Bolted to the side of the mountain, about hip high above the ground, is a bronze plaque, weathered grey-green, like the colour of mould on cheese. The words on it read:

AN ETERNALLY CHANGING
WORLD OFFERS NO FUTURE FOR
WHICH YOU MUST AIM. WITH NO
FUTURE TO ASPIRE TO, YOU ARE
FREE TO LIVE FULLY IN THE
HERE AND NOW.

AUGUST 1868

Below the plaque is a conspicuous pile of rocks. Six of the rocks have been painted green and are as big as ostrich eggs. Cautiously, Sonia picks up the top rock, intending to examine it. As I look at the rest of the pile, I suddenly notice through the spaces between the remaining green rocks a dull piece of metal. "*Sonia!*" I exclaim tensely, and begin to remove the remaining green stones. My heart quickens as I see, nestled in a hollow, a tin box. The box is dented and scratched and about the size of a dictionary. I pull it out of the cavity and pop off the lid.

Inside the box, wrapped in a clear plastic bag, is a weathered notebook. Sonia is close beside me—I can feel the heat of her skin and the beat of her heart. She is as excited as I am, as I pull the notebook out of the plastic. Two short green pencils, golf pencils, drop onto the rocks at my feet. The notebook, we see, is in rather awful condition, worse than even Jenner and Kimberly's old journal.

"It looks as though it was dropped in a pool of water and then left to dry in the sun," Sonia observes.

It opens like an accordion as I carefully turn to the first cracked page. Someone has traced over faded words. I think I recognize the writing. I pass the dilapidated notebook to

Sonia, then take the Heracs' photocopied journal from the backpack. Incredulously, I look at the writing in the 1867 entry and the writing in the dilapidated notebook. Both were written by the same person.

"I don't understand," I say, puzzled, and show Sonia the two sets of writing. "The writing in the notebook is the same as the writing in the journal—but that man died sailing from India. I don't get it."

We begin to read:

August 22nd, 1868

This register has been established in order that visitors to this place should learn of the authentic history of the journal that led them here.

In the winter of 1865, my wife and daughter became consumptive. On March 30th, my darling little daughter, Astrid, just two years of age, died. A month-and-a-half later, on May 22nd, my beloved Inga breathed her last. Their deaths quenched the fire I once felt burn so fiercely within. For more than a year, I locked myself away in my home and paid no heed to the outside world. During that year, by virtue of neglect, the businesses to which I had dedicated my life came to ruin.

Attempting to escape a life that now hung heavy upon my hands, I departed Halifax and went abroad with friends. Over the course of many months, I travelled through India, hoping to discover a healing balm to ease the pain I felt so deeply. Unable to rest my weary mind, I parted from my companions. In the town of Chindah, I crossed paths with a woman named Ritika, who allowed me to dwell on her farm. It was at that farm that I met her grandfather, Abhay, and learned of his uncommon convictions. As wise as he was, however, I was beyond consolation and found myself contemplating my death. But death—in the jaws of a tiger—was not to be my fate. As it happened, my brush with death actually brought me renewed life.

Aboard the Friedrich, on the voyage home to Halifax, I found myself writing in a journal to my dearest Inga as if she were still alive, for I felt only she would understand me. While sharing my experiences with my departed wife, I came to better understand Abhay's beliefs and realized that the dead make poor companions for the living.

Back at home, with my grief finally easing, I began to believe that the wisdom Abhay had imparted to me might interest others. But how could I give you, my readers, the same opportunity to reflect upon Abhay's teachings as I once had? I felt I needed to tempt you to leave your everyday surroundings, which would provide you time to consider unusual ideas. For it was proven to me, through my own long, solitary meditations aboard the Friedrich that, in order to digest new thoughts, one needs time to contemplate and a new environment in which to do so.

With this in mind, I rewrote my journal, deliberately making it appear as if I, the man who had journeyed across India, had died after entrusting my friend, Torvus Sumac, to hide a treasure for my daughter, Astrid. Since a journal was given to you by Torvus Sumac, you undoubtedly assumed that my daughter never received the journal intended for her and therefore a treasure remains unclaimed.

Let me now correct three deceptions. The first deception is that I, the man who wrote of his journey in India, died on board the Friedrich. That did not happen. As of this date, August 22nd, 1868, I am alive and well. The second deception was that Torvus Sumac was a good friend. Actually, it is I who am Torvus Sumac. The third deception, I am sorry to say, concerns the treasure. If you imagine something resembling a pirate's booty, you may be disappointed. The treasure consists only of the plaque and this notebook.

You may have surmised by now, I have not given away only one fallacious journal; I created copies and offered them, and will continue to offer them, to those I deem capable of experiencing the world in Abhay's unique way.

I only partly regret my ruse, for I believe that those who make the journey to find the treasure will understand my duplicitous actions and will forgive a foolish man his whims. As for the plaque, it is a reproduction of the words Abhay left in a letter to me, which to this day, I carry as a reminder of his lesson.

I remain your obedient servant,

Torvus L. Sumac

P. S. Visitors are respectfully requested to register such observations and remarks as they may desire, in this notebook. I also invite you who have travelled so far to make your own additions in the empty pages of the journal that led you here.

When Sonia and I left Montreal, we had no idea what we would find. Certainly, we did not expect to discover a mouldy notebook and a weathered plaque.

I imagine the enormous task this man, Torvus, undertook. Not only did he have the plaque made, he carried it across the country, all the way from Halifax in the east to the Rockies in the west, hiked up the mountain, and affixed the plaque to the cliffside. He did it all, if I correctly remember the history of Canadian railroads, fifteen years before the first train ever travelled this far.

The journey must have taken him many months when one considers that a canoe or a horse would have been his mode of transport. Then for years, he judiciously handed out copies of his adventures in India, in the hope that some people might be sufficiently intrigued to search out this place. All this effort for the sake of an idea Torvus may have surmised only a few people had the potential to understand. I wondered if he would have been astonished to know that 140 years after he wrote it, at least one of his journals was still being handed down from generation to generation.

Holding the notebook, I suddenly laugh. Sonia laughs too—though at what, I don't know. The sound of our voices is at odds somehow with the silence of the mountainside. After a moment, I turn my attention back to the notebook. On the page after Sumac's note, the writing almost completely washed away, is a note written by a new author. It reads:

July 22nd, 1875

Imagination and fascination have drawn me to this distant spot, where I am delighted to find myself in the company of golden sunshine, jagged rocks of long-dead volcanoes, and drifting vapours weaving and parting through the alpine summits. Such views remind me that I am of subordinate interest to the universe and that I shall find peace if I recall this experience in times of trouble.

Patrick Witt
Charlottetown, Prince Edward Island

The second supplementary entry comprises a dozen Oriental characters, Chinese or Japanese, and is signed in a spidery script: *Sun Ling 1883*.

The next entry is dated 26/5/84. It's signed by William and Lynn Mach, but though I manage to read their names, I can barely understand what is written: only something about a chance encounter with Torvus.

There are other names, dates, short notes, mostly impossible to read. I scan them quickly, until I come to handwriting I recognize.

1890 August 18

In the company of she who is dearest to me, I find myself in wonder of all that lies in the past. The man I once knew, the respect with which he treated me, and the lessons I learned from him by example rather than by dictation are still with me. Is it possible I would have known such contentment had I not encountered him? I have no answer, for who can guess at the randomness of our existence? I say only this, if one day you should return to this spot, Mr. Sumac, please know that your friend retains fond memories of you that will only be effaced by death.

Alexandre Arouet
Fredericton, New Brunswick

Below Alexandre's note is a short entry.

1890 August 18

To tread in steps seldom attempted by others and among scenes that can hardly be surpassed is reward enough for the journey on which we find ourselves.

Alethea Arouet
Fredericton, New Brunswick

Further on are entries in what appears to be Spanish, German, Arabic, and more Japanese or Chinese. Some of the authors are from such places as Bulawayo, Rhodesia; Aix-la-Chapelle, Germany; Al Madinah, Saudi Arabia; and St. Louis, Missouri.

While Sonia and I eat lunch, we continue reading the notebook, taking care not to stain the pages. Most of the comments are serious, but not all. A 1963 humorist asks if an enthusiastic engineer can install a slippery slide from the plaque to the highway. Another writes in 1970, "Disappointing view—could only see mountains." Several business cards drop from the weathered pages of the notebook. A card dated 1929 reads *Rudolf Aemmor, Swiss Guide, Golden, B.C.* Another from 1949 reads *Thomas Lomack, Certified Mountain Guide, Canmore, Alberta.*

Sonia and I also come across names we remember from the photocopied journal: Viktoria Linck, Emily Herac, and Maximilian Herac. We see many other Heracs and Lincks.

I count almost two hundred names in the notebook, and I wonder how many journals Torvus gave away and whether others have survived like the one belonging to Jenner and Kimberly.

Sonia finishes her sandwich and brushes crumbs from her hands. "I want to add something to the notebook," she says then.

"I think I will too," I say thoughtfully. I take out my pocket knife, sharpen the little golf pencils, and hand one to Sonia.

After entries dated just a month earlier by Jenner and Kimberly—his deals with their journey across the country, hers with her feelings for this special mountain—Sonia adds her own note:

Beside peaks bold, ragged, and bare,
Beneath million spaced blue,
Mindful thoughts I do dare,
To see again new.

I gaze out across the valley to the mountains north of me. Although we are far from the summit, we still have an outstanding view. Off to the east, the flat prairies blend with the horizon. To the south and the north, pine trees cover the lower slopes of these granite castles, while at higher elevations, inclined at various angles, are layers of brown, black, and grey rock, which, an aeon ago, were thrust violently from the oceans and now reach through the clouds above us.

As I take pleasure in the grandeur of the mountains, I gaze at the plaque and recall the journal, with its personal records spanning parts of three centuries. I realize that everyone who wrote in the journal, though all from different eras, experienced personal pain and unique challenges. Although I have often felt that life dealt me a poorer hand than everyone else, I was mistaken. Pain, loneliness, and confusion are not unique to me. I realize, too, that all who wrote in the journal

shared something else. Something I should have learned long
ago. "The here and now," I murmur to myself.

With a clarity of thought I have rarely experienced before,
I make a decision.

I remove my jeans, pick up my pocket knife, and cut off
the pant legs just above the knees.

Sonia looks at me in astonishment. "What are you
doing?"

"Making shorts," I answer simply.

The legs are not even, but they will serve their intended
purpose. I put on the jean shorts and feel the sun on my
white legs. "Could you pass me the notebook?" I say then.

Sonia's jaw hangs open in astonishment.

"Please," I say.

Still astonished, Sonia slowly hands it to me. She watches
silently as I add an entry of my own. Satisfied, I carefully
replace the notebook and pencils in the clear plastic bag and
place it in the tin box, which I cover with the green-painted
stones.

I turn to a still-baffled Sonia and reach for the water
bottle. I take a long drink, and then, after offering it to
her—she only shakes her head imperceptibly—I put it back
in the backpack.

I smile at her. "Ready to go down, honey?" I haven't
spoken the endearment in more than a year.

Sonia's look of confusion disappears; she smiles back at
me. A radiant smile, which brings a rosy glow to her soft
cheeks and a moist glimmer to her lovely, hazel eyes.

"Yes, love," she says, her voice quivering with such
emotion that for a moment, I think she is going to cry.

At last I decide to start the hike back down to the car.
When I don't hear the scraping of shoes behind me, I turn.

She stands by the plaque; she almost looks rooted to the mountain.

"Something wrong?" I ask.

"What did you write?"

I wrote what I now understand about myself. "I am a lucky man."

As she steps towards me, she reaches for my hand. A jolt of pleasure runs down my spine, as it did the first time Sonia and I touched at the Halloween party at McGill all those years ago.

"Let's go home," she says.

Little does she know it—I am already home.

Author's Note

The plaque is located on the eastern side of the face of Mount Yamnuska. The exact coordinates are 51° 07' 47" N and 115° 06' 25" W at an elevation of 1887 metres or 6190 feet. To view photos of the plaque, please go to www.theimpact.ca/plaque. When you have visited the plaque, please leave your thoughts at www.theimpact.ca/postclimbcomments.

R. L. (Rod) Prendergast, who grew up in Alberta and Nova Scotia, has worked in sales and marketing for a number of companies. He began writing during a year-long sabbatical in New Zealand. Rod's first novel, *The Impact of a Single Event*, was long-listed for the 2009 Independent Publisher Book Award for literary fiction. Rod lives with his wife and son in Edmonton.